W9-AGO-130

Marcus pressed his lips softly against hers

Desire built inside Christine, like a wave slamming again and again. She could feel how much Marcus wanted her, too, could sense his struggle, and she was so aroused she felt like she'd levitated.

He put his arms around her and pulled her against his chest, inundating her with the delicious smell of cologne mixed with sun-dried cotton. His fingers pressed into her back, kneading her muscles, starting up a trembling in them both.

He broke off the kiss. "Christine," he whispered near her ear as if he'd been dying for this moment. He pressed her face against his. He kissed the side of her neck, tucking his hand beneath her hair to cradle her head.

Oh, she wanted this. Needed it. His arms around her, his desire obvious, his struggle for restraint obvious in the tension and quiver of his every muscle.

A white-hot ribbon of desire twisted through her body. She wanted more, much more of him burying his mouth in her neck. "I want us to try."

Dear Reader,

What makes a home a home, a family a family and love love? The question fascinates me. In this story, Christine Waters gets surprising answers to each. This book has special significance to me. I've worked on it off and on for several years, so I'm thrilled to finally see it on the shelves.

The journey home to Harmony turned Christine's expectations and beliefs about her mother, her father, her son, her lover, even her ex-husband upside down and backward before she'd finished sorting it all out. Her struggle with her teen son David was particularly difficult for me to write. What mother hasn't lain awake at night wondering if she's raised her child right?

Marcus was such a gift to Christine, helping her see clearly who she was and could be. Christine saved Marcus from the numb isolation he'd sunk into due to past tragedies. These two needed each other. I mean *needed.* As to physical chemistry, Marcus was lighter-fluid and cool water to Christine's crackling bonfire, intensifying and soothing in exactly the right way. I was so happy when they earned their happily-ever-after.

I hope you enjoy Christine and Marcus's story as much as I enjoyed writing it. Please visit me online at www.dawnatkins.com.

Best,

Dawn Atkins

Home to Harmony
Dawn Atkins

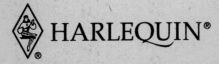

TORONTO • NEW YORK • LONDON
AMSTERDAM • PARIS • SYDNEY • HAMBURG
STOCKHOLM • ATHENS • TOKYO • MILAN • MADRID
PRAGUE • WARSAW • BUDAPEST • AUCKLAND

If you purchased this book without a cover you should be aware
that this book is stolen property. It was reported as "unsold and
destroyed" to the publisher, and neither the author nor the
publisher has received any payment for this "stripped book."

Recycling programs
for this product may
not exist in your area.

ISBN-13: 978-0-373-78428-8

HOME TO HARMONY

Copyright © 2011 by Daphne Atkeson

All rights reserved. Except for use in any review, the reproduction or
utilization of this work in whole or in part in any form by any electronic,
mechanical or other means, now known or hereafter invented, including
xerography, photocopying and recording, or in any information storage
or retrieval system, is forbidden without the written permission of the
publisher, Harlequin Enterprises Limited, 225 Duncan Mill Road,
Don Mills, Ontario, Canada M3B 3K9.

This is a work of fiction. Names, characters, places and incidents are
either the product of the author's imagination or are used fictitiously,
and any resemblance to actual persons, living or dead, business
establishments, events or locales is entirely coincidental.

This edition published by arrangement with Harlequin Books S.A.

For questions and comments about the quality of this book
please contact us at Customer_eCare@Harlequin.ca.

® and TM are trademarks of the publisher. Trademarks indicated with
® are registered in the United States Patent and Trademark Office, the
Canadian Trade Marks Office and in other countries.

www.eHarlequin.com

Printed in U.S.A.

ABOUT THE AUTHOR

Award-winning author Dawn Atkins has written more than twenty novels for Harlequin Books. Known for her funny, poignant romance stories, she's won a Golden Quill Award and has been a several-times *RT Book Reviews* Reviewers' Choice Award finalist. Dawn lives in Arizona with her husband and son.

Books by Dawn Atkins

Don't miss any of our special offers. Write to us at the following address for information on our newest releases.

Harlequin Reader Service
U.S.: 3010 Walden Ave., P.O. Box 1325, Buffalo, NY 14269
Canadian: P.O. Box 609, Fort Erie, Ont. L2A 5X3

To Wanda Ottewell,
who believed in this story from the beginning
and understood it better than I

ACKNOWLEDGMENTS

A world of thanks to Laurie Schnebly Campbell
and Laura Emileanne
for sharing their therapy expertise.
Any errors, distortions or inaccuracies
are completely my own.

CHAPTER ONE

CHRISTINE WATERS PARKED her sturdy Volvo in front of the main building of Harmony House, the commune where she'd grown up, her heart pinched as tight as her hands on the steering wheel, a spurt of panic overriding her determination.

What the hell was she doing back here? When she'd left this place at seventeen, it had been for good.

She knew why she'd come, of course. She had two good reasons: to give her fifteen-year-old son a fresh start and to help her mother recover from heart surgery.

Simple. Easy.

Except nothing about David, her mother or Harmony House itself was simple or easy. Ever.

David shoved off his ever-present headphones, which shut out the world—especially her—and jumped out of the car, enthusiastic for the first time since Christine had announced they would be here for the summer.

"It's like an old-time hotel," David said, surveying

the two-story building surrounded by gardens, the clay works barn and the animal stable.

"It was a boarding house back in the thirties, I think," she said, joining him. In the years she'd been gone—eighteen of them—the place had become stooped with age, the yellow paint gone as faint as cream and the different-colored doors were milky pale. The wraparound terraces looked as though they'd give way in a breeze.

This shocked and saddened her, like seeing a lively friend wan and weak in a hospital bed. She'd never liked the place, but it had always seemed bright and vibrant.

"Cool," David said, nodding.

Cool? Christine hid her smile of relief. The one thing in her favor was that David's girlfriend, who shaped his every opinion, *approved* of communes.

Well, la-di-dah.

"Check out the school bus," David said, indicating the ancient vehicle painted with hippie rainbows and peace signs.

"I can't believe Bogie still has that monster. Wonder if it even runs." She used to hate when it broke down on the winding road to town. Being late for school had been mortifying, not to mention all the stares at her homemade clothes. Christine was seven when Bogie had talked her mother into moving out of the cozy apartment in Phoenix to the commune in the middle of nowhere. To Christine's young eyes, beyond the bright paint, the place was all mud, stink and chaos.

Now, weary after the four-hour drive from Phoenix, Christine peeled her sweat-drenched tank top off her back. The cooler air in the hills was a relief, at least, though there would be many hot hours in the clay works, as well as tending the gardens, the animals and the kitchen, helping out until her mother and Bogie were back on their feet. Bogie, her mother's old friend and partner in the commune, was recovering from prostate cancer.

Absently, Christine scratched the back of one arm, then examined the itchy red bump. Mosquitoes already? The flying pests bred in stagnant irrigation water or at the nearby river's edge and they'd eaten her alive as a kid.

As if on cue, both her legs began to itch, too. She bent down to scratch them. "Remind me to get bug spray in town."

"No way. Too toxic. Just cover yourself up," David said. He would say that, dressed in his usual flannel shirt over a ratty T-shirt and shapeless cords, all too hot for early May in Arizona.

"We'll see. Grab a suitcase, okay?"

He went for the backseat, crammed with luggage, his too-long straw-colored hair hanging over his face, hiding his gorgeous eyes. Dragging out one of the bigger bags, he stumbled a little. The two inches he'd grown in the past year had made him as gangly as Pinocchio, not quite able to work the long limbs he'd suddenly gotten.

How she missed the old David. They used to be Team Waters against the world, as close as a mother and son could be. She'd been so proud of the way she'd raised him. She'd been open, direct, affectionate and accepting, and always, always talking things out. So different from the way she'd been raised, with all her questions unanswered, Aurora mute or dismissive.

From the moment she found herself pregnant she'd sworn to be a better mother than Aurora and she'd succeeded.

Until David slipped into puberty's stew of hormones and hostility. After that, and so much worse, came Brigitte. Two years older and snottier than David, she'd wrapped him around her sexually active little finger in no time flat.

He was too young. Only fifteen. Too young for sex, for drugs, for dangerous friends, for any of it. Christine's anxious heart lurched with sorrow.

Watching him drag the bag across the gravel, she made a vow: *I will not lose you.*

"What? What's wrong?" he demanded, letting the suitcase drop to the dirt. He assumed she was criticizing him.

"Nothing's wrong," she said, managing a smile. *Not so far, anyway.* Away from Brigitte and drugs, David's head would clear. He'd get involved in the commune, finish his schoolwork, talk to a counselor and, eventually, to her, and gradually get back on track.

That was Christine's plan, along with helping Aurora without damaging their fragile relationship.

Oh, and doing some ad agency projects on the side.

She would make this work. She had to.

A goat's *baa* drew her attention to a side garden, where a man in a straw hat was pulling weeds, watched over by a black-and-white sheep dog perched on its haunches. Bogie?

She headed over to see, lifting her bag because of the gravel. When he shooed the goat with his hat, Christine saw the gardener wasn't Bogie. Not at all. He was mid-thirties, not mid-sixties, and tanned, not leathery. He was also handsome.

Strikingly so.

The goat trotted past her and Christine caught the sour stench that had gotten her labeled "Goat Stink Girl" at New Mirage Elementary. Ah, the good times.

The sheepdog gave an excited woof and galloped at David as if he knew him. Once he got close, though, the dog drew back, turned and shot off toward the cottonwood grove.

"Did we scare your dog?" Christine asked.

"Lady's shy. She tolerates me only because I feed her." The gardener smiled at her so quickly she wasn't sure she'd seen it, but when he looked at David his face went tight, as if in unpleasant recognition. Odd.

"I'm Christine Waters. This is David."

"Marcus Barnard," he said, whipping off a leather glove to shake her hand. He looked her over with cool green eyes that held a glimmer of masculine interest...or maybe that was a trick of sunlight. It hardly mattered. She was not about to reciprocate.

"You're Aurora's daughter," he said, nodding. "She said you'd be coming."

"How is she doing?" Bogie had told her the prognosis was good, but Christine was anxious to see for herself. The news that her mother was ill had hollowed her out. Aurora had always seemed indestructible.

"She seems weak, but managing. I've done whatever extra Aurora will allow." He shot her a brief smile.

"Allow? That sounds like my mother. Bogie asked me to say I'm here because *he* needed help, not her." She smiled, but she felt far from happy. If Bogie hadn't called, she was certain Aurora never would have. That hurt deeply, though Christine told herself it was Aurora's way and always would be.

"People as self-sufficient as your mother often find it difficult to accept help," Marcus said.

"Self-sufficient, huh? That's one way to put it, I guess." It irked her that this stranger felt the need to explain her mother. Over the years, Christine had tried to bridge the chasm between them, but her mother hated questions and wasn't much for phone calls. E-mail was out, too, since Aurora didn't approve of computers. Christine sent cards and called, but made no headway.

"So how long have you been a guest, Marcus?" She figured him for a short-timer. He carried himself like a business guy dressed for a hike in a neat chambray shirt and newish jeans, not a bit like the grubbier, weather-worn and laid-back commune residents.

"Almost three months, I guess." His eyes were piercing, but cool, lasering in, but warning you away at the same time.

As striking in demeanor as he was in good looks, he seemed wound tight, watchful, and there was a stillness about him….

Not a man easy to ignore. That was clear.

"Can I help you with your bags?" he asked.

"We don't know where we'll be yet, so, thank you, no."

"When you do, I'm here." He settled his straw hat onto his head in a firm, deliberate way. Sexy. Definitely sexy. "And good luck in there." He flashed her a smile.

"Can you tell I'll need it?" When she walked away, following David to the porch, she stupidly wondered if Marcus Barnard was watching her go.

At the door to Harmony House, all thoughts of anything but what she faced fled. Christine paused to collect herself. *Ready or not, here I come.* For better or worse, Christine was home.

Once inside, she was startled by how everything looked the same as she remembered. There was the same hammered-tin ceiling, dark carved paneling, marble fireplace and antique furniture. It even smelled the same—like smoke, old wood and mildew. She was swamped with memories, her feelings a jumble of fondness, nostalgia, dread and anxiety.

She followed David down the hall into the big kitchen, which was empty and eerily quiet, unlike the old days when it was always crammed with people cooking, talking, eating or drinking. Christine had loved mealtimes, when everyone was in a good mood, not too high or drunk or argumentative. As a child, Christine had stayed alert to the vibe, braced to scoot when it got ugly. Remembering made her pulse race the way it used to. Ridiculous, really.

The back door opened and Bogie entered with a canvas holder of firewood in his arms. "Bogie." Christine's heart leaped at the sight of him. Bogie had always been kind to Christine, offering a gentle word on her behalf during the daily arguments with Aurora over food, clothes, toys and Christine's free time.

"Crystal!" He dropped the wood into the box by the woodstove and approached her, a grin filling his gaunt face, which was sun-brown and webbed with wrinkles. His ponytail had gone completely gray. He'd aged so much, though his cancer treatment might have temporarily set him back.

"Who's Crystal?" David asked her.

"I'll explain later," she murmured. God. She'd forgotten about the name thing.

Bogie shifted his weight from side to side, lifted then dropped his arms, as if not knowing whether or not to give her a hug. She decided for him, throwing her arms around him. *He was skin and bones.* "It's good to see you," she said.

He ended the embrace fast, blushing beneath his tan, and studied her. "You're so pretty, like I expected, but your eyes look tired. We'll help you with that for sure."

She flushed at his close attention, surprised and warmed by his obvious affection for her. He'd always been in the background here. "Bogie, this is my son, David."

"Nice to meet you, young man," Bogie said, ducking his head. So humble. He'd organized the commune, yet he'd let the much younger Aurora take charge. "Aurora's lying down. Let me tell her you're here."

"Oh, no, let her sleep. Please." Feeling as rattled as she did, she wouldn't mind delaying her first contact with her irascible mother.

"She'd never forgive me." Bogie thudded down the wooden floor of the back hall.

Christine was dripping with sweat, ridiculously

nervous. Her mother needed her help and she was here to give it. Maybe it would be as simple as it sounded.

"So…Crystal? What's that about?" David asked.

"Lord. Aurora changed our names when we got here."

"She named you *Crystal Waters?*"

"And she wasn't joking, either. She wanted it to be a spiritual rebirth, like a baptism. I was to be *sharp and true and sweet as the truth.*" She'd resisted at first, but her mother had been so excited and happy, she'd given in.

"That is so whack."

"You're telling me." Seeing David so amused, she told more of the story. "Picture the whole second grade laughing their heads off when I got introduced that first day."

"That would be harsh for sure." He smiled his old smile and Christine's heart lifted. So far, so good. "What about Grandma's name? *Aurora* sounds made up."

"It was. Her real name's Marie. *Aurora* means *dawn.* She wanted to *experience daybreak as a bright new woman.*" The words had stayed with Christine. When her mother had been that happy, Christine had felt swept away on a merry current. When she turned sad or angry, the trip became a churning tumble over sharp rocks. Probably how all kids felt.

"That's so trippy," David said, just as Aurora tromped in from the hall, Bogie on her heels.

"I can get out of bed on my own, dammit. Quit treating me like an invalid, Bogart."

Christine sucked in a breath at how small and frail her mother looked. Aurora had always seemed larger than life and tough as an Amazon warrior, even once Christine became an adult. When David was five, Aurora had come to Phoenix for a short, awkward visit and seemed as substantial and strong as ever.

Christine hid her alarm with a smile. "Aurora, hi."

As always, her mother's brown eyes slid away without making contact. "It's about time you got here. Bogie, get them iced tea. It's rose hip," she said to Christine.

"No need to fuss. We snacked the whole trip." But Bogie was already in the fridge.

"You look wrung out to me," Aurora insisted. "What are you doing in a silk top out here?"

"I don't know. It's light and cool." She smoothed her hair as if to prove how fresh she was. God. She'd automatically defended herself against her mother's tossed-off criticism.

"Look at you, David, tall as hell." Aurora started to move forward—to hug him perhaps?—but instead sank into a chair, breathing heavily.

"Should you be resting?" Christine asked, alarmed at her mother's weakness.

Aurora drilled her with a look. "Don't you start the invalid treatment, too." She swung her gaze to David. "Nice tat." She meant the ring of yin-yang symbols around David's heartbreakingly thin upper arm.

"I think it's awful," Christine said. It was a Brigitte idea, along with the eyebrow stud.

"It's a kid's job to rebel," Aurora said. "That's how they individuate. *You* rebelled by conforming." She turned to David. "Your mother loved to iron. Can you imagine that around here?" She winked at him. "She brushed her hair a hundred strokes, flossed her teeth every night, followed every rule. We didn't have many, so she made up some of her own."

"She still loves rules, that's for sure," David said.

"I'm not that bad, am I?" If being the butt of a joke or two helped David get comfortable here, Christine would dance around the room with boxer shorts on her head.

"Get the herbed goat cheese and some pita, Bogart," Aurora said gruffly. Bogie had already set out four mason jars of iced tea. "So, David, how'd you get kicked out of school anyway?"

"He wasn't expelled, Aurora. We talked the principal down to a suspension. As long as David keeps his side of the bargain."

Her son colored, not pleased about being reminded.

"So what kind of hell did you raise?" Aurora asked. "Back talk? Independent thought? Authority figures in institutions hate people who think for themselves."

"No shit," he said.

"Language," Christine warned. "It was for fighting, disrespecting teachers and—other things." Suspected marijuana possession, which was the part that most worried Christine. He *had* been using pot, she knew. Stopping was part of their deal.

David had promised to finish his schoolwork online and return in the fall with a new attitude. And Christine would do everything in her power to make that happen, including getting David some counseling. Aurora had told her about a therapist in nearby New Mirage, which was a lucky break in such a minuscule town.

"Christ, kids are kids, Crystal. They're not all taking Uzis into social studies class."

"Aurora…" Christine shot her mother a look. They'd discussed this over the phone, since Christine was concerned about her mother's permissive style and the free-to-be atmosphere at Harmony House.

"Okay," Aurora said. "Your mother wants me to remind you to obey the rules. There aren't many, but the ones we have we mean. No fighting. No smarting off…well, maybe a little smarting off. No drugs, of course. A fresh start, right? Pull your weight with chores. We all share and care. That's our motto. Always has been."

She nodded at the commune rules posted next to the chore board, where everyone was assigned duties. It looked as though there were only a half-dozen residents at the moment.

"Are we agreed?" Christine said to David. They had to be on the same page if they had any hope of her plan working.

"Chill, okay?" David said. "I got it."

"We'll have fun anyway," Aurora pretended to whisper behind her hand. That was typical Aurora. When she'd visited, she'd let David sip mescal, skip dinner and stay up all night watching vampire movies that gave him nightmares for a week.

David, of course, had adored her.

"Here we go." Bogie set down a plate of creamy cheese and big triangles of pita bread.

"Sit down, you two," Aurora said, spreading blobs of the cheese onto the pita, then handing them out. "Eat, Bogie," she said. "Since the radiation, he hardly eats."

"I do fine," he said. "I have…uh…medicine."

Christine felt a twinge of worry. Bogie grew a few marijuana plants for medicinal use, since pot was good for pain suppression, nausea and poor appetite. He'd promised to never smoke around David and to keep his half-hidden grow-room locked.

In the old days pot had been everywhere at Harmony House, a fact that had annoyed Christine immensely, since it led to so much silly, lazy behavior in the grown-ups.

Christine took a bite of the pita. The cheese was lemony and so delicate it melted like butter on her tongue. "Mmm," she said, then sipped the rose-hip tea, which tasted fresh and healthy.

David grimaced at the tea and barely nibbled the pita. He was a junk-food maniac, so the grow-your-own meals would be an adjustment for him. She'd take him to Parsons Foods in town for a stash of processed sugar and sodium nitrates. She had enough issues with David. Nutrition could wait.

"You'll love Doctor Mike, David," Aurora said. "He's brilliant. So intuitive. He sees right into you."

David shrugged, not enthused about the counseling. The guy would have to be good to get through to him.

"If you don't like him, we've got Doctor B.," Aurora said.

"Doctor B.?" Christine asked.

"Marcus Barnard. He's a big shrink in LA. He's working on a book while he's here."

So the man in the garden was a psychiatrist. That certainly explained his cool formality and intense gaze, along with his attempt to interpret Aurora's obstinacy for her.

"He's a hard worker, too," Bogie said. "A good thing since we're low on residents right now.

Lucy—she runs the clay works operation—thinks you should hire part-time kids, Crystal."

"Crystal doesn't need to mess with any hiring," Aurora grumbled. "I'll be back in a week."

"The heart doctor said six weeks," Bogie said quietly.

"We're here to work, Aurora," Christine said. Bogie had warned her that her mother might resist help.

"You'll have your hands full with the animals, the gardens and Bogie's greenhouse," Aurora said.

"Let's just see how it goes." If she had to hog-tie her mother to her bed to make her take it easy, she would. She'd need her A game to manage Aurora, that was clear.

Christine was a pro at finessing difficult clients, but here with her mother in the Harmony House kitchen, she felt herself shrinking into her childhood self, like Alice in Wonderland eating the cake that made her very small.

"If that travel article brings more folks out, we'll have more hands," Bogie said.

"There was an article?" Christine asked.

"It was about out-of-the-way travel spots. It said we're the oldest continuously inhabited commune in the western U.S. We got a couple of hikers from Tucson due to the story."

"Harmony House is the oldest?" That fact fired up Christine's professional instincts. "We could market that in ads, up your census, then raise your rates." It was a relief to talk about something she knew how to do.

"We don't have *rates*," Aurora said. "We ask for a contribution to cover food and laundry services and whatnot."

"What about your cash flow? Is it predictable?" Christine's mind was spinning with the key questions she'd ask a client.

"This is a commune," David said. "It's about living off what you produce and being sustainable. It's not about cash."

Thank you, Brigitte. "Even Harmony House needs income." She pointed at the Parsons Foods bag on the counter. "I doubt the grocery story lets them barter."

"They do buy our eggs and goat cheese," Bogie said.

David made an impatient sound. "Just because your job is getting people to buy crap they don't need, doesn't mean the rest of us want to live that way." He was showing off for Aurora and Bogie, she could tell.

"It was my evil capitalist job that paid for your cell phone, laptop and Xbox," she said, hoping he would joke back.

"Whatever, Christine."

She winced. Calling her by her first name was another Brigitte brainstorm: *We're all peers on this planet.* But Christine was not about to object at the moment. She had to pick her battles or they'd be in a never-ending war.

"Hell, we all start where we are and do what we can, right, Crystal?" Aurora said, surprising Christine with her kindness. Maybe her mother's brush with death had softened her a little. "Your boss is cool with you taking off the summer?"

"I've brought projects to do from here." If the commune work tied her up too much, she'd have to dip into savings, but that would be fine. Within a year, she intended to leave Vance Advertising and open her own agency. "The main thing is for you to get your strength back."

Her mother bristled. "I am not an—"

"Invalid, yeah. That's what you said."

"And I mean it," her mother said sharply. Except the emotion that flashed in her eyes wasn't anger. It was *fear*. A chill climbed Christine's spine. She'd never seen Aurora afraid and it made the world tilt on its axis. Aurora was clearly weaker than she wanted to be. *Oh, dear.*

"How about we get you settled in now and tomorrow Aurora can show you around the clay works?" Bogie said, evidently trying to smooth the moment.

"That sounds great," Christine said before her mother could object. "So I'll stay in my old room and put David in the spare one next door?" Christine and Aurora had lived in the old boarding house owners' quarters at the back of the building.

"The spare's got furniture at the moment," Bogie said. "We could move it if you like."

"Nonsense," Aurora said. "David can pick one of the empty rooms on the far end of the second floor. Once you've picked it, grab a key." She nodded at a rack by the kitchen door.

"Okay. Cool."

He'd be too far away from her, but seeing the delight on David's face, Christine wouldn't object.

"We never used to lock a door," Bogie said, shaking his head sadly. "People insist these days. Your room's open, Crystal. I figured you'd want to stay there."

Outside, David barreled up the stairs to pick out his room. Christine grinned at his eagerness. Of course, dragging buckets of table scraps to the compost heap might chill his excitement, not to mention the lack of cell service or high-speed Internet, but Christine hoped he'd be so busy learning and exploring that he'd forget all about Brigitte.

She caught up with him halfway down the terrace, opening doors. When he reached a faded blue one, Christine got a jolt of electric memory. That was Dylan's room, where she'd lost her virginity not exactly on purpose.

"Not that one!" she called, then saw that David had opened the door to Marcus Barnard, who was buttoning up a blue shirt.

"Sorry," David said, the moved on to the next room.

"He didn't realize the room was occupied," she

said, watching Marcus's fingers on the buttons. His ring finger had a pale indentation. He was divorced or widowed and not long ago. Hmmm.

"No problem," he said, tucking in his shirt. "I'll get the dolly." Before she could object, he was loping down the terrace.

"Thanks!" she called as he took the stairs down to the yard. Leaning on the terrace rail, she watched him cross to the clay barn, moving with the easy grace of an athlete, strong, but not showy about it. Easy on the eyes. Maybe she shouldn't stare, but, heck, window-shopping didn't cost a dime, did it?

CHAPTER TWO

MARCUS ROLLED THE clay-spattered dolly toward Christine's car, not certain what bothered him more: how much David looked like Nathan or how abruptly he'd been caught by Christine.

She was pretty, of course, and lively, a coil of energy ready to spring into action. It had to be the contrast to his quiet life. She was like an explosion of confetti, a surprise that made you smile.

And when she'd burst in on him dressing, he'd all but expected her. He'd felt abruptly *alert*. Awake.

Which made him realize he'd been numb for a while, since long before the divorce. The sensation almost hurt, like the tingling ache of a sleep-numbed arm regaining circulation.

Then there was her son. The last thing Marcus needed was a walking, talking reminder of his stepson. His memories and regrets were difficult enough.

He got to the car as Christine staggered beneath the huge suitcase she'd dragged from the overhead luggage rack. He lunged to catch it before it hit the gravel. If she'd waited… But, then, Christine Waters didn't strike him as the kind of woman who *waited* for much at all.

She jumped in with both feet, which at the moment were clad in heeled sandals, not exactly stable on uneven ground. She was dressed for the city in a filmy top, white shorts and flashy jewelry. It was as if she hadn't wanted to admit she was coming to a commune. Her mother was clearly a source of tension, too.

What the hell was he doing analyzing the woman anyway?

"That's David's bag," she said, nodding at the one he held, her face flushed from exertion. "Let's load his stuff first."

Marcus put the bag on the cart and David added an electric guitar case. "You play?" Marcus asked.

David nodded. He had the same long blond hair, scrawny frame, soulful eyes and narrow face as Nathan. Even Lady had been fooled, barreling at him with joy, her owner home at last.

"His teacher says he's gifted, but he hardly practices," Christine said. "He'll have time when we're here to—"

"I'm not gifted," David blurted, glaring at his mother.

"I didn't practice much until I got into a band," Marcus said to smooth the moment.

"You play, too?" Christine locked gazes with him. Her eyes were an unusual color—a soft gray.

"Acoustic these days, but yes, I play."

"Maybe you and David could jam." Her face lit up, but her son's fell, clearly mortified.

"God, Mom."

"If you're interested, of course." But he was certain the boy would decline. A good thing. Marcus would prefer to keep his distance.

"David...? Answer the man!"

Easy, Mom, Marcus wanted to warn her.

"Maybe, whatever," David mumbled, clearly fuming. He yanked the cart forward just as Christine tossed a bag. When it hit the ground, she teetered and Marcus steadied her arm.

Balance restored, Christine stepped back, her cheeks pink. He noticed that in the swelter of early summer the woman smelled like spring.

"Sorry," David muttered, tossing the fallen suitcase onto his load and shoving the cart toward the house.

"Everything I say pisses him off," she said with a light laugh, though she looked sad and confused.

"That's not uncommon with teenagers."

"Really? So, in your opinion, he's normal?" She faced him dead on, standing too close, digging in with her eyes. "Aurora told us you were a psychiatrist."

"I'm a partner at a mental health institute near L.A., yes." Until they offered to buy him out, which he expected when he returned. Better for everyone.

"But you've treated clients, though, right?"

"In the past, yes, but—"

"I mean, I wasn't asking for free therapy...well, not yet anyway." Another grin. "I bet that happens at parties a lot, huh? People hitting you up for advice?"

"At times." Not that there had been any parties after all that had happened—the controversy over his research, Nathan, his crumbling marriage. Fewer phone calls. A handful of e-mails and cards. Mostly silence.

Christine had turned to watch David drag the dolly to the terrace. "He'll be seeing a counselor in New Mirage, which I hope will help. Michael Lang? Do you know him? Is he good?"

"I don't know him, no." It surprised him to learn the tiny town had a therapist of any kind. His friend Carlos Montoya, a GP, offered the only medical care, a three-day-a-week clinic, with Carlos driving over from Preston.

"It should help, right? I mean, the counseling?"

"It can," he said. "If the therapist's style suits the client. Assuming your son wants to be treated."

"I was afraid you'd say that. David's not exactly into it. He agreed to it to keep from getting expelled. Plus, it was my idea and he hates me lately." She sighed.

"The transition to adulthood can be difficult," he said, moving to the trunk, wanting to get on with the task.

"We never used to fight like this," she said,

joining him in surveying the load of office equipment, again standing too close. "We always talked, you know? About everything. He came to me with his problems, talked about school and friends. Now every conversation is a minefield. One wrong word and he explodes."

"It can be that way." And so much worse. He leaned in to shift a computer into position.

"Do you have kids, Marcus?"

The question startled him and he jerked upward, banging his head on the trunk lid. "Not of my own, no."

"I didn't mean to pry."

He realized he'd spoken sharply. "It's fine." He braced the CPU on the rim of the trunk with his hip so he could rub the knot on his head.

"Sorry about that. Wait, we need the cart." It sat empty outside the room David had chosen. "David, the cart!" she called. "I swear I taught him better manners."

She dashed after it. It was impossible not to watch her run, graceful and quick, even in heels. The sight of her firm curves and long legs in motion set off an unwelcome reaction below the belt. He was human, of course. And a man.

No excuse to gawk. He started emptying the trunk.

The rattle of wheels told him she'd returned and he began stacking items onto the cart. "He's excited about the room," she said, as if he'd asked the question. "This is just a rough patch, you know? Most parents and their kids survive the teen years, right?"

"Most, yes." *But not all.*

Not all.

She stared at him, clearly wondering what he meant.

Afraid she'd pry—the woman seemed to have no boundaries—he put the last item, a fax machine, on top and pushed the cart toward Harmony House. "Where to now?"

"Toward the back of the house. Through the courtyard."

They walked together, with Christine placing a steadying hand on the stack. "I hate that David's room is so far from mine. Of course, you're next door, so can I count on you to make sure he keeps curfew?"

He stopped moving and blinked at her.

"Joking. I'm joking, Marcus. Jeez." She laughed, then her smile went rueful. "I just wish I could get in his head and make him make better choices."

"How does David feel he's doing?" The question was an automatic one, something he'd have said to a client.

"Fine, of course. Everyone else has the problem, not him. When he's disrespectful at school, it's the teacher's fault. When he loses his temper, someone else made him. Smoking pot is no big deal, so that's my problem, not his."

She shifted to block the cart from moving and faced him. "I can't get through to him. I feel so helpless, you know?"

"I do." Marcus had been as close as Nathan would permit him to be, but he'd never forgive himself for not doing more, for not intervening somehow, no matter what Elizabeth wanted, no matter what his own training and intellect told him was possible.

Christine resumed walking. "I can't believe I dumped all that on you." She shook her head and her dark hair shivered over her shoulders. "You're easy to talk to."

"I don't mind." Not as much as he'd expect to. Christine was so direct, so in-your-face. Elizabeth had been intense, but quietly so. Angry, Elizabeth smoldered. Christine would no doubt burst into flames. The idea made him smile.

"Probably all that listening training, huh?" She stopped to scratch her calf. He noticed insect bites on both her legs and her arms. He could mention the salve he had upstairs, but then she'd know he'd been staring at her body. He sighed.

"What I really need is a shower," she said, shaking her top as if to fan herself. "How's the water pressure these days?"

"Acceptable. Not strong, but steady."

"In the old days it was a hopeless trickle. Which made it no picnic trying to wash off the smell of goats. This way." She turned them toward the rear entrance to the courtyard.

"I can imagine. So you grew up here?"

"I was seven when we came and when I left ten years later, I was all Scarlett O'Hara about it— 'As God is my witness, I'll never go *smelly* again!'"

Marcus smiled. She joked about things that he could tell clearly troubled her. "And you haven't been back since?"

"No. It's been eighteen years. That sounds bad, I know, but Aurora and I have a rocky history." The cart stalled in the grass of the courtyard. Chickens squawked their objection to the interruption. He used force to get it moving again.

"My whole goal is to help her without getting into heavy battle." She bit her lip, clearly worried. "I'll be walking on eggshells—free-range eggshells."

He smiled at her quip. "She clearly needs your help, so maybe if you focus on what you're here to do…"

"'Busy hands are happy hands'?" She grinned. "Is that your professional advice?"

"It works." He paused. "Frankly, a psychology practice built around folk wisdom is as sound as any other."

"So, 'a stitch in time saves nine…people who live in glass houses shouldn't throw stones…an apple a day keeps the doctor away'? Like that?"

"All valid, depending on the issue."

"Interesting, Doctor B." She tapped her lips. "Got one for David? 'Straighten up and fly right' maybe?"

"Too directive perhaps."

"Also very military-schoolish. Then how about a parenting one for me?"

"Hmm. Maybe 'a watched pot never boils.'"

"Nice try. Patience is not one of my virtues."

"Something to work on then."

"You shrinks, always with the assignments." She sighed. "So how much do I owe you for the session?"

"No charge. Consider it part of the bell service at Harmony House." He held the door for her to step into the hallway. He realized he was enjoying talking with her. Other than lunches in town with Carlos, he didn't have many lighthearted social contacts, so this was…pleasant. And she smelled like spring.

STEPPING INTO THE COOL hallway of the owners' quarters, Christine's smile felt easy for the first time since she'd arrived. Joking around with Marcus had been fun. He'd been taken aback at first. She came on strong, she knew, loud and chatty and nosy, while Marcus was quiet and self-contained, a still pool happy to remain ripple free. He'd joked back, though.

The wooden floor creaked in a familiar way as they walked past the tiny kitchen, Aurora's bedroom—its door closed—the bathroom, the spare room, then Christine's old room.

"This is it," she said, turning the cracked ceramic

knob, her heart doing a peculiar hip-hop. The room would be different, of course, after eighteen years. Countless residents had stayed here, she'd bet. But when she stepped inside, she saw it was exactly the same as when she'd left it.

"Oh, my God. Nothing's changed."

"It's very…pink," Marcus said, pulling the cart inside.

"Bogie painted it for me. It was my princess room, like what I figured Susan Parsons would have. She was the most popular girl at school."

"Susan from Parsons Foods? She's married to the mayor, I believe."

"She was queen back then, so of *course* she'd marry the mayor." She ruled the girls who mocked Christine and the other commune kids.

Christine ran her hand over the pink polyester bedspread with the ruffles she'd sewn herself. "I made this, you know." She touched the sagging canopy netting attached to four broom handles. It looked ridiculous, as did the papier-mâché French Provençal frame around the bureau mirror and the pink fur-padded stool she'd made. "This was my haven. Aurora called me Rapunzel and made fun of me for expecting a prince to save me."

"Is that what you wanted?"

"Not really, but that didn't matter to Aurora. Fairy tales were sexist—the girls passive chattel to be bought or rescued."

"Pretty heavy rhetoric for a seven-year-old to absorb."

"All I wanted was our cute apartment, my little Catholic school with the neat plaid uniforms and the strict nuns." Everything squared-off, peaceful, predictable.

"What brought you here?"

"Bogie talked Aurora into it. They'd been friends years before and ran into each other and he got her all fired up."

"But you not so much?"

"God, no. There were power-outs constantly. No TV. No privacy. People moving in and out."

"Not to mention no water pressure."

"You're getting it, yeah." She'd been babbling, but it helped ease how strange she felt being here again. She liked how Marcus honed in on her while she talked, really listened, as if the details were vital to him.

"Everything okay?" Bogie stood in the door-way.

"My room's the same," she said, still amazed.

"That's Aurora. She sits in here and thinks about you."

"You're kidding. She always laughed at my princess stuff."

"We're sure glad to have you home again, Crystal," Bogie said. The affection in his gray eyes tugged at her. He sounded as though she was here to stay. That made her stomach jump.

Just for the summer, she wanted to remind him, but couldn't, not with that happy look on his face.

"Well, I'll let you get settled." He ducked his gaze, then retreated. That was Bogie's way, to slip off, disappear, as if he wasn't worthy of people's time or attention. How sad. She would spend as much time with him as she could, she decided.

Marcus helped her off-load the bags and equipment.

"The office stuff looks ridiculous in here, huh?" she said, looking around at the desk, computer and printer. "Actually, the only phone is in the kitchen. I'll have to set up in that alcove if I want to be online at all."

"The drugstore in New Mirage has computer terminals at the back where the post office is. It's DSL. That's what I use."

"I wonder how hard it would be to get DSL out here. Of course, Aurora thinks computers are a plot to destroy our minds."

"Should we move the equipment to the alcove?" he asked.

"I've kept you too long already. Thanks for the help, Marcus. And for listening to me jabber."

"It was my pleasure."

"Oh, I doubt that," she said, studying him. "I make you jumpy, don't I? You keep backing away."

"No." He looked surprised at her words, then seemed to ponder them. "I haven't had much social interaction lately...."

"And you prefer it that way?"

He didn't answer, but she was curious. "Why? Because of the book you're writing?"

"Aurora mentioned that, too?"

"What's it about? Psychiatry?"

He nodded.

"So how's it going?"

"It's…going." But distress flared in his eyes and he eased toward the door. "I'll see you at supper then," he said and was gone. So he didn't want to talk about *that,* either.

What was the deal with him and kids? *None of my own, no.* Stepkids then maybe? Why not say so?

The man had a lot on his mind, evidently. She wondered why he'd quit seeing clients. Maybe one too many female patients hitting on him. Didn't every woman crave a man who knew her inside-out, but stayed all the same? Marcus Barnard was a mystery, that was certain. At another place, another time, she might want to solve it.

DAVID STUMBLED INTO the Harmony House kitchen, so frustrated he wanted to smash a mason jar or one of those big pottery plates. His legs ached and he was dying of thirst from climbing hill after hill looking for a cell signal to call Brigitte. He'd failed. No bars. No signal. No Brigitte.

"How'd the exploring go?" his mother asked, all eager and excited. Like he was out having *fun,* not sweating his balls off for no good reason. "What did you see?"

"I can't get a cell signal!" He tossed his phone to the floor, instantly sorry he had. If he broke it, Christine wouldn't replace another one. Why did he get so mad?

"Just use the house phone," his grandmother said, pointing at a squat black one so old it had finger holes.

"Get permission first," his mother just *had* to add, looking up from her laptop. "Toll calls add up fast." *And we're not made of money.* That was always the next line.

"Did you know there was no cell service here?" he asked.

"We can live a few weeks without mobile phones and broadband connections," she said, holding out a glass of water.

"Wait. You mean there's no Internet?" That would kill him.

"Dial-up only and we don't want to tie up the phone a lot."

"Dial-up's too slow."

"Drink the water. You look dehydrated."

"You're not one of those computer addicts, are you, David?" his grandmother said, sewing a hole in some overalls. "That's no way to relate to the world."

"May I please use your phone, Grandma," he said, ignoring her jab, being so polite it hurt his throat.

"Anytime you want," she said. "And call me Aurora, for God's sake."

"You can call Brigitte once a day, but keep it brief," his mother said.

One call a day with the love of his life? No texts, no phone photos, barely e-mail? He was so mad he might explode.

Shaking, he dialed Brigitte's number one digit at a time, rattle, rattle, rattle. It took forever. This was what they meant by *dialing a phone*. He carried the handset around the corner into the little den for privacy. Brigitte should be between classes right now. He had to talk to her. Had to.

He listened for a ring, his heart racing, but the call went straight to her voice mail. Her phone was off. David's insides seemed to empty out. He squeezed his eyes shut and forced himself to calm down. Hanging up, he headed straight for his room. At least he had a room to escape to.

He hated that he was here. His mother had used Grandma Waters's surgery as an excuse to drag him away from Brigitte.

Brigitte. Her name was a wail in his head.

Up the stairs, he saw Lady was sitting outside his door. Was she waiting for him? He slowed as he approached to keep from scaring her, then crouched and held out his hand. She took a gingerly sniff. "You lonely, girl?" *Me, too.*

The dog watched him, rigid and wary, but her tail

made one flop onto the wood. A *yes* that warmed his heart.

"I should warn you that she howls at night."

He turned to look at Marcus Barnard, who'd come up behind him. "I wouldn't blame you if you wanted a different room."

"It's all right." David knew how the dog felt. He'd howl, too, if they wouldn't put him in a mental hospital for it. Already, he had to see a shrink. "Why is she so sad?"

"She misses her owner."

"Where is he?"

"He died. About a year ago."

"Wow." Looking again into Lady's sad eyes, he felt his own sorrow well up and his eyes start to water. "Sorry, girl."

Marcus cleared his throat. "She could use a friend and she seems to like you."

"Yeah?" Would she come into his room? He opened his door and stepped inside. "Want in, girl?"

Lady shivered, whined and stepped toward him, then back. She sat again. David's heart sank.

"Give her time." Marcus acted so calm, like nothing could shock him. He was a psychiatrist, so maybe nothing did.

"Yeah. Sure. Thanks." He closed the door, leaving Lady outside. Maybe she thought he needed guarding.

Inside his room, David felt worse. He'd thought it

would be cool to have his own place, like in a hotel, but it smelled dusty and neglected and the bed was creaky-ancient and he didn't have any of his posters. This wasn't his place. It was a beat-up cell in a nowhere prison. He didn't even have Internet.

To calm down, he fished a joint from his small stash, then the bag of Cheetos he'd brought from home. He meant to eat only organic from the commune like he and Brigitte had discussed, but that goat cheese had tasted like ass.

He took a giant hit, then flopped onto the bed. From the ice chest he'd put beside his bed he popped a can of Dr Pepper. He would quit junk food once he felt better.

He wanted back to Phoenix *now*. Brigitte was going to a bunch of parties this weekend. He'd miss the whole summer with her. In August, she was doing a backpack-hitchhike deal, heading to Seattle, then across the country. By Thanksgiving, she'd be in Europe. If he didn't lose his nerve, he'd go with her, screw school. It was all a fascist factory of mind control anyway.

He took another toke, holding it in a long time, but the pot didn't erase how raw he felt inside. He should run. Hitch a ride to the pathetic town and take the bus home. If a bus even came to New Mirage.

If he knew how to drive, he'd borrow the Volvo, or one of the commune's pickups or, hell, maybe that school bus of Bogie's painted with hippie crap.

Brigitte would love how retro it was. But he didn't know how to drive because Christine said no permit until his grades went up.

She killed every hope every time.

David studied the smoke curling up from the spliff. His mom would go nuts if she knew he'd brought weed. *Every*thing freaked her out. She always had her eye on him, making him nuts with questions: *Where are you going? Who will be there? How's school? Do you like your English teacher? Are you using drugs? Promise me this, swear that, agree to x, never do y.*

His thoughts smeared and echoed. The bud was doing its trick. Good. He needed the world to blur. He took a long swallow of soda and a handful of the cheesy curls, which now tasted creamy and tangy and melted amazingly on his tongue.

Christine didn't know anything that went on inside him. Whenever he tried to say something real to her, she went pale and scared or red and mad.

At times like this, loaded, he thought about his father. If he only knew where he was. Christine refused to find him. She claimed he would disappoint David, hurt him, that he had a terrible temper, that he was a flake and a jerk.

David didn't believe that. His dad would relate to him. He would know that smoking a little dope was no big deal. David wasn't a druggie, he wasn't "using" like his mother claimed. Like he was on meth or heroin.

He'd done mushrooms a couple times, Ecstasy once and a kid at a party had some Vicodin, but that was just recreation. And he didn't do booze. Too harsh. He didn't *need* drugs.

All he needed was Brigitte. His mother hated her because she was older, because she had ideas of her own. So unfair. Thinking that sent the red flood into his head and he wanted to break something—a wall, a door, a window.

It scared him when he got this angry. His mother said that was how his father was. Even if it was true, he probably had good ways to handle it he could teach David.

Brigitte could always talk him down. Brigitte was his steady center. Brigitte was his life. He had to get to her.

So much burned inside him. He wrote stuff— poetry, mostly, like Brigitte, but also song lyrics. He should practice guitar. Once he got better he could compose. Except it took so long to get better. So, so long… And he'd be here so, so long….

He remembered Christine asking Marcus if he would jam with David, like David was a needy geek. He loved his mom, but she wanted to stroke his hair and read him bedtime stories like he was still five and scared of the dark.

He couldn't take her anymore. And he hated being mean to her. She'd be sad when he left with

Brigitte, but she should get it. She'd left home when she was a teenager, too.

Knock, knock. "Can we talk?" Christine again. He put on his headphones for her own good. If he opened the door he'd just hurt her again.

CHAPTER THREE

THE NEXT MORNING, when Christine opened her eyes and saw gauze over her bed, she shot bolt upright. *Where am I?*

Then her mosquito bites kicked in, itching madly, and it all came back to her. She flopped back onto the creaky, saggy mattress of her childhood bed.

Her cheek itched with a new bite. So did both elbows. Damn. Mosquito repellant and calamine lotion were going on her grocery list, no matter what David thought.

"We said breakfast, not lunch," Aurora grumbled when Christine met her in the kitchen for their visit to the clay works barn.

"It's only seven-thirty, Aurora," she said on a sigh.

"Well, let's go then," Aurora huffed.

Christine grabbed a slice of fruit bread and joined her mother, who was walking so slowly it seemed painful. Worry tightened Christine's chest. Twice, she reached to support her, but gave up, knowing her mother would slap her hand away.

The barn that housed Harmony House Clay

Works was cool and dim and smelled of moist earth. Sunlight slanting in from windows lit wide swaths of thick dust in the air. A crew of four young men shifted items from potter's wheels to shelves that already held drying pots, bowls and bells.

"Hey there." A woman in a red-paisley do-rag left the clay she was kneading, wiped her hands on her overalls and came close. "You must be Crystal," she said, holding out a callused hand. "I'm Lucy. Pleased to meecha."

"Happy to meet you, too."

"Lucy runs the show when I'm not here," Aurora said. "She'll tell you what she needs you to do. Lucy?"

"Mostly you'll handle the orders. Also make sure I got crew and clay. Help us load and carry when we're in a bind and such. I'll show you the books."

Lucy led Aurora and Christine to a makeshift table at the rear of the barn—plywood resting on sawhorses with beat-up bar stools for chairs. On top were a ledger, a small invoice pad, an index-card box and a clay-grimy calculator. Not much of an office, Christine thought with dismay.

"Is the income steady?" She flipped through the handwritten ledger.

"About half the year," Lucy said. "Trouble is we turn down jobs when it gets too busy."

"We get backed up," Aurora said, shrugging. "No big thing."

"That's a shame," Christine said, hating the idea of inefficiency or lost profits. Maybe this was an area she could help. "Do you have a Web site?"

"No. And no computers," Aurora said. "We're not a factory, Crystal."

"I've been telling her we could do a lot better with a Web site," Lucy said, her eyes lit with energy.

"That's absolutely true," Christine said. Aurora snorted.

"Take this order for wind chimes." Lucy motioned at a cardboard box full of ceramic bells. "This guy has a gift shop in Sedona. He looked for our Web site but no luck. He stuck to it and tried the phone book, but who knows how many sales we lose that way?"

"The kiln only holds so many pieces," Aurora said.

"Not if we add more shelves," Lucy insisted.

"And what about the crew? Huh?"

"We hire more when we need them," Lucy said. This was obviously an argument they'd had before.

"Maybe I could help with that," Christine said, not wanting Aurora to get upset. "I can probably get the design guy at my agency to put up a simple Web site for free. If we buy a cheap computer, you could see how it would work."

"Let's just get through a week or so," Aurora grumbled, shooting her a look. "Bogie's not up to much in the gardens and someone should supervise the animals—feeding, milking, collecting eggs. Plus, you have your own work, don't you?"

"If I can help your business, I want to." Aurora's dismissal of her ideas hurt, but she refused to let that show.

"We're fine as we are, Crystal."

Behind Aurora, Lucy shook her head. *No, we're not.*

"We were fine before you came, we'll be fine after you're gone. Because you *are* going…right?"

Before she could answer, the plea in her mother's question stopped her cold. *Her mother wanted her to stay?*

Christine felt her jaw drop. That made no sense. Aurora was as uncomfortable around Christine as Christine was around her. They'd be lucky to survive the summer without tearing into each other and Aurora wanted her to *stay?* She must be more frightened than Christine realized. Her heart squeezed at the thought.

"How about this? Before I leave, I'll be certain any change is dialed in tight. What do you say?"

"I don't know…." Her mother's pride surely would keep her from admitting she needed help.

"Marketing is my profession, Aurora," she said gently. "I'm good at it. Why not let me see what I can do for you?"

Aurora heaved a sigh. "No changes without approval from me or Lucy. We can't have a bunch of crazy stuff disrupting our operation."

"Of course not," she said, irritated by her mother's insult. *Crazy stuff.* Really. Enough already. She wanted to say so, but then she remembered what Marcus had said.

Focus on the work. He was right. The important thing was that there were improvements she could make here. And Aurora was feeling weak and out of control in the place she usually ran. "I won't do anything you don't approve of, Aurora," she said.

"As long as we're clear, then all right."

Behind Aurora, Lucy did a *yes* fist pump, which made Christine smile. Aurora lowered herself onto one of the benches, her breathing shaky. Was she too tired? "Lucy can show me the operation from here," Christine said. "Maybe you need to head back inside." To bed, to rest. *Please.*

Aurora waved off the idea. "You ever throw a pot, Crystal?"

"Throw a…?"

"Work with clay. Create something with your own two hands." Her mother's eyes were bright now, and full of mischief. "You want to see the operation, you gotta get your hands dirty."

"Okaaay…"

"I didn't start in until after you left, you know. It took a while to develop my style. Better late than never for you." Her mother pushed to her feet, arms trembling, and led Christine to a half-dozen pedal-powered potter wheels and motioned Christine onto a clay-splattered stool. "Now sit."

In for a penny, in for a pound, Christine thought, sitting. She'd have to share that with Marcus, when she told him his advice had worked.

"BUT I CAN'T *do* MY homework," David whined as Christine drove him into New Mirage for his first appointment with Dr. Mike. "Dial-up's too slow. It freezes all the time."

"You don't need the Internet once you've downloaded the assignments. Look, do you want to be a junior when school starts or not?" She gritted her teeth and twisted her hands on the steering wheel. Losing her temper wouldn't help a bit. "You made a deal, David."

"I'm sick of the deal. Let's go home. I hate it here. It's boring and stupid. There's nothing to do."

"There's plenty to do. You're just not doing any of it." He'd been assigned to work in the garden with Marcus and help Bogie in the greenhouse, but he was constantly wandering off. Sullen with her, full of complaints, he stayed mostly in his room, except when he talked to Brigitte, and he was sneaking in extra calls, Christine was certain.

David showed no improvement, but at least Christine had made progress at the clay works in the past week. The agency's designer was putting together the Web site using digital shots Christine had sent of Aurora's most beautiful pieces and Christine had been contacting previous clients about new orders, as well as generating new business with cold calls to tourist boutiques around the state. Maybe boosting the commune's income made Christine a slave to the capitalist overlords, but she didn't care. Aurora and Bogie must have huge medical bills to handle. This was a way Christine could help.

Aurora came out to the barn each morning to issue opinions, question everything and generally slow things down. The first two days, Christine steamed with annoyance, barely holding her tongue. But she gradually saw this was Aurora's way to hang on to the place a little. She looked so relieved when Christine would suggest Aurora head back to "handle things in the house," which was code for lying down.

Christine had downloaded heart surgery post-operative instructions and read them out loud to Aurora, over her strenuous objections. She was supposed to rest every day, take breaks between activities, avoid stairs, not cross her legs, not lift anything over five pounds and not drive.

The good news was that if she followed the rules, in six to eight weeks, she'd be back to normal, with decades of life ahead of her, which relieved Christine immensely.

Christine parked in front of Dr. Mike's office, which used to be a Laundromat, crossing her fingers that this visit would change things.

Dr. Mike wore an Indian tunic and flowing pants, and his office smelled of patchouli and was ringed with shelves of crystals, stoppered bottles of herbal remedies and books on alternative medicine. Okay, so not traditional therapy, but if the man helped David, Christine didn't care if he used a Ouija board and danced under a full moon.

Leaving David in his hands, Christine headed to Parsons Foods to pick up a few things. She saw that Susan Parsons was "filling in" at the register again and she reminded Christine of the dinner at her house Saturday night.

On her second day, Christine and Marcus had gone on a grocery run together and Susan had insisted they both come to supper and bring David to meet her twin sixteen-year-old sons. To get David friends, Christine would endure a night of Susan showing off her husband—she'd mentioned that he was *the mayor* at least five times before the groceries got bagged—and her, no doubt, perfect princess home.

Back at Dr. Mike's office, Christine wrote a check and walked a smiling David out to the car. Her hopes soared. Maybe this would help. In the car, she asked, "So how was it?"

"He looked into my eyes and told me my nutrition is bad."

"He what?" Christine's hopes dropped like stones. "Didn't you talk about your problems?"

"I don't have any problems. He said my irises were muddy, which means my bowels are blocked."

"Just great."

"He gave me some breathing exercises to clear

my heart chakra." He demonstrated, huffing while patting his stomach. "Then we talked about the Phoenix Coyotes. He likes hockey."

Dammit, Aurora. Dr. Mike was no more capable of counseling David than he was of doing Aurora's heart surgery.

"You're not going back there."

"Why not? It'll get the principal off your back."

"More roughage is not going to help us here. We'll have to find someone in Preston." Which meant a two-hour round-trip.

"Come on. He said he'd hypnotize me next time." David was clearly loving this. Christine shook her head. Now what?

"NOT THAT PLATTER, the swirled glaze one," Aurora ordered Christine, whose only wish was to keep the couscous as moist as her own skin in this boiling-hot kitchen.

She and Marcus had kitchen duty, instructed by Bogie and Aurora, who were supposedly resting, though Bogie had been up and down seasoning things and Aurora had been barking commands.

"If you'd keep the trays in the same place, it would be easier," Christine said, forcing herself not to snap at her mother. She was dying to say, *Go lie down, for Pete's sake.*

"Here you go." Marcus handed Christine the tray. It was one of her mother's surreal creations in green, blue and turquoise. "And the serving utensil and leftover pita she's about to tell you about." He winked. "Saving you time."

"Thanks," she said, vividly aware of how close he stood.

After a week of seeing Marcus, mostly at meals, Christine could no longer deny how attracted she was. Whenever he was near, she felt a low electric hum start up inside. It was delicious. She wasn't going to *do* anything about it, it was just...fun.

She rarely dated, but when she did she kept it casual and mostly physical. She had David and engrossing work, of course. Plus she'd been burned the few times she'd gotten serious by charmers who let her down—like David's father, Skip—or pursued her relentlessly until she fell for them, then disappeared or went cold on her.

Not good. Her judgment when it came to relationships plain reeked. Short-term hookups were fine for now. Maybe some day, when she got smarter, less emotional or developed better mating instincts, she'd go for more, the whole picket-fence deal.

Marcus felt the attraction, too, she could tell. It was thrilling to get a man as restrained as Marcus all charged up. She liked making him laugh, too. And talking to him. She realized she didn't spend much relaxed social time with men, so this was a nice change.

It was all good fun. She enjoyed the tease and retreat and he seemed to, too. She had too much on her hands with David, her mother and her work to even think about sex. Well, she could think about it. But that was *it*.

Marcus seemed equally reluctant, pulling back from any accidental contact, when they brushed hips in the entry to the dining room or tangled fingers over the dishes they washed.

Marcus had the goulash pot in both hands and gestured for her to pass in front of him. She did, then glanced over her shoulder to catch him watching her backside.

She got that roller-coaster dip in her stomach. "Watch your step," she said, nodding at the bump in the floorboard, but she was grinning and he cleared his throat.

This was such a kick.

At the entrance to the dining room, Christine paused to admire the rough-wood table holding the ceramic plates in her mother's singular style, the pewter flatware and Mason jar water glasses. Bogie had let David choose the cuttings for the bouquet of fragrant herbs, river bamboo and exotic amaryllis in the center of the table. There were ten people at the table tonight.

Aurora and Bogie emerged with the salad and bread and Christine handed the couscous to the wife of the hiking couple, Lisa Manwell, who loaded up, then passed to Carl, a scary guy with the smeared ink of a prison tattoo. Aurora said he was a teddy bear and Bogie declared him a wizard of a mechanic who kept the school bus purring. If he didn't murder them all in their sleep, Christine would be grateful.

The good karma here is too strong for anything negative, Aurora had told her. Lord. No wonder her mother liked Dr. Mike.

"Enjoy the bounty of the earth through our hands," Aurora said, head down. "May we all find here what we need."

Carl mumbled an amen. Silently, Christine put in her own request: *Please bring David back. Make us a family again.*

The commune food was grainy and dense, made with whole grains, lentils and beans, with Middle Eastern spices, fresh and healthy and there was always plenty. It had taken Christine forever to get the dirt off the tender lettuce and celery Marcus had picked for the salad that afternoon.

"So you're in high school?" The question for David came from Gretchen, across the table, a pretty twentysomething poet on retreat. Beside her were two college students, Mitch and Louis, researching sustainable living for a college project.

"I'll be a junior," David answered, his face aflame, "but school's bullshit."

"David!" Christine said, embarrassed by the swear word. The Manwells exchanged disapproving glances.

"Creativity can suffer in school, for sure," Gretchen said.

"That's what my girlfriend says. She writes poetry. Also political pieces. She's really good."

Christine's heart clutched at his wistful tone and lovesick look. A week hadn't eased his feelings for Brigitte at all.

"Do you drive?" Gretchen asked him.

"Not yet." He glared at Christine. Learning to drive had been a sore subject. She'd said no permit without a B average.

"Hell, you can learn while you're here," Aurora said.

"He doesn't have a permit," Christine said.

"Who cares?"

"I care. It's illegal."

"We rarely see a deputy, so who'd write the ticket?" Aurora waved away the issue like a gnat over her plate.

"Aurora…"

"I might as well learn. I've got nothing else to do."

"Now isn't the time to talk about this," she said quietly.

"It's *never* the time with *you*," David blurted. He'd been in a bad mood since his call to Brigitte. He looked around, clearly aware of how rude he'd sounded, jerked to his feet, knocking off his knife and loudly scraping his chair before he stomped away.

"Teenagers," Christine finally said into the awkward silence. Heads nodded. Forks clicked, water glasses clinked.

"Kids are so out of control these days," Lisa Manwell said. "It's shameful. My sister's teens rule the house."

Christine bit her tongue to keep from suggesting Lisa try a stroll in her sister's Free Spirits before she criticized her.

"Since Socrates, adults have thought kids ran wild and parents were lax," Aurora said, winking at Christine. "That's how you know you're old, when you start saying, *kids today....*"

Lisa sniffed at the insult.

"David's a good kid," Aurora said.

"Thank you." Christine was touched by her mother's kindness. Aurora really was trying to do what they'd agreed—support Christine's parenting of David.

"He's at loose ends out here in the country," she said. "So let him drive, Crystal. Where's the harm?"

Lord. So much for Aurora's good intentions. "How about if I get the dessert?" Christine said, happy to escape to the kitchen. Marcus stood and began gathering plates.

Taking a knife from the cupboard to slice the cinnamon carrot bread, she noticed the phone was missing its handset. The cord stretched around the corner into her office alcove.

David sat on the floor there, knees up, back to

her, his voice low and fervent. "I've got to see you. I'm so alone here. Christine's such a…she's so… Exactly. Controlling. I hate her."

Christine's cheeks stung, as if she'd been slapped. He didn't really mean that, but it still hurt. She tried to back away without being seen, but when he saw her, she knew she had to say something about the rule. "You already called today. You need to hang up."

He covered the phone and gave her a desperate look. "This is all I have. Do you want me to go psycho?" He said into the phone, "Yeah, she's making me hang up. I'm sorry. 'Bye." He jerked to his feet, charged around the corner and slammed down the receiver. "Are you happy? You made my life a complete hell."

Marcus was slicing the bread, so he'd heard.

"I'm simply asking you to keep your word, David."

"No, you're not. You hate Brigitte and you want to break us up. You can cut me off from everyone I care about, but you can't change me. I'll never be your perfect son with straight As and straight friends, on the student freaking council."

"That's not what I want and you know it."

His eyes flashed with a hatred that scared her. "I don't have to stay here, you know. I can leave."

"That wouldn't solve anything." This was the first time he'd threatened to run away and it terrified her.

"If I found my father it would."

"What?" Skip was the last thing David needed at the moment. Angry, flaky and mean, Skip would break David's heart for sure.

"Just because you won't look for him, doesn't mean I can't." Skip's bad credit history meant he never had a listed number, thank God, but still...

"That's not what you want, David," she said as kindly as she could manage.

"You don't know what I want." He brushed past her, pausing when he noticed Marcus holding the tray of bread, then barreled out the back door.

She wanted to go after him, but she knew better. David needed to cool off before they talked. *Talked.* Right. It had become a pointless exercise. He stonewalled every question. Christine fought despair.

"I can take over," she said to Marcus, putting her hands beneath the tray, enjoying the comfort of his warm fingers for an instant. She liked that his face showed neither pity nor embarrassment over the outburst.

Together they served the dessert and when it was over started on the dishes, since *cooking means cleanup* was a commune rule. She tried to stay cheerful, but David's anger was wearing her down. She'd begun to become discouraged.

"I'm sorry you heard that fight," she said, glancing at Marcus. "Living with his father would be a disaster for David."

"'The grass always seems greener...'"

"More folk-saying therapy?" She couldn't quite

smile. "You probably think it's bad that I won't let him see his father, but if you knew Skip..."

"You don't need to justify yourself to me, Christine."

"He would break David's heart." She scrubbed fiercely at the plate she was cleaning, then plopped it into the rinsing sink so hard that water splashed Marcus's face. "Sorry, sorry." She brushed away the drops from his smooth cheek.

"I'm fine, Christine," he said, low and reassuring, catching her hand in his.

The touch felt so good, she just stood there letting him hold her hand and look into her eyes, sending calm all the way through her.

She blew out a breath, then went back to the dishes, more gently this time. "Skip calls now and then, drunk or stoned, wanting to *connect* with David. I used to set up a day and time for him, but he always bailed. Thank God I never told David in advance. The man is an overgrown child, so distractible, with a scary temper—" She wiped a blob of lentils from a plate.

"Lately, I just let the machine take his calls." A month before, he'd left her his most recent number and address.

She paused for Marcus to comment, but he kept rinsing and stacking, allowing her to fill the silence if she chose.

"Even if Skip did show up, he'd throw out piein-the-sky promises, then break them. David is too vulnerable now."

She stopped washing and turned to him. "Don't you think waiting until he's eighteen is better? He'll have more maturity to put the hurt in perspective and by then he'll be done hating me." She managed a half smile.

"Are you asking for my professional opinion again?"

"Would you give it to me? In an emergency?"

"I'm in no position to give advice," he said. A shadow crossed his face and she realized her request disturbed him more than he had let on. "Want to hand me those?" he said, indicating the dishes she'd let pile up while she talked.

She wanted to ask him about that, but he was sending out leave-it-alone signals like mad, so she stuck to the dishes, glancing at him now and then. He had such a strong face—straight nose, solid jaw and a great mouth, sensual and masculine. His hair brushed his collar, as if he'd been too busy for a haircut and he smelled of a lime aftershave with a hint of sandalwood.

His presence calmed her, as well as the slow, sure movements of his strong hands. He was so *quiet*. "If I didn't talk, would you ever break the silence?" she finally said.

"Excuse me?" He stopped rinsing and looked at her.

"You hardly ever talk," she said.

"When I need to, I do."

"So is it that after all those years of listening to people bitch and moan, you've had enough?"

His mouth twitched. She'd amused him. That felt like a prize.

"Meanwhile, I hate silence. I say whatever comes into my head. I'm probably annoying the hell out of you, huh?"

"No. I enjoy you. Kitchen duty is flying by."

"That's flattering. I'm more amusing than greasy plates."

He laughed, looking almost boyish. "I didn't mean it quite like that, no."

"You have a great laugh," she said. "You should do it more."

He pondered that. "You think I'm too serious?"

"At times, I guess. But I like how you are, Marcus." She touched his forearm and felt another, stronger frisson of desire. "You're…soothing."

"I *soothe* you?" He lifted an eyebrow, looking wry. "That's not exactly flattering, either."

"Well, you have other effects on me, too," she said softly, moving closer. "The opposite of soothing."

"I see." Heat sparked in his eyes, but only for an instant. Then his eyes went sad, almost haunted, and she sucked in a breath. Something awful had happened to Marcus. She wondered if she'd ever find out what it was.

CHAPTER FOUR

MARCUS LEFT THE KITCHEN as soon as the dishes were done, saying he needed to work on his book, but he was clearly avoiding more sexual byplay or, perhaps, thoughts of the old hurt he'd remembered. Possibly his ex-wife?

What if he withdrew altogether? Christine would hate that. He provided the only spice and spark to her time at Harmony House. Dammit. For all its thrills, sex could be such a pain. If she lost Marcus's friendship because of her stupid libido…

What did he think about her anyway? Men were a puzzle to her. Maybe because she'd never really known her father and had only Harmony House's hippies and drifters as examples of manhood. There was Bogie, of course, who was sweet, but mostly a ghost in her life.

Her first sex with Dylan had confused and kind of scared her. After that came Skip, a smooth operator who'd promised much and given little, then one, two, three more screwups before she finally learned her lesson—hold back her heart, stick with short-term fun and friendship.

She didn't blame her past or anything. She'd screwed up all on her own. But she wished to hell she was better with men.

Christine closed the last cupboard and sighed. Time to try to talk with David.

Outside the front door, the porch smelled of sunscorched wood, reminding her of summer, returning wet and shivery from a swim in the river to dig into a slice of watermelon warm from the garden, spitting seeds at the other kids, letting the juice run down her chin, not caring about being neat at all.

The porch, with its rockers, wooden swing and cable spool tables had always been a popular hangout for talk, cards, music or watching people play Frisbee or dance in the yard.

"Nice night." Aurora's voice, from a rocking chair, startled her out of her reverie.

"Yes, it is."

"Where you headed?" her mother asked, sipping iced tea, the ice cubes rattling gently in her glass.

"To check on David. We had an argument."

"I'd leave him be if I were you."

Christine bit back a sharp response. Aurora had hardly been Parent of the Year and now she was dishing out advice? Christine forced down her spike of outrage and sank into the fabric hammock for a moment. Now was as good a time as any to update Aurora on the clay works.

Organizing her thoughts, she ran her hands over

the colorful braids that formed the hammock. "I recognize this cloth. Where's it from?"

"It used to be my bedspread. Bogie made the hammock. He can make you one if you like. He does that for people."

"Maybe we could sell them. Handcrafted at a commune? I bet the gift shops where we're placing our ceramics would buy tons."

Her mother chuckled. "You *are* a slave to profit. David's right." She was in a good mood at least.

"We all have our gifts." Christine fingered the familiar cloth, lost in memory for a moment. She'd loved her mother's bed, the smell of vanilla and patchouli, the orange light through the Indian-print curtains on the window.

"I liked your waterbed…the way it jiggled. You used to tell me stories sometimes." When Aurora allowed it, Christine would cuddle up to her, toying with her mother's thick braid while Aurora talked and talked.

"You and your endless questions," Aurora said. "You were relentless."

"They were mostly about my father," she said, remembering vividly. "You would never tell me much about him."

"It wasn't relevant." She locked gazes with Christine. "Do you tell David all about Skip?"

"Skip is a train wreck. My father was a good man." A police officer who died in the line of duty when Christine was three.

"I told you he loved you. That should have been enough."

"I wanted to know everything." She remembered the gold buttons on his blue uniform, and the smell of leather and aftershave. "You didn't even save a picture."

Aurora shrugged. That was that. End of topic.

Christine felt a stab of the helpless feeling she used to get over Aurora's stubborn silences—wanting so much to know about her father and having Aurora lock him away and toss the key. At least Christine had grown out of that pointless pain.

All she wanted now was to keep this fragile peace with her mother until it was time to leave. They were too different, her mother too shut down for them to ever be close, which had been her old stupid fantasy.

"You went ahead and bought that computer, didn't you?" Aurora said gruffly.

"It was a good price, so, yes."

"But you didn't clear it with me. We agreed—"

"It was the one you chose, Aurora, with the features you liked, remember?" Her mother had pored over the catalog Christine had searched out on her laptop. "Tomorrow I want to show you the draft of the Web site. Also the PayPal account."

"PayPal? This is the first I've heard of that," she snapped, eyes sparking in the dim light of the porch.

"You wanted something easy to manage, remember? Lucy and I worked out the details. If you don't like it we'll change it."

Her mother rocked angrily for a few seconds.

Christine took a slow breath and blew it out. Why did this bother her so much? She never got testy with clients when they second-guessed her. Only Aurora made her temper flare. "Also, I can get agency rates for some advertising at key venues that I know will generate more orders. If that's all right, I'd like to set that up."

"I told you before we're not an assembly line."

Calm, calm, calm. Lucy had asked her to push this issue with Aurora, so Christine would do her best. "Lucy and I worked out a plan. By enhancing the kiln, adding a second shift, plus some on-call part-timers, it'll be easy. No worries for you or pressure. In your condition, you need low stress, so—"

"You let *me* worry about my *condition*." Her mother glared at her. "You could stand to lower your stress, too. You act like if you hold still for one minute the world will stop turning."

Christine closed her eyes to collect herself. She tried to rise above, but her mother's digs and grumbles stung like sandpaper on a sunburn. "It's your show, Aurora. If you don't want ads, we won't buy ads. But Lucy is getting frustrated. If you don't watch it, you'll lose her."

Her mother stopped rocking and seemed to consider that. "Just be sure you stick around until every kink is worked out, like you said you would." There was that underlying plea again: *Please stay.*

The request felt like a weight on Christine's chest, making it hard to breathe. She couldn't stay. No way. David hated it here, for one thing. He had school and she had plans to open her own agency. She had a life in Phoenix. Here was an awkward limbo.

She comforted herself with the thought that Aurora must be feeling weak still. As soon as she was herself again, she'd probably pack Christine's bags herself.

"I'll stay until you boot me out. How's that?" she said, using the cheery voice of a nurse with a grumpy patient.

"See that you do," Aurora said, as if she'd won a fight. "And do something with your room before you go. Paint it, replace that god-awful furniture with stuff from the spare room. That pink-and-gingham mess depresses the hell out of me."

Great. Another mean zing to Christine's heart. So much for Bogie's claim that Aurora meditated about Christine in the room she'd kept the same all these years. The man lived in a sunny-side-up haze.

"Well, I like my old room," Christine said just to be stubborn. "It's darling. It makes me think of fairy tales." She grinned.

"Good God," her mother groused, looking off across the yard in the dark to where mesquite trees were silhouetted by moonlight. Was she smiling? Maybe.

Mission accomplished, more or less, so Christine rose from the hammock to go to David.

"You do need to cut David some slack," Aurora said.

Anger spiked in Christine. *Do not yell. Stay calm.* "Excuse me, Aurora, but you have no idea what I've been through with him this last year."

"I see what I see."

Christine made herself count to ten—twice. "You promised to back me up with him."

"I *am* backing you up. I told him to follow the rules."

"And urged him to drive a car without a license."

Aurora shrugged. "It's summer vacation. He's away from his friends. Give him a break."

"*A break?* I had to beg the principal not to expel him. He's got schoolwork he has to do if there's any hope he can rescue enough credits to be a junior. Plus, we agreed to therapy. Real therapy, not crackpot tips from Doctor Mike, who got his doctorate from Wacko State University."

"Doctor Mike is a great guy."

"He's a joke. Now I have to find someone in Preston."

"Anything else I did wrong?"

"Since you asked, I don't like David in such a faraway room. The last thing he needs is more freedom."

"You weren't much older when you left home, you know."

"You think that was a good thing?" It was the loneliest she'd ever felt.

"It was what you wanted." Her mother rocked back and forth.

She so much wanted to yell, but she kept her voice level. "I was a *kid*. I didn't know what I wanted." Aurora hadn't even tried to stop her. Christine had hung back for a good hour before buying her bus ticket, secretly hoping Aurora would come to get her. But Aurora had let her go. Just like that.

"I will not leave my son to struggle on his own."

"Like I did you?" Aurora said. Christine was startled to see hurt flicker in her mother's brown eyes. "It was your life, Crystal. Holding you back would have made me a hypocrite after all I preached about choice and self-determination."

"Sorry, but I was your daughter, not a political statement," she said fiercely. Bitter hurt rose from deep within her. Maybe Aurora loved her, but it wasn't any love Christine recognized—then or now.

Aurora didn't speak for a long moment and when she did, her tone was softer. "All I know is that my folks tried to lock me in and it made me desperate to escape. I did, but I had a weak moment when I found I was pregnant. The best thing they ever did was not let me back in. It made me stronger. That's what leaving did for you. It made you independent."

Not even close. Christine had been lost and scared

and lonely until she'd latched on to Skip, a life raft in rough waters, she'd thought…until he dumped her into the deep again.

But that was old news. She'd learned and grown, so what was the point in rehashing it? What mattered now was David. "David's growing up too fast. He needs to catch up with himself."

"It's the nature of kids to break away."

"It's the nature of kids to change their minds on a dime."

Her mother sighed. "You were always so sure you were right. You had these pictures in your head of home, family, work, life, and nothing ever measured up. You wore me out."

The feeling's mutual. But saying so would not help. "All I ask is that you don't undercut my authority with my son and—"

Aurora bent forward and coughed, holding on to her chest, her face tight with pain.

"Are you all right?" Panic surged inside Christine. She'd let her anger show and it had upset her ill mother. "Can I get you water? A pain pill?" She felt sick. She'd picked a fight with a fragile woman, not the hard-as-nails, blunt mother she'd grown up with. Shame on her.

"Stop that. My stitches burn when I cough, that's all."

"I didn't mean to agitate you. I'm here to help and—"

"I said stop it, dammit. I'm not dying. I'm fine.

Better than ever." Aurora pushed up from her chair and stomped toward the door. Reaching it, she hesitated, then turned around. "Hell, that's not how I meant that to go."

She lifted a hand as if to reach out to Christine, then dropped it. "So…just…good night then," she said, disappearing without waiting for Christine's response.

When they next got together, Aurora would behave as if they'd never quarreled. That was how she handled conflict—stir it up, then let it simmer forever.

Christine should never have argued with her. What folk saying would Marcus offer? *Think before you speak? Respect your elders?* Something like that. Dammit. She ought to be better at this by now.

She headed down the porch steps to try to talk to David, hoping she wouldn't blow it with him, too. At his door, she heard loud music, so she knew he wasn't wearing headphones, but when she knocked and called his name, he didn't answer. "I'm sorry about the phone," she called to him through the door. "Can we talk a little?"

Nothing.

Oooh, so frustrating. She wanted to break down the door, *make* him talk to her, anything but suffer this sullen stew of tension that would last for days. His closed door was a cry for help, she knew. She was here to answer it, but he'd locked her out. Again.

A sharp sensation at her neck had her slapping at a mosquito. Further exploration revealed three new bites on her neck. Also her upper arm and her shin, she realized, scratching both places. So much for the bug spray. Worse, the lotion she'd bought at Parsons didn't soothe the itching one bit.

"David!" she called one last time, resting her forehead on the unmoving door. Hopeless.

Then she noticed guitar music coming from downstairs. It had to be Marcus. Surely he wouldn't refuse to talk to her. She'd be careful not to chase him off by flirting too much.

She found him on the top step of the side porch and sat close by, bracing her back against a post.

He shot her a quick smile, taking her in with his eyes, while still playing. "David all right?"

"I have no idea. He won't let me in, he won't answer me, he won't talk." She kicked off her athletic shoes and pressed her toes into the warm wood, worn smooth by passing years and feet.

"He knows you care. He might need privacy to think."

"When I was his age, I'd have given anything for Aurora to come to me to talk through a quarrel." She shrugged. "So you're saying it's a good thing I didn't use a battering ram on his door?"

"Very wise move."

She sighed. "Meanwhile, I picked a fight with Aurora."

"One step forward…" He lifted an eyebrow.

"Two steps back? Thank you Dr. Folk Wisdom. I keep trying to not let her hurt my feelings, but I can't seem to resist." She glanced at him, but he was focusing on his guitar, playing the Beatles' song "Blackbird."

"That sounds so nice," she said, breathing out. "Wish you'd been there when I was talking to her. What's that saying? Music hath charm to soothe the savage…daughter?"

He laughed his low, masculine laugh and sexual desire washed through her. Jeez, all the man had to do was laugh to turn her on. *Get over it.*

"I definitely need to be more Zen." She crossed her legs, hands upturned on her knees in a lotus pose, eyes closed.

"Sorry. I don't see that happening." When she opened her eyes, his were teasing and twinkling. More lust washed through her. What would Marcus be like in bed? Quiet or noisy? Fire or ice? Gentle or rough?

Stop that this minute.

"You're probably right. I'm so not Zen." She broke the gaze and dropped her pose. "David's problem is Brigitte. And it's my fault they even met. I nagged him into this writer's club and there she was, too old, too smart, and David hung on her every word."

She scratched the bites on her neck, then the one on her shin.

Marcus kept playing.

"You know what she told me once? She doesn't wear underwear because it blocks the root chakra. Can you believe that?"

Marcus laughed.

"You wouldn't find it so funny if you were the parent."

"Perhaps not. No."

"Do you think David might run away?" The thought sent a jolt of fear through her.

Marcus stopped playing. "He seems to be exploring the power he wields in your relationship."

"By scaring the crap out of me?"

"Typically, an outburst like the one in the kitchen relieves the tension, especially if the parent doesn't escalate the stressors."

"You mean if I keep my mouth shut?"

He just smiled.

"Okay, I'll try not to overreact. Any more advice? And, please, no folk sayings. I'm serious."

"A couple of things, I guess. When he erupts, acknowledge the emotion he's displaying without criticism. *You seem angry…. You sound hurt…. I can hear how upset you are….* Once he feels heard, he'll calm down and handle the problem more reasonably."

"That makes sense…until I'm in the middle of it with him. He pushes all my buttons."

"That's because he installed them," he said.

"I thought we agreed no more folk wisdom tonight."

"Sorry. Also, you might try not engaging over every poorly chosen word in an argument. If you can take a moment to catch your breath, you'll be less likely to exacerbate the conflict."

"Easier said than done."

"If it were easy, there would be no psychiatrists."

"Ah, so this is job security for you?" She smiled.

"I'm not telling you anything you don't already know or do, Christine. Trust your instincts and you'll be fine."

She liked Marcus's attitude. He didn't judge her or discount her ideas, or make too much of her mistakes. And when she talked, he listened so closely, tracking each hesitation, every change in her tone.

She'd bet he'd been a damn good shrink. Which reminded her of David and Dr. Mike. "By the way, Dr. Mike turned out to be a bust, so do you know any therapists in Preston?"

"Sorry, no. My friend Carlos lives there though. He runs the New Mirage clinic. I can ask him for you."

"That would be great," she said, then decided to take a stab at Plan B. "I was thinking, though, about what you said about the therapist needing to be someone David relates to…?"

"Yes…?"

"I've seen David talking with you in the garden and I know he likes you, so I was wondering if you'd consider maybe—"

"Treating him? I don't see clients, Christine. I told you that."

"It wouldn't be official or anything. An informal chat, you know? Every few days maybe?"

"Listen to me. I'm not who you want for your son. Period." His words were abrupt, almost angry, which startled her.

"Okay," she said. "I guess I have a hard time with no."

"Yes, you do." He shot her a brief smile to ease the moment. "I'm sure there are fine therapists in Preston."

"And plenty of quacks, too."

"Most therapists will set up a phone interview so you can assess their approach. You'll find someone, I'm sure."

That was that. Worth a try, but no dice.

Marcus went back to his guitar, playing something Celtic, fast and wild, the melody line flying from deep despair to soaring ecstasy.

It was wonderfully distracting, she realized, and sank into the moment, the music, the man beside her. She smelled eucalyptus, the metallic scent of the river and traces of creosote. River toads were carrying on, croaking and chirping and groaning out their needs. Crickets rasped away from beneath the porch.

Moonlight cascaded over the front yard, making it look exotic instead of dusty and abandoned as it had when she'd arrived. She felt better, she realized. "It's nice out here, huh? I was so miserable as a kid, I never noticed."

"Home always seems different when we've changed."

She blinked. "Wow, good one. That was yours, right?"

He shrugged.

"I have changed, I guess. Grown up some anyway. Though around Aurora my thirty-five years seem to melt away."

She focused on Marcus's fingers, so confident on the strings. There was that empty ring finger again. Was he seeing someone? It was only natural to wonder. "Do you get lonely way out here?" she asked. "I mean compared to L.A.?"

"Why would I? There's plenty to do."

"You can be busy and lonely at the same time, Marcus."

He didn't respond, merely played something quieter.

"I liked what Aurora said at dinner tonight. *May we all find here what we need.*" She studied him. "What about you, Marcus? I know you're working on a book and all, but why here?"

He dropped his fingers from the strings and

looked at her. "It was Carlos, I guess. I needed a quiet place and he thought I'd like Harmony House. The physical labor clears my head and at night I have the time and space to think and write. The stars are nice." He looked up at the sky.

She looked up, too. "Kind of scary," she said. "All that space and blackness, the stars so tiny. It makes me feel small."

"Yeah?" When she looked over, he was watching her face.

"What do you want from Harmony House? You're here for your mother and David, I know, but what about for you?"

"Me? I don't know…." His close attention made her want to really think about her answer. "I want to make a difference here, make things better. I'm in advertising and I love when my work boosts a company's profits, so I'd like that. Mainly it's David I'm concerned about."

She scratched absently at her new mosquito bites. "I feel so at sea with him. In the old days, we got along great. David was kind and thoughtful, a good friend, reasonably responsible, and he *talked* to me…about everything. Now…" She shrugged, feeling as lost and small as she did surveying the cold black sky with its icy spikes of stars.

Marcus watched her, waiting for her to speak.

"I'd heard puberty was hell, but I didn't expect this. It's like someone switched off the lights in a strange room. I keep banging my knees on sharp corners I can't see."

"That's an interesting image."

"I wish it weren't so apt." She slapped at a mosquito that had landed on her upper arm, then scratched at the other bites. "Mosquitoes are driving me nuts."

"You've got quite a collection of bites, I see." Marcus reached for her arm, turning it this way and that. "Six just on your forearm." She liked the gentle warmth of his fingers.

"Only the beginning. Twenty-five yesterday, plus five news ones tonight." She showed him the places. "And the calamine I bought is useless."

"In that case…I make a salve that works pretty well."

"You *make* a salve? Really?"

"I grow some herbs at home and mix a remedy or two."

"You have some with you? Here?"

"In my room, yes."

"Then let's go." She jumped to her feet.

Marcus sat there blinking at her.

"Come on. This is an emergency."

CHAPTER FIVE

WHY DIDN'T HE JUST bring the ointment down to her? Marcus asked himself, following Christine up the stairs, his gaze caught by the lift of her calves, the curve of her backside.

He knew when she got into his room, she'd treat his belongings like she treated him—poking, prodding, asking too many questions. The woman was so full of heat and crackle, she made him want lie in the dark under an ice pack.

Upstairs, Lady waited outside his door. When they approached, she let out a gut-wrenching howl, then galloped away, down the stairs and across the yard toward the trees.

"What was that about?" Christine asked.

"She misses...her previous owner." He opened the door and strode inside.

"So how did you get her?" She moved in front of him, wanting the whole story. There was no point evading her.

"Lady belonged to my stepson, Nathan. He died a year ago and my ex-wife couldn't bear to have her around."

"Oh, I'm so sorry." She looked as though she'd been punched.

"It's all right. You had no way to know." He shouldn't have been so blunt. "So, about the salve…"

"How terrible for you both. Were you close to Nathan?"

"As close as he'd allow me to be. He was thirteen when I began dating his mother. He was fifteen when he died."

"Fifteen?" She covered her mouth. "That's David's age."

"Yes. And, actually, David resembles Nathan in physical appearance. I think that might be why Lady was so drawn to him. Since Nathan's death, she's been inconsolable."

He wouldn't tell her the rest—that Lady's mournful cries burned through him like fire-tipped arrows, a fitting punishment for believing he had anything to offer Elizabeth or Nathan in the first place.

"Let me get the salve." He started forward, but she stopped him with a hand at his elbow.

"I'm so sorry, Marcus. What happened? A car accident? Illness? I mean, unless you don't want to talk about it…"

Of course he didn't. But after all the nights he'd lain awake rehashing the events while Lady howled, telling the story could hardly make him feel worse.

"It was an accidental drug overdose. Heroin and

fentanyl, which is very easy to OD on, especially for a new user."

"Oh, no. Was he living at home at the time?"

"Yes. I broke down the door to the bathroom to get to him. Elizabeth was away, thank God."

"I can't imagine how awful that must have been."

"I had no idea he was using needles. He'd had a scare snorting heroin and talked to me about it, so I thought he'd turned a corner. I was wrong."

"You can't read their minds, I know that for sure."

He should have done more, intervened somehow. Irrational as it was, the idea hounded him. "It was much harder on Elizabeth. She didn't want to believe he'd been using drugs at all, let alone heroin." His throat tightened. Enough of this. "Let me get the cream."

He went to the cabinet over the sink, where he kept the salve, and handed her the jar, tilting his head toward the door, suggesting they leave. She studied him, absorbing what he'd told her, no doubt, looking concerned.

"Here. Let's give it a try." He took the jar, opened it and held it out to her.

It took her a few seconds to notice. She scooped some onto a finger and sniffed it. "It smells good. Green. Herbal."

All he smelled was Christine's spring scent.

She rubbed a little on the bites on her forearm.

"Oooh, that's better," she said, breathing out in relief.

She scooped more and applied it to her other arm, moaning the whole time. After that she braced one bare foot on his chair to rub it into her long, long leg. To avoid the hypnotic sight of all that stroking of attractive body parts, he pretended to study the items on his desk.

Eventually she finished with her legs. "Oh, this really helps!" She bobbed on the balls of her feet. "Would you get my neck and back?" She handed him the jar, spun around and lifted her hair off her shoulders.

He groaned inwardly.

"Marcus?"

"Yes, uh, certainly." He lifted a blob of salve and rubbed over the red areas on the back of her slender neck, her skin supple and soft.

She gave a little moan, something like how she might sound making love. "That's so *niiice*," she said.

"Glad to hear it," he said and cleared his throat.

She dropped her hair, sending a wave of sweet smell his way, then lifted the back of her top, revealing a black bra.

He sighed and scooped out more salve and began to gingerly apply it to the crop of bumps on her upper back.

"Hang on," she said, fingering the clasp. "Underneath are more." She flicked the thing apart, exposing three more bites and her entire back to his gaze. "That's easier, right?"

"Mmm-hmm." *And so much harder.* He used his entire palm to smooth the balm over her back, using circular motions, the muscles sliding beneath his fingers. She relaxed into the pressure, making appreciative sounds, hums and moans and breathy sighs. He found himself rubbing longer than strictly necessary, picturing her naked with him, imagining the sounds she might make then....

"Thanks," she said breathlessly, stepping away from his hand, which felt as warm as if he'd been clutching a hot coffee.

He had to clear his throat again to speak. "Very welcome."

She pulled the two sides of her bra together, but struggled with the hooks, so he took over, aware that this was the kind of intimate favor that lovers did for each other.

He did miss holding a woman close.

He pulled her top down and gave her a chaste pat. Physical needs merely complicated things. He was far better off keeping his distance. He never wanted to hurt anyone again. The medical directive fit him perfectly: Above all, do no harm.

She turned toward him, her eyes shining, her pupils dilated, her color up. "That felt great," she breathed. "I can't believe how much better I feel." She swayed closer, so near he could kiss her with the slightest dip of his mouth.

"I've been testing various, um, ratios of aloe to unguent," he said slowly, caught by her closeness, how lovely she was, how the pigment in her irises seemed to swirl with the same energy he felt pulsing in his veins.

"You nailed it," she said softly. "The formula's perfect."

He broke her gaze to screw the jar lid on and hold it out. "You can keep this."

"But what about your bites?"

"I don't seem to be as irresistible," he said.

"That depends on who you ask," she murmured, then seemed to catch herself and turned away. She seemed to inventory the room—his made bed, desk and computer, shelves of books and reports and file boxes of research. "It's so weird," she said. "The paint's darker and the posters are gone, but I think the furniture's the same as back then."

"You stayed in this room?"

She gave a short laugh. "I've been here, let's say. This was the room of a guy who was here for a while when I was sixteen. Dylan. He was older—twenty, I think." Her features tightened, but she forced a smile. "I lost my virginity on that very bed."

"Oh. Well." Her words startled him.

"It was kind of an accident. I was flirting, but he took me seriously. It kind of happened faster than, um, I intended."

"You were assaulted?"

"I didn't say no. And I didn't want to chicken out. Afterward, I cried. Which was dumb. I mean what was the big deal? At a certain point, virginity is stupid. Dylan took off the next day. I guess he was afraid I'd make a fuss."

"Did you talk to anyone about what happened? Your mother?" The experience was clearly more traumatic than she was letting on. Her smile was tight with pain.

"Are you kidding? She would have lectured me about how stupid it was to give up my power to a man."

"I find that unlikely."

"Let's put it this way, when I was ten I begged for a Barbie doll and she ranted about how the dolls distort a girl's body image, portraying women as nipple-less, dehumanized sluts and she would not allow one anywhere near her or me."

"She would not have blamed you, Christine." In difficult relationships, memories could be distorted, negative incidents mythologized. That seemed to be how Christine felt about her mother. "She would have wanted to reassure and comfort you."

"Well, anyway, I survived. And, believe me, ever after, no meant no." She laughed, but her eyes held sadness. "You know, Bogie secretly bought me that Barbie doll. He felt sorry for me." She shrugged, then looked at the ceiling over his bed. "Dylan had a poster of the Doors taped up there. I do remember that."

He wanted to ask a question, give her time to let deeper feelings surface, but that was not his place. She was not a client. Worse, he had the primitive urge to find this Dylan and beat the crap out of him for hurting her.

Christine moved on—to his desk, where he'd printed out the seventy-five pages he'd eked out after all these weeks. "So this is where the magic happens?" she asked.

"Not so much lately." Why admit that? Something about Christine. How open she was, how direct. She seemed to have conquered his usual reticence as neatly as his salve had soothed her insect bites.

"What? You've got writer's block?"

"I'll work through it." The truth was, he was dead-on stalled. Just sitting down at the desk made his skin crawl and his muscles itch to move.

Back in L.A., after the firestorm over his journal report, fury had driven him through a first draft. Once the dust settled on his anger, his momentum slowed, then ground to a halt.

"So tell me about the book. That's what I do when I get stuck on an ad project. Maybe that will help."

If it were only so simple. "It's about the stranglehold the insurance companies have on mental health care in this country. Therapists are virtually irrelevant to the treatment plan, almost to the point where they're committing malpractice."

"Malpractice? Really? That sounds extreme."

"It's a controversial premise. The research I published last year created a stir, so the book will more comprehensively lay out my ideas." *Stir* was an understatement. *Tsunami* was more like it. He'd been prepared for the insurance companies to squawk, but the attacks from his colleagues had shocked and wounded him.

"So what's your solution?" she asked.

"Reform. I want to put control of care where it belongs—in the hands of practitioners in consultation with their clients."

"That's certainly a big issue in Washington. How are you organizing the book?"

"I'm using an extensive literature search, in addition to my own research. I've examined shifts in suicide rates, psychiatric hospitalizations, relapse rates, malpractice cases due to misdiagnosis and—" He stopped. "I'm boring you."

"Not at all. We have to get you unstuck."

"It'll take more than a conversation for that, but thanks for—"

"You said your research caused a stir? In what way?"

He should end this, walk Christine out of his room—and his troubles—but he found himself wanting to answer. Her earnest concern touched him. "I was criticized extensively and from unexpected quarters."

"What do you mean?"

"I expected insurance companies to try to discredit me, but I was also attacked by colleagues I expected to support my theories. And, even worse, Nathan's death occurred in the middle of the storm and it was used to defame me in the media."

"You're kidding! That's outrageous."

He shook his head. "I was portrayed as a self-named savior of psychiatry who callously ignored my stepson's deadly drug use."

"But that's so unfair."

"Fairness is rarely the point in these situations. The media exposure was torture for Elizabeth. Nathan's picture in the paper, his death rehashed on TV over and over."

"Torture for you, too, Marcus."

"But Elizabeth was blameless. It was actually a relief when she asked me to leave." He no longer had to wake up to her stricken face, the resentment in her eyes.

"Jesus, Marcus. Look at what you've been through—Nathan's death, a divorce, your work attacked. No wonder you're stalled. You're not a writer on retreat. You're a refugee seeking sanctuary."

"That's melodramatic. I'm hardly innocent here. I made mistakes. I should have shored up defenders before I released my report. I failed both Elizabeth and Nathan. I was arrogant and bullheaded and—"

She put a finger to his lips. "You've been through hell. You get to feel bad about it. Really bad." He couldn't take his eyes from her face. She was so pretty and she smelled so good and he wanted to kiss the finger she'd pressed to his mouth.

To resist, he gripped her hand and held it against his chest, though that only made him want to wrap her in his arms and hold all of her. "I don't know why I told you all that."

"Because I asked." Her eyes swirled with emotion. "Because you needed to talk to someone. I'm glad I was here."

Was she right? He'd talked with Carlos about what happened, but only superficially. Evidently, he was still in turmoil or he wouldn't have told her the sordid details.

"I know how it is to fail someone you love. I joke about it, but I'm really scared I'm losing David. This trip feels like my last chance. Part of me believes he could end up—" she swallowed hard "—like your stepson."

"David may look like Nathan, but he doesn't act like him."

"You can't know that," she said, her eyes full of anguish.

He knew then that he had to help her. "I'll talk with David for you," he said. "An informal conversation or two."

"Really?" A smile burst out on her face, a blaze of light in a dark room. "That would be wonderful. You have no idea what this means to me. I know he'll talk to you. This is perfect."

She surprised him with a hug, swamping him in

her spring sweetness. His entire body warmed to the contact, the flutter of her heart against his ribs. He raised his arms to return the embrace, but would that suggest more than he intended?

Ah, hell. He encircled her with his arms and buried his nose in her curls to breathe her in, stealing a moment of pleasure for the lonely hours ahead.

They stayed like that, wrapped in each other's arms, for long seconds. It was a time-out for both of them...from loneliness, from doubt, from letting down a loved one.

Finally, Christine loosened her arms and stepped back. "That was nice." Her eyes chased his, worrying about his response. "But I'd better go." She eased toward the door, seeming embarrassed—as he was—that they'd held on to each other so urgently.

"Don't forget what you came for," he said, grabbing the jar of salve from his desk, where she'd placed it.

She took it, then stepped quickly to him to press his cheek with a soft palm. "Thank you for this. And for David. I know this will help him."

"He may not cooperate, Christine."

"I can hope, can't I?"

"Something tells me you will, no matter what I say." For a moment, an unexpected yearning rose in him, a desire to make her happy, to smooth her path, to be there for her, come hell or high water.

Completely unrealistic, but he felt it all the same. Trying to help David could be a painful reminder of how badly he'd failed Nathan.

Still, the warmth of her hand lingered on his skin and for hours he could still smell spring.

DAVID LEFT THE GARDEN to fill his metal water bottle from the pump under the mesquite trees. His blisters had healed, but his hands still cramped up and his back ached from the work. He wasn't really thirsty, but he needed a break.

As usual, when he had a quiet moment, his thoughts turned to Brigitte. He decided to go into the house for ice so he could call her. His grandma had said he could use the phone anytime, hadn't she?

It was Saturday so Brigitte should answer. He'd been trapped here for almost two weeks now. The only payoff was he was getting tanned and muscular. Brigitte would like that.

He didn't mind working with Marcus, who was quiet and never nagged David when he took breaks for water or to coax Lady over. Marcus said Lady needed a friend. David did, too.

"I'm getting ice. Want some?" he yelled.

Marcus shook his head, carrying weeds to the compost pile.

He felt bad leaving Marcus to work alone. The short-timers did more talking than working and

David had gotten up too late to help him feed the animals. The "care and share" bit got old.

Inside, he raced to the kitchen and dialed the number, taking the handset into the alcove his mom used as an office in the afternoons. She spent the mornings in the clay works, so he knew he'd have privacy.

David lived for these calls. He'd started to be afraid he was forgetting Brigitte—her smile, the way the beads in her blond cornrows rattled when she shook her head, the click of her tongue stud against his teeth when they made out, the way she tasted of Juicy Fruit even when she wasn't chewing any.

"'Lo?" Brigitte answered on the first ring, her voice breathy and as sweet as she tasted.

"'Sme," he said, going for a sexy whisper.

"Who is this?" she said loudly. "Hello?"

That sort of ruined the moment. "It's me. David."

"Oh. Hi." She didn't sound too glad, which made him feel like he'd been punched.

"What's wrong?" he asked.

"Nothing. I was just on the way out is all."

"To where?" He felt stupidly left out.

"To listen to a new band practice for a gig at the MainLiner with Melissa and Speel."

"Oh. Wish I was there."

"Me, too," she said, her voice warm again.

Relief blew through him. He closed his eyes and leaned against the wall. "I want you...so much."

"It's a drag you're so far away."

A drag? It was a tragedy that had ripped them apart. They'd both agreed. Now she sounded resigned to it.

"I'm going to try to come see you," he blurted. "I'll take the bus...or borrow a car." He needed to learn to drive first, of course, but he had to get to her somehow.

"That's cool," she said.

"Don't you want me there?" Ice froze his veins.

"Sure. It'd be great. Really great." Her voice went muffled as she spoke to someone. Laughter in the background made him burn with jealousy. She was half out the door already.

"You want to hang up, I can tell."

"Don't pout. You know I'm not good on the phone."

"It's just hard to be away from you—"

"I know, but you're having this incredible experience out there. How's the bud? You've got homegrown from a commune. Wow."

He'd found the tiny grow room the day he'd first helped in the greenhouse. Bogie'd got all panicked and told him he had to leave because he'd promised Crystal to keep it locked—it was medicine for his cancer and all—but David had asked about the plants and Bogie got into explaining his hybrids and forgot about chasing him out. Bogie wasn't big on arguments.

Since then, David had only helped himself to a joint's worth now and then, not enough that Bogie would notice. Even if he did, David doubted Bogie would narc to Christine, who thought one blunt required rehab. Bogie was cool.

"He's got these amazing plants with so much resin you wouldn't believe. And the smell…" It was so strong, David had had to air out the nuggets before hiding them beneath his mattress.

"Bring us some when you come, okay?" she said.

"If I can." That would be stealing, and David would never do that to Bogie. She sounded more into the weed than seeing him again.

"Gotta jet. Everyone's waiting. I wish you got cell reception so I could call you when I'm more in the mood."

And like that she was gone. She didn't even play their *I love you more…. No, I love you more* game with him.

She was slipping away. Adrenaline prickled through him. He had to get back to her before she was altogether gone.

When he returned to the garden, Marcus stopped working and braced an arm on one knee, looking at him. "Where's your ice?"

"Uh, I forgot. I'm not thirsty now." He felt like a jerk for lying. Lady nudged his hand, so he petted her.

"She seems to really like you," Marcus said.

"I heard her howling last night." It was such a lonely sound, but it made David feel like he wasn't the only one suffering. "What happened to her owner, anyway?"

Marcus looked David in the eye like this would be important. "Nathan, my stepson, died of a drug overdose. He injected 'magic.' Have you heard of it?"

"Not really." He didn't want to sound like he knew too much, though he hadn't heard of that drug.

"It's heroin mixed with fentanyl, a strong pain-killer. Both suppress heart rate and respiration so it's easy to get too much, especially by injection."

"Needles are stupid."

"That's how I thought Nathan felt." The dude looked so sad all of a sudden. So did Lady, which was weird, and it made David's own sorrow well up. He blinked hard.

"You okay?" Marcus said, looking closer at him.

"Life is sad sometimes."

"You feel sad right now?" His eyes looked deep, catching secrets David would rather keep to himself.

"Yeah." He swallowed. "It's my girlfriend. She's with all our friends in Phoenix and I'm stuck out here." He swallowed the emotion that flooded his throat.

"Separations can be difficult."

At least he didn't say *you'll get over it* or *you're too young for a girlfriend* the way his mother would have.

"You want to help me out here while we talk?" Marcus smiled, waving his spade over the row of onions beside him.

"Okay. Yeah." He went through the gate and started yanking weeds, the dense, green smell of the onions filling his nose.

"What helps with your sadness?" Marcus asked.

"What do you mean?"

"What do you enjoy doing here?"

"Nothing. I talk to Brigitte. Sleep. Try to get online, but dial-up sucks." *Spark up a bowl*, but the guy wasn't cool enough to say *that*.

"Music? Sometimes music is a good escape."

He shrugged. He would like to get better at his guitar so he could write music to go with the lyrics he'd written.

"It seems like time drags when you're watching the clock. Why don't you distract yourself with things you enjoy doing?"

"I guess."

"You'll meet the Barlow twins tonight at dinner, right? School will be out soon, so they'll have more time to hang out."

"That sounds like my mom. 'Go on and play with

your little friends.'" He shook his head. She was clueless.

"Christine is concerned about you."

He yanked at some weeds. "She dragged me here to break me and Brigitte up. She hates Brigitte."

Marcus didn't dispute what he was saying, so he kept going. "She can't stand that I have opinions, that I want my own life. She hates how I look, what I say, how I think…everything."

"What do you want from her, David?"

"For her to leave me alone, get off my back." He breathed hard, getting angry thinking about how she harassed him.

"What would it take?"

"Huh?"

"To get her off your back? What does she want from you?"

"Everything. She wants me to slave in the gardens all day, then do schoolwork, go to bed early, get up all smiley about feeding chickens at the crack of dawn. Then she wants me to spill my guts to a shrink who'll tell me what a screwup I am."

Like he didn't know already. Like he could change that.

"She wants me to get straight As, be class president, eat spinach, hate drugs, never drive a car or have sex ever." His throat tightened at how hopeless it was. "I can't make her happy and I'm sick of making her cry."

Dammit. He'd spewed at Marcus like a dill hole. He yanked at the weeds to hide his emotions.

Marcus let the silence between them hang. The only sound was the chuff of his spade, the tearing of the weeds, a birdcall. "Which are you willing to do?" he finally said.

"None of them. There's no point. Nothing's ever enough for her." He yanked hard and saw he'd ripped up some onion shoots. *Whoops.*

"If you want her to back off, you'll have to do something she wants. Which make the most sense to you?"

The guy wouldn't leave this alone. "I don't know." He paused, thinking it through. "The schoolwork, I guess. No way will I repeat those classes."

"What's holding you back?"

"The Internet. I don't know. I don't feel like it, is all."

"Is it a lot of work?"

"Not really," he muttered. The math was a pain, but the history was reading and answering questions and the English was mostly writing. He was good at that.

"Some visible progress would make your mother feel a lot less worried. You have to do it anyway, correct?"

"Yeah. I guess."

"Anything else you could do? To get her off your back?"

"I could be nicer, I guess. You think if I do the

work and act less sarcastic, she won't make me go to a shrink?"

"For what it's worth, no therapist will tell you you're a screwup. They usually leave that up to you."

David smiled at the joke. After saying all that he felt lighter inside, not as angry as usual. Marcus hadn't given him any attitude, just the facts. Cut and dried. He liked that.

And Marcus had a point. If David did his homework and stopped fighting with her, Christine might chill out and he'd have more freedom to figure out how to get to Brigitte.

CHAPTER SIX

CHRISTINE SET THE LAST load of bowls on the drying shelf. Mitch and Louis and two new part-timers from town were helping Lucy build the extra kiln shelves to accommodate the larger orders Christine had coming in.

Christine rubbed her lower back, not really minding how sore she was. Physical labor was rewarding. And she enjoyed working with her hands. Her first attempts with clay had failed miserably, but she'd been practicing at the wheel during breaks and she was definitely improving.

She looked at the four goblets she'd thrown and grinned. She couldn't wait to see how they'd look glazed. Aurora had even said they were decent— right before she demanded that Christine write up a *full and complete* procedures manual before she even *thought* about leaving. The biggest proof that Aurora was on the mend would be when she stopped cooking up tasks to keep Christine at Harmony House longer.

Christine stepped to the barn door to get some fresh air and noticed Marcus and David together in the garden. This must be the first "talk." She felt a spike of excitement.

Watching Marcus tilt his head to listen to David, then laugh, made something in Christine's chest go loose and tight at once. It was as though she had a partner, someone who understood her struggle, something that as a single mother she'd never experienced. These were only informal chats, but still...

Christine couldn't stop thinking about being in Marcus's room the other night. She'd basically clung to the man. The only thing that relieved her embarrassment was how tightly he'd held on to her. She hadn't realized how lonely she'd been.

For that blip of time, she'd felt how it might be to be truly intimate with a man, to open her heart, to share the daily joys and sorrows, to trust him, depend on him, and to let him know he could trust and depend on her.

She definitely saw the appeal. It was stupid to deny that deep down she wanted that. Even if she found a decent guy, she'd probably foul it up. She was a flawed pain in the ass, intense, emotional, in your face. It would take a special man—sturdy and calm, with a generous and patient heart—to put up with her for very long. Men like that didn't grow on trees.

Hell, would she even know one when she saw him?

She looked out at Marcus, remembering his strong

arms around her. He'd smelled of sweet lime, fresh laundry and a woodsy spice. He had some of those traits she needed, but he was so…uptight. She'd practically had to torture him to get him to tell her what had happened to him. She would drive him nuts for sure. And who wanted to work that hard anyway?

What was she doing? Thinking about getting with Marcus? She practically laughed out loud. Talk about counting your chickens before they hatched. That was like counting your chickens before you had a rooster in the coop.

Still, it was lovely to watch him talk with her son. He gave her hope. Way better than a relationship. Right?

DAVID TOOK ONE LOOK at Todd and Robert Barlow's room with the matching plaid bedspreads, NBA and NFL posters, chessboard and sports trophies and wanted to get the hell out of there. These preppy jocks were from a galaxy far, far away.

He was appeasing Christine, though, part of his plan to get her off his back, so he'd gut out the evening and hope the food was at least good. He dropped into one of the desk chairs.

Todd, who seemed to be lead dog on the team, said, "So, David, got any bud?"

Huh? "You two smoke?" he asked.

They sneered, like *duh*, but he didn't buy it.

"We figured you'd have killer weed from the commune."

"Sorry." He had an emergency joint in his pocket, but he wouldn't get these two stoned in front of their parents in a million years.

Their faces fell. "Just get it," Todd muttered to his brother, who upended a trophy and pulled out a baggie and a pipe. "It's just ditch weed…." Todd shrugged.

"I'm cool," he said, raising his hands to decline. He needed a clear head in this alien land.

There was a knock at the door, so Robert put the trophy back and went to answer. The maid handed him a tray with soup and enchiladas, along with plates and silverware.

It smelled amazing.

"You sure you don't want to smoke?" Todd asked him. "Carmen's tortilla soup is *awesome* when you're stoned."

"I'm good," he said, digging into the soup. It was as tasty as it smelled. Meanwhile, the twins went through their dope-smoking-prep routine. Todd lit incense, while Robert shoved a towel along the door crack and opened the window.

They sat on the backs of desk chairs and blew the smoke outdoors, grinning at each other like baboons.

Get me out of here, David thought, digging into an enchilada. It practically melted in his mouth.

Once the twins had a buzz on, they joined him

with the food, apologizing about how they had to act so scrubbed for their parents. They made their mom sound more neurotic than Christine and their dad was a bully.

"What do you do for fun around here?" he asked them.

"We drive the BMW to Preston when Dad lets us," Robert said.

David's ears perked up. *Drivers' licenses and a car.* Jackpot. "What about Phoenix? Ever go there?"

"On our own? No way," Robert said. "Our dad's an asshole about his car. He checks mileage every time we drive."

"Dad's an asshole about everything," Todd said.

"Mainly when he drinks, though," Robert said, shrugging.

Okay, no ride to Phoenix, but David would bet there'd be a bus station in Preston. The twins could drive him that far.

"Think it's Ginger time?" Todd asked his brother.

"Ginger time?" David asked.

The boys snorted with baked laughter. "It's this amazing porn chick. For free...well, five minutes' worth anyway."

That was the last thing he needed. David spotted a phone on the nightstand. "Can I use your phone?" The ache for Brigitte was like a live animal chewing him up inside.

"Go ahead," Todd said. While David dialed Brigitte's number, lying between the beds for privacy, the twins sat side by side at the computer and clicked their way into porn land.

"Hello?" Brigitte yelled into the phone. David could hardly hear her over the background wall of noise and music.

"It's David," he said. "Where are you?"

"At a club. It's loud. Sorry."

"Can you step outside?"

"I might not get back in."

"I miss you so much—"

"It's crazy here," she yelled. "I'll tell you when you call tomorrow. I can't hear you. I love you. 'Bye."

David felt sick. Brigitte was going to clubs, meeting guys who didn't know she had a boyfriend and hardly talking to him.

He had to get to her. *Had to.*

"She's got the longest tongue ever," Robert said.

"It's a biological miracle," Todd said, equally amazed.

God. These two chuckleheads were content to gawk at pixilated female flesh, while David's whole soul had been packed into a stolen phone call that Brigitte had cut short.

His chest ached and his throat was so tight he could hardly swallow. He wanted to hit something hard, anything to stop feeling the pain in his brain and chest.

He slugged the bed frame with all his might, glad when pain sliced through his rage and hurt. He squeezed his bruised hand and gasped for air. When the burning faded to a dull ache, he fished out his iPod, lifted the sound-canceling headphones from his neck and played fierce metal full blast, more determined than ever to get home.

If the twins couldn't drive him to Preston, he'd teach himself to drive after everyone was in bed at night.

He was just starting to calm down when he became aware of a commotion around him. He pulled off his headphones and sat up. Mrs. Barlow stood in the doorway with a tray of little bowls with a crusty white pudding, Christine behind her. They both looked upset.

"But we're *not* smoking," Todd said. "That's incense."

"What's that window doing open? Our A/C bill has been through the roof." Their mother set the tray on one of the beds and went for the window, but Robert lunged in front of her, while Todd scrambled to hide the pipe and weed.

"What in the name of goodness are you boys looking at?" Mrs. Barlow gasped. They'd been so stoner clueless, they'd forgotten the porn on the computer screen.

"What's the trouble in here?" The moment their

father appeared, both twins stiffened, clearly afraid of the guy.

"Explain!" he snapped, sounding like a drill sergeant in a bad war movie. He also sounded drunk.

"We accidentally clicked the wrong link, Dad, and—"

"That's it. The Internet is done in this house." He ripped the cord from the back of the computer. "Cancel our service on Monday, Susan."

"Dad, come on. It was a mistake. Don't do that." Jumping up to object, Todd's elbow knocked the pipe and pot to the floor. Everyone's eyes shot to the small glass tube and bag of weed.

"Is that what I think it is?" Mrs. Barlow said. Her gaze shot instantly to David. "Did *you* bring *drugs* into *our house?*"

So he had to be the druggie, not her angel sons. Disgusting. David opened his mouth to object. Then he noticed the twins, white as ghosts, cowering together, shooting fearful looks at their dad, the bully. Robert caught David's eye and put his finger to his mouth. *Don't tell.* If David ratted out the twins, they sure as hell wouldn't be driving him to Preston anytime soon. The porn might get them smacked around already by their butthole father.

He just couldn't do it to the doofuses. He could take the hit easier than they could anyway. His mom would be proud of him for being kind. Plus he hadn't even smoked. He reached down and grabbed the goods.

"Why, never in my life—" Mrs. Barlow gasped. "You gave our boys *drugs?*"

"Give me that and get out to the car," Christine said, holding out a trembling hand, her face pale, lips tight, eyes full of shame.

She might not believe me, he realized. That made him mad. He handed over the stash and stalked out.

The one good moment was seeing the amazed gratitude and relief on the twins' faces. They owed him now. Big-time.

A LITTLE WHILE LATER, David watched his mother and Marcus head down the sidewalk toward him. He sat in the backseat of Marcus's Acura. Christine walked very fast, clearly furious. He didn't want her to yell at him in front of Marcus, so the minute she sat down, he said, "The pot's not mine. I was just covering for the twins with their asshole parents."

"Don't lie to me!" she yelled. "Do you think I'm an idiot?"

"Forget it." Figured she'd expect the worst.

"How could you do this? How? You promised me no drugs. It's bad enough *you* use pot, but you talked those boys into it? You sabotage everything! How could you?" Her voice shook and she was about to cry. He hated when she cried.

"I'm sure David will explain what happened when

you're able to hear him," Marcus said in a strong voice. "For now, take a moment to catch your breath, Christine."

"Catch my breath? Are you kidding me?" She glared at the guy, opened her mouth to give him hell, then suddenly sagged in her seat, blowing out a huge breath.

Good one, Doctor B., David thought, amazed the shrink-talk had actually worked on his mother.

They drove for a few minutes in tense silence, until Marcus spoke. "You seemed angry at more than David, Christine."

She jerked to face him. "What? More than…?" She paused. "I guess I didn't appreciate how self-righteous Susan got. Like we'd polluted her house or something. 'I have *never* in my *life*… I can't believe you gave our boys *drugs.*' Well, la-di-dah. Welcome to the real world, lady."

David felt his mouth fall open. His mother was defending him against the snooty bitch she'd been trying to impress. Wow.

"Meanwhile, her husband, the big-shot *mayor,* was drunk on his ass. I swear he drank that second bottle of wine all by himself. They're both hypocrites, that's all I can say."

Marcus said nothing. In the quiet pause, David realized this might be his chance to say his piece. "I know you won't believe me, but the pot was theirs. I didn't smoke any of it."

"What?" His mother twisted to look at him.

"They asked me if I wanted some and I said no. Their dad's an asshole and they were busted about the porn already. They were begging me not to narc on them, so I took the hit. The parents thought I was druggie scum anyway." He shrugged.

"They did not think that," Christine said, but in a softer, more thoughtful voice. "Susan thinks you're handsome and you have nice hair. If you'd just get it out of your eyes…" She looked out the window. She seemed more sad than pissed now.

She believed him. Marcus had made her calm down and hear him for once.

"What am I supposed to say to Susan now?" she said.

"Who cares? Those people are assholes."

"Stop saying the *A* word," she said, but she wasn't really that upset. In fact, he figured she agreed with him.

"I mean they spent the whole night showing off how rich they were," David responded. "Like they needed a cook. Come on. And that golf course in the backyard? The guy's a dill hole."

Marcus coughed to hide a laugh.

"I hate that Susan and Winston think you dragged their angel boys into doing drugs. It's not right."

"Who cares? You just called her self-righteous and him a drunk. Don't be a hypocrite yourself."

Marcus caught his eye in the mirror, trying to remind David about keeping his mother off his back.

He shot back a *yeah, yeah* look. "Anyway, I didn't

do anything wrong. I was helping my friends." He paused. "Plus I'm almost done with English."

"Really? You are?" She whipped around again, all hopeful.

"Yeah. In a couple days. Then it's only math and history."

"That's good, David. Really good." She faced forward with a happy sigh. For now. It wouldn't last, he knew, with sinking dread. To her he'd always be a screwup and a disappointment. The only person who understood him was Brigitte and she was slipping away. He had to get to her. And soon.

WHEN THEY GOT BACK to Harmony House, Marcus watched David take off for his room. The kid had done a brave thing for the Barlow boys. He was making an effort with his mother, too, clearly taking Marcus's advice. He liked David a lot. He was smart and sensitive and he had a big heart.

Keep your distance. The warning rang like a bell in his head. Without distance, his judgment would be impaired, as it had been with Nathan. He'd reacted with his heart, not his head, hoping for the best instead of digging for the harder truth.

He opened Christine's car door for her. She was so pretty in the soft clingy top that dipped enough to tease the eye. "Did I do okay once I caught my breath?" she asked, looking up at him in the moonlight.

"What do you think?" he said.

"God. Is that a shrink trick? Turning around

the question? Okay, I'll bite. I think I did pretty good."

"I was watching David in the mirror when you defended him against Susan and his jaw dropped."

"Really?"

"He clearly felt you were on his side there. The important thing was he felt heard. That means a lot."

"So I did do good. Plus, he's finishing school stuff, too."

"Sounds like progress to me."

"It does. Yeah." She smiled. "Whatever you said to him out in the garden did the trick, I guess. So what *did* you say?"

"I told David that whatever he told me would stay between the two of us unless he wanted me to speak to you."

"Sure, but if there's something bad I should know—"

"Then I'll ask his permission to tell you or urge him to talk to you about it himself."

"God. You're so ethical." She was pretending to be annoyed. "Do you believe him about the pot not being his?"

"Do you?"

She groaned. "I don't know what to believe. I'm afraid to believe. The drugs worry me the most, you know. He promised to stop, but I don't know if he has. Or if I should make him take a drug test or what."

"Drugs are part of the culture, Christine. He'll face drug decisions the rest of his life. The best thing you can do is keep talking. Ask questions and really listen to his answers. How authoritarian or invasive you choose to be is up to you."

"In other words, it all depends." She sighed.

"I wish there were easy answers, but there never are when it counts."

"No kidding. No one tells you how hard parenthood will be. I never know when to push, when to trust, when to hang on, when to let go." She shook her hair off her shoulder. "I just want to do it the right way, you know?" Her eyes shone with urgency.

"There are lots of right ways, Christine."

"And a million wrong ones." She smiled wryly. "Want to sit and talk?" She motioned toward the porch. She was so eager he could hardly decline, so he followed her up the stairs. "How about a nightcap? I've got beer, I think," she said.

"I'm fine, thanks. I managed to pry the bottle out of Winston's hands long enough to get a glass."

"Oh, you're bad." She grinned, then dropped into the hammock, kicking off her shoes as she lay against the stretchy expanse. She looked so good lying there.

Desire surged through him again, as it had all evening. The more he knew her, the more his attraction grew, which was not at all helpful.

He sat in a nearby rocking chair, caught by the

sight of her calves tightening and releasing as she pushed the hammock back and forth. Damned pretty feet, too.

To end that thought, he lifted his gaze to the sky.

"So the endless black of the night sky doesn't scare you, does it?" she asked.

"It makes me feel free." As if he could disappear and no one would know or care.

"We're different that way, I guess."

"We're different in lots of ways."

"Is that a bad thing?"

"Not at all. I find you…refreshing."

"And annoying?"

"Not at all."

"I'll take that." He enjoyed making her smile. In fact he found himself making mental notes of things that might amuse her all during the day.

As blunt and direct as she could be, he was relieved not to have to second-guess her emotions or coax out the truth as he'd had to do with Elizabeth.

"That was good what you said, Marcus. I mean pointing out that I was angry at Susan, too. And you didn't even infuriate me telling me to take a breath. I promise you, the last thing an upset person wants to hear is 'calm down.'"

"Is that so?"

"Absolutely. But coming from you, somehow, I don't know, it works." She surveyed him, head tilted.

"I bet you were great with clients. What made you stop seeing them?"

"I needed a change and I was invited into the institute partnership where I could do the research I wanted."

"Do you miss seeing patients?"

"At times. When it works, when you help people improve their lives, therapy can be very rewarding."

"Maybe working with David will get you back into it."

"I'm not *working* with David. We're talking, that's all."

"You're helping him and that's what counts."

"But I'm not his therapist. We need to be clear about that. David may benefit from a formal therapeutic relationship and you might want to pursue one here or back in Phoenix."

"Calm down. I'm not going to sue you. You're not exactly Dr. Optimistic, are you, Marcus?"

"You sound like Elizabeth. She considered me too negative." He felt a stab of regret. "She wasn't fond of hard truths."

"Really?" She stopped the hammock's sway with one toe. "What was she like anyway? Elizabeth."

"I don't see the point in getting into that." But he knew full well Christine would not let that go, so before she could ask again, he answered her. "She is intelligent. Brilliant, really. She's an administrator at the state health department. A serious person, quiet and thoughtful."

"She sounds a lot like you."

He smiled, but felt empty inside. "That's what I believed. She seemed more self-sufficient than she turned out to be. She needed more support than I realized. I let her down in the end."

"How? Did she blame you for Nathan? I know when a child dies marriages often fall apart. I know I'm being nosy." She gave an apologetic laugh.

"I'm getting used to that," he said, surprised to realize it was true. He felt less guarded with her since that night when they'd embraced. "To some degree, she blamed me. With a senseless death, it's natural to want an explanation, to find reasons, to assign blame." He blamed himself and always would.

"You said she couldn't stand the sight of Lady… did she feel the same about you? Is that what went wrong?"

"It was a blow to our marriage, certainly, but the truth is I wasn't the husband Elizabeth needed."

You're never really here, Marcus, she'd said to him, her face ravaged by grief. *You're always in your head, obsessing about your research, your blessed work. Do you even know how to be with another person?*

"Simply put, she needed more than I had to give."

"So you were wrong for each other?" Christine frowned, intent on understanding, it seemed, making sense of the senseless.

"I'm not sure I'd be right for anyone." He gave a short laugh, surprised he'd confessed his deepest truth. "I'm not made for the kind of emotional engagement required by marriage."

He should never have taken the chance with Elizabeth, no matter how alike they'd seemed. It had been cruel to her and Nathan.

Christine shook her head. "Oh, I don't believe that, Marcus." She sat up abruptly and leaned over to pat his arm. "The trauma you went through would mess up any marriage."

"That's kind of you, but—"

She laughed. "Who am I to talk? I'm no relationship expert." She shook her head, her curls shivering across her shoulder, then threw herself back into the hammock, sending it flying. "My marriage to Skip was a disaster. I pick the wrong men and scare off the right ones."

"Frankly, I'm amazed any relationship survives. There are so many crossed wires, misunderstood impulses and bad judgment calls that an enduring bond seems like a miracle."

"Jesus, Dr. Optimist. You were smart not to go into marriage counseling."

He laughed, surprised at how good-naturedly Christine had reacted to truths that gnawed at his core.

"So you're skittish on marriage. How do you

deal with sex? You don't strike me as the booty-call type." She stopped the hammock again and bore down on him. "I bet when you're in, you're *all* in. Am I right?"

He smiled. "Let's just say I'm better off out."

"Yeah, but everyone needs sex, Marcus." She was teasing him, but his body was taking her very seriously.

"Including you?" he teased back.

She sighed, pushing off with that plump big toe of hers. "I work a lot. And there's David." She shrugged. "I'm all talk, no action."

"Is that so?" He watched her sway back and forth, lying there looking so available. He had the urge to prove her wrong, prove them both wrong, lift her out of that hammock into his arms, take her to his bed and—

"Go for it," she breathed.

He jolted. Had she read his mind? "Excuse me?"

"The hammock. Get in it. There's room." She patted the space beside her. "You look like you're dying to try it. It feels good, like a great big body hug. You know you want to." The words hit him low and she clearly knew it.

He should decline, of course, but she would never let him hear the end of it, so he got out of the chair and lowered himself into the curve of the hammock. It creaked under his weight as he lifted his legs and shifted more fully in place.

He wobbled, then rolled against Christine. "Sorry," he said, attempting to retreat.

She stopped him. "Don't be. It's nice like this."

It was. Dangerously so. The hammock held them together, swaying back and forth. Christine dipped her nose to his chest. "Mmm. You smell like lime and the woods and clean cotton."

"And that's…good?" he asked.

"Oh, yes…." She took an exaggerated sniff. "Very good."

"You, uh, smell good, too," he ventured. "Like spring."

"I smell like spring? That's a lovely thing to say."

"I noticed it the first day." He felt like an idiot and a kid saying that.

"You smelled me then?" She grinned. "That's so sweet."

He settled against her softness, aroused, but hoped it wasn't evident. They were held, as if in the palm of a fabric hand. He settled into the physicality of the moment, the way she was pressed against the side of his body, her breast soft on his chest, her curls brushing his cheek, impossible to ignore.

After a bit, she rose on an elbow to look at him. "Anyway, I'm sorry we dragged you into that drama at Susan's."

"My only regret is missing the crème brûlee."

She laughed. "How funny. Could you believe her saying right in front of Carmen that even though she was *only* Guatemalan, she had a *gift* for French cuisine. Gawd."

"Carmen rolled her eyes when she said that."

"She did? Oh, good for her. Then when Winston said he liked being mayor because it was an easy gig that didn't interfere with his golf game, Susan gave that speech about how he'd sacrificed his big law practice in the city for a safe place to raise kids and so Susan could be near her family."

"She did seem anxious to impress you."

"I can't believe I used to envy her."

"You were young. She was popular."

"But at least I grew up." She stabbed his chest with a finger. "And, by the way, Susan was seriously *after* you."

"Excuse me?"

"I thought she was going to slam you against a wall and unzip your jeans when we first got there."

He arched an eyebrow. "Please."

"Oh, yes. You were what's for dinner, no question."

"You're exaggerating." He found it tough to focus on their conversation, being so aware of her warmth beside him, the way her breasts shivered as she gestured, the weight of her leg.

"Of course. You're the total package—hot, buff, smart, a successful doctor. Mainly, you're not Winston."

"Speaking of Winston, what was his excuse to get you to stop by his office?"

"Oh, some packet from a tourism convention about the trend toward 'experience' vacations—people who want to help build schools in Africa or work on a cattle ranch or an organic farm, instead of lounging around at the beach. Actually, a commune would have a lot of appeal with that market."

"Well, grab the brochure and run, that's all I'm saying. I recommend pepper spray."

She laughed. Shifting her position, her elbow slipped and she fell on top of him.

"Easy," he said, not sorry to have her body draped over his, her breasts against his chest, their legs overlapping.

"This is nice, huh?" she murmured, heat flaring in her eyes.

"Too nice." He wanted her more than he remembered wanting a woman in a long, long time.

"Oh, what the hell," she whispered and lowered her lips to his.

Her mouth was sweet and pliant and he deepened the kiss, as she moved fully over him, a blanket of soft, warm woman. This felt so good, like an escape from everything but pleasure.

A sharp bark made them break apart. Lady sat on her haunches beside them.

"Looks like your chaperone is here," Christine said.

"Great work," he said to the dog, as the heat of the moment dissipated like so much smoke.

Christine untangled herself from him and sat up. "Close one, huh?" She smiled shakily.

He nodded, helped her to her feet and stood beside her. Sex sounded simple, but too easily became complicated. And she was probably right about him. As a young man, he'd been fine with sex alone. At thirty-seven he supposed he *was* an all-in guy.

Christine scooped up her shoes. "He's all yours," she said to Lady, then stood on tiptoe to kiss Marcus on the cheek. "Thanks for tonight. I had fun." And with that, she danced away, leaving him uncomfortably erect.

Duty fulfilled, Lady accompanied him upstairs, curling up on the terrace between his room and David's.

Too agitated to sleep, Marcus sat at his desk and woke his sleeping hard drive with a touch. He'd done this often when sleep eluded him, but rarely did more than read over a few chapters.

Tonight, however, was different. He felt alert and clearheaded. He saw what the opening paragraph needed and added it. Then he realized what the rest of the page required. His fingers moved over the keyboard, almost of their own will, his thoughts flying from brain to finger to screen.

Was this reaction due to endorphins from sexual arousal? Or maybe the result of Christine reminding him of the emotional toll the last year had taken on him.

Whatever it was, he'd been shaken awake and he liked it.

Before he looked up, Marcus had revised ten pages, then fifteen. What the hell had he been waiting for?

Christine. Evidently he'd been waiting for her.

Smiling, he moved on to page sixteen.

CHAPTER SEVEN

CHRISTINE LAY DOWN and turned off the light, her lips still buzzing from kissing Marcus. She turned on her side, searched with her leg for a cool place on the sheet, but got nothing.

She was too riled to sleep. She wanted Marcus, dammit. She'd acted like stopping was no big deal, but it was. Very big.

She positively *yearned* for him now. She'd bet he'd be a great lover, slow and thorough and sweet. She wiggled against the sheets, imagining his hands being slow and thorough and sweet all over her body.

Why was she so desperate? She had normal sexual needs, of course, but she'd never felt so out of control. It had to be because they'd denied themselves. Usually, if she wanted a guy, she went for it. But this…this was *torture*.

Why not have sex? They'd discussed their attitudes. Neither of them wanted a relationship, or even felt equipped for one. Why couldn't they have a simple physical connection? Maybe they'd get it out of their system and be friends. Sure. Why not? Why hadn't she thought of that before?

Dammit, she was going for it. She jumped out of bed, threw on some clothes and took off after Marcus. She would quietly tap on his door and then, well, jump him….

Silently, of course, because David was next door.

Down the hall she scooted, then across the courtyard and outside. Then she noticed lights on in the greenhouse and someone moving around. It was Bogie, judging from the shape of the figure. So late at night? Was he okay?

She'd been so concerned about Aurora, she'd neglected the man completely, breaking her vow to spend time with him.

Guilt stopped her in her tracks. She blew out a breath, reining in her impulses, her needs. It took a minute or so of fighting her urges, but eventually her head cleared.

She'd been running off to Marcus's room like a sex-crazed teenager. Completely nuts. He'd be dead asleep by now anyway, so he'd come to the door all rumpled and puzzled and she'd end up looking like an idiot and a nympho.

Not to mention the fact that David *was* next door. What if he heard her knock? Or saw her? The horror burned through her like acid. David had begun to bond with Marcus. If he saw his mother panting outside the man's door it would ruin everything.

Thank God she'd noticed Bogie and remembered her mission here. She headed for the greenhouse to check on him.

The instant she stepped inside, Christine got that peaceful feeling she remembered. She took in the special air, dense with earthy smells and heavy with humidity. It felt like a health-giving elixir.

"Crystal! Welcome." Bogie smiled so broadly she wanted to hug him. "What brings you out here?"

"I wondered how you were doing is all."

"I'm doing just fine. I get stronger in here." He did seem younger and more energetic to her.

The atmosphere was almost like a church, the light extra white, with the plants confident worshippers who expected to be blessed, no penance required. And there was the surprise of fresh growth and new blooms. Everything coming up so brave and proud: *Look at me, look at me!*

"I used to love being in here," she said.

"You always had the touch, Crystal."

The compliment gave her a spike of unreasonable delight. "I've been so preoccupied with Aurora and the clay works I haven't asked how your recovery is going."

"Much better since you came. You've gotten Aurora to rest more, so you've taken a big worry from me. She's so glad you're here, that's for sure."

"I don't know about that. I think I upset her more than soothe her." She paused. "You know she asked me to fix up my room since it depresses her so much."

Bogie smiled. "Aurora doesn't always mean quite what she says. Don't let her fool you."

"I guess not." That drove Christine nuts. She wanted to shake the woman half the time. *Tell me what you really mean.* But, of course, that would never happen.

"Your mother has her reasons. You have to wait a bit and it will come to you."

Wait…. Calm down…. Let it be. That was Bogie's way, all right. He'd seemed almost invisible to her in the old days here. Even now, when she thought about it. Had he ever had a girlfriend? She didn't remember seeing him with anyone.

That was sad. He was such a kind and gentle soul. He could make someone very happy.

"Would you like to help me plant these anemone seeds?" Bogie asked, tilting his head at her.

"Sure. Yeah." She walked down the aisle with him, flashing on how as a girl she would trail him as he moved from plant to plant, touching, pinching, spreading soil and nutrients like a green-thumbed wizard.

He took her to fresh bedding trays and showed her how deeply to push in the seeds. "They grow quickly, so we don't want to pack the dirt too tight."

It felt good to work her fingers into the soil. Time slowed and so did she. She became aware of her breathing and her heartbeat. She'd always liked how Bogie talked about what was growing, what was struggling, what was root-bound, what was not.

"So, how has it been here for you so far?" he asked.

She told him about the improvements in the clay barn, the Web site and the new orders, working with him as she talked.

"Does that make you happy, Crystal?" He searched her face with his gray eyes. "What you're doing here, I mean?"

"It makes me feel useful. I want to help you and Aurora."

"But what about for yourself? What do you want for you?" Bogie slowly drizzled water over the bedding trays.

"The main thing is David. I want him to be okay."

Bogie nodded sagely. "A child is big. You want your child to be happy. That's the most important thing." Something flickered in his eyes. Concern? Sadness? Then he smiled. "But how about for you on your own? What would make you happy?"

"I do okay, Bogie. Everyone could be happier, I think." She smiled. "But once David's fine, what do I want? For me...?"

Watching Bogie gently separate the roots of a houseplant, then situate it in its pot, she let her deeper wishes shape themselves into words in her mind. "I guess I'd like to feel that I'm settled in, safe, surrounded by people I love who love me back, doing work that feels important, that matters."

She ran her finger along the smooth surface of a leaf as she talked. "I like advertising and I'm good at it and all, but it can seem…well…pointless at times. I'm fine financially. I've put away savings, but I'm always afraid I won't be, you know?"

She paused, thinking how neurotic she sounded.

"Then that's your work here."

"My work here is to help you guys."

"I mean your soul's work."

Good grief. Aurora wasn't the only woo-woo person on the place. Selling wind chimes could hardly solve her existential crisis, but she let that go for now. Bogie meant well and she was touched by his concern. "I guess I'll have to see how that turns out."

"I'm just glad you're here at last." He patted her arm with surprising force. "There's time to fix everything."

"What do you mean? What's to be fixed?"

He simply looked at her and she was too tired to probe further. She left the greenhouse with dirt under her nails, but feeling peaceful and calm. Which was pretty impressive considering how riled up and desperate for Marcus she'd been before she spotted Bogie. The gentle man had given her a philosophy lesson and saved her from a foolish mistake.

THE MONDAY AFTER CHRISTINE and the hammock, Marcus slid into the booth across from Carlos Montoya at Sammy's Cocina for lunch. They ordered Sammy's specialty—goat tamales with a nopalitos salad on the side.

"So what's shakin', *jefe?*" Carlos asked, sliding his menu behind the napkin holder where Marcus had put his.

"Not much." Carlos had given Marcus the nickname *jefe*—meaning *chief*—because Marcus had organized their study groups throughout med school. "Something is rollin' for you. I see that. You got color and your eyes are alive." He leaned forward and whispered, "*Oye, ese,* you get laid?"

Marcus laughed, the sound rising from deep inside, as if it had broken out of jail or something. "Not quite, no."

"Not quite? What does that mean? Who's the female?"

"Christine Waters, Aurora's daughter. She's here for the summer. We had a…moment, that's all."

"A moment? That code for *blue balls?*"

"If I were sixteen, I suppose."

"Too bad. But why the *payaso* grin, *hombre?*"

"*Payaso?*"

"*Clown.* All that's missing is the red nose."

"I'm going strong on the book again, I guess. The dopamine rush seemed to have given me the kick-start I needed."

"So being horny helps you work? Maybe I should

suggest that to Rosemary. She's pissed that I crash before we get busy."

"Are you putting in too many hours?"

"I guess. Plus all the driving for the New Mirage clinic. Rosemary wants me to quit when my contract comes due."

"Any chance of getting some help here?"

"Not without funds. If I could get the damned mayor to stop golfing long enough to return a call, I might get somewhere."

"I'm sorry to hear that."

"Ah, no big deal. That's how it goes in the boondocks." Their food arrived and they dug in. "So, you're writing again. Good on you, *hombre*." He gave Marcus a high five. "I have to say, why not go for the whole package—write *and* score?"

"It's complicated. Christine has a son. David. He's had some troubles, so I told her I'd talk to him."

"You're treating him?"

"Just talking." He paused, sliding his water glass forward and back. "He's the same age as Nathan was. He even looks like him. David's not shut down like Nathan, but…"

Carlos set down his fork. "You cool with that? The reminder and all?"

"I have to be."

"Okay," his friend said, not quite convinced. He took another bite of tamale, chewing slowly. "So after you finish the book, what then?"

"Then I'll talk to the partners. Let them buy me

out. Hopefully sell the book. And after that…I don't know." He hadn't said this out loud, but his future was a void, white noise in his head. He'd never before not had a plan for his life and he wasn't sure how he felt about that.

"What about opening up a practice again? You were good."

"That's over for me." He missed it, as he'd told Christine, but he no longer possessed the optimism or the emotional distance for a clinical practice. That part of his career seemed finished. "For now, I'm glad to be writing again."

He felt more human these days. More alive. That felt damn good. He refused to question it for now.

Carlos aimed a loaded fork at him. "You should go for it with this woman. Christine. If frustration fires you up, imagine what regular orgasms could do."

"I'll stick with this for now." It was far better to keep a level head. Self-control had been his byword through the domino fall of disasters last year and it had saved his dignity and contained the fallout. He would keep himself in check.

"What about you?" he asked Carlos. "What are your plans?"

"Hard to say. Truth is, I don't feel finished here. I don't want to walk away, *entiendes?*"

"I do." Marcus looked at his friend. "If you did get funding, what would you do?"

"That's easy. Hire a couple nurse practitioners to

keep the clinic going all week, get some basic E.R. equipment, set up a portable clinic to take out to the fields."

"You need grant money," Marcus said. "I wrote a proposal for mental health care for the indigent a couple years back. I could see what's out there. Assuming I can get anyone to take my calls."

"Anything you can do, Marcus, would be great. Seriously."

"I'll talk to Elizabeth. She's on several charity boards."

"You two are speaking?"

"Of course." They'd been too numb to tear at each other. She'd wanted a divorce and he saw no reason to fight her. "I should have asked you before now." He couldn't believe he'd been so fogged in by his own crisis he'd been oblivious to Carlos's.

"You could save me, *jefe*." Carlos slapped Marcus's shoulder. "And thank Christine for me, would you?"

"Excuse me?"

"She got you all horny and helpful, bro. Hell, sleep with her. You might come up with a cure for cancer."

IT WAS NERVE-WRACKING in the dark, but it was the only way David could practice driving without being seen. Since chores began at the crack of dawn, everyone was in bed by ten. He had a flashlight and Lady at his side, so he headed for the side of the clay works barn where the trucks were parked, keys in the ignition. No vehicle on the place was worth stealing and they were out in the middle of nowhere.

He'd talked Mitch, one of the college dudes, into showing him the basics one night when he was headed to town for a beer. He'd let David drive halfway to town and back.

It had been so scary on the winding roads that David's heart had been in his throat the whole time. When he'd parked, he'd been so sweaty he slipped right off the seat.

Now all he had to do was practice. As soon as he could make it all the way to New Mirage without passing out from hyperventilating, he'd be ready to head for Phoenix.

Heart pounding, he climbed into the cab of the truck. "Come on, girl," he whispered, patting the passenger seat for Lady to jump up. She walked backward, as if she didn't feel safe. He hoped she was wrong.

The engine would be noisy starting up, so he decided to push the pickup to the gate before turning the key. He used his flashlight to read the gear panel, set the truck in Neutral and, with the door open, put his weight into getting the heavy Ford rolling forward. He would make a slow curve away from the mesquite trees, then have a straight shot to the gate.

Lady whined at him and paced, clearly wondering

what he was doing. He'd only gone ten feet or so when he hit a gravel hump and had to rock back and forth to get enough momentum to bounce over it. He was breathing hard and his arm muscles throbbed when the truck finally made it. Whew.

Except the truck picked up speed and he realized they were on a slope. David's heart lurched. He leaned back, holding the door, dragging his heels to slow the truck, but it was too heavy and going too fast, headed straight for some trees.

Lady gave a sharp bark.

Running to keep up, David lost his footing, stumbled and dropped to the ground, scraping his knees, forearms and palms in the gravel. Lady hovered over him, whining. He watched as, with a sickening thud, the truck slammed into a mesquite tree.

Oh, no. He'd crashed the truck. Ignoring the sting and burn of his road rash, he ran to see how much damage he'd done, Lady at his heels. Leaning over the seat to get the flashlight, he bumped the horn, which gave a loud blast into the quiet night.

His heart in his throat, he ran the flashlight over the front of the truck to check the damage. It looked bad. Very bad.

"What the hell are you up to, David?"

He jumped at the sound of his grandmother's voice. Lady barked in surprise, too. He whipped around.

"Ouch." She blocked the flashlight beam with a hand. "Put that down, for God's sake."

"Sorry," he said, dropping it to his side. Lady nudged his thigh, as if to comfort him.

"You crashed the Ford?" His grandmother scratched her tangled hair. She wore a baggie T-shirt and sweatpants.

"I was trying not to wake anyone up."

"By honking the horn and making the dog bark? Here. Give me that." She yanked the flashlight from him and stomped to the other side of the tree to shine it on the front of the truck. "Well, the grille's destroyed. The radiator...maybe."

"Will it still drive?"

"Let's find out." She climbed into the driver's seat. This time Lady leaped right up and over her to the passenger seat.

"Are you supposed to be doing this?" he asked. "With your heart surgery and all?"

"*Now* you're worried? Like you didn't about give me a heart attack wrecking my truck? I'm fine. You're as bad as your mother and Bogie." She seemed just the usual grouchy, at least. She left the door hanging open and turned the key. The engine started, then died. She tried again. It rattled, turned, but didn't catch, dying again.

She shook her head. "I don't know, David. Doesn't sound too good. Let's hope Carl can repair it. God knows if they even make parts for this old thing anymore."

"I can help him fix it."

"You've done a lot of engine work, have you?"

He hung his head, feeling like he might cry.

"Maybe you can bring him lemonade or wipe the sweat out of his eyes." Her words sounded mean but he could tell she was trying to distract him from crying.

It didn't work. Tears were running down his cheeks. He'd wrecked the truck and he was further from seeing Brigitte than ever. Plus, now that the shock was over, his arms, palms and legs burned like hell. He peeled back his sleeve to examine his injury.

"You get hurt?"

"Just scraped, I think," he mumbled.

"You're better off than the pickup. There's peroxide in our medicine cabinet. Put some on when you get in. What were you doing driving? Your mother said no way."

"Mitch showed me how and I was practicing." His stomach felt like he was about to puke. "I'll pay for the repair." But it would have to be Christine's cash. How would he get it?

"Just say a prayer to the god of auto parts."

"Are you going to tell my mom?" She'd never let him out of her sight again. All his efforts to chill her out would be down the drain.

"Now how would that fix this?" Aurora shook her head and stared through the windshield at the mass of branches. "I guess I'll have to say I did it." She looked down at him. "I'll keep this between us on one condition—you tell me what this dead-of-night learn-to-drive thing is all about."

"You won't tell Mom?"

"Tell me what you're up to and we'll see."

He swallowed hard. "I was going to borrow the truck to get back to Phoenix."

"For the girlfriend, right? Barbara?"

"Brigitte. I have to see her." Lady whined, as if she felt the same urgency. "I really do."

"So, let me see if I got this. You were stealing my truck without knowing how to drive, planning to take a twisting mountain road to the highway, then drive eighty miles an hour to Phoenix in the middle of the night. What do you think Highway Patrol does when they see a kid weaving around? They stop him. And when they find out you have no license? Let's just say HP cops have no sense of humor. Trust me, I know."

"I was only practicing, okay? I wasn't leaving yet." He hated how stupid she'd made him sound.

"And what about gas money? Got any?" He shrugged. "This thing leaks oil like crazy. It can barely make it to town, let alone three hundred miles."

"I didn't figure that out yet."

She shook her head like he was a hopeless kid. "Okay, so you're desperate to see this girl. She desperate to see you?"

"I think so…. Maybe. I'm not sure anymore."

"She's older, right? She have a license? Invite her here."

"She doesn't own a car. Public transportation is green."

"She too green to *borrow* a car?"

"It doesn't matter. Christine would never let her come."

"Sometimes seeing a person in a different place changes how you feel about them. Maybe they'd get along better out here."

"Not Christine. No way."

"Give your mom more credit."

He couldn't believe she was saying that, since she picked on Christine every chance she got. Still, his mind was racing. What if Brigitte did drive here? She *was* interested in Harmony House. He could hide her in his room….

"You really love this girl?"

"Yeah." It felt good to let it out, like a balloon about to burst getting suddenly released. "She's, like, my life."

"You'll love a lot of people, David. Don't hold on so tight to one. Attachment isn't healthy. It breeds jealousy and possessiveness and a lot of poison you don't want inside you."

"Not with Brigitte." Not if you were lucky enough to find the one person who understood you. "Being away from her mixes me up."

"Then invite her to visit," she said. "I'll talk to your mother if you want me to."

"It wouldn't help. She doesn't get it at all." Bitterness welled up inside him and he blurted his secret wish. "I should be with my dad. She's always telling me that I'm like him, so that's where I should go."

The words scared him a little. He felt uneasy about his dad. Why hadn't he reached out to David in all these years?

"It would kill your mother if you left," Aurora said.

"She should understand. She left, too, right?"

His grandmother only looked at him. "That's a long story, David. It was a different time. And she was older than you."

"Just two years." He didn't see the difference at all.

His grandmother sighed. "All I know is your mother will think I've lost my mind when I tell her I crashed into a tree."

"I don't get what she has against you." She was always huffing and rolling her eyes and all the stories she'd told him about Aurora made his grandmother look bad. He'd loved it when she visited him when he was five, but his mom had bitched about all the fun stuff they'd done.

"Like I said, David. It's a long story."

"Anyway, I'm sorry I took the truck without permission."

"What's mine is everyone's here, you know that."

"Thanks, Grandma—uh, Aurora—for not telling her."

She waved away his gratitude and started back to the house. Lady jumped from the truck and stood with him, watching her go. Despite how much his scrapes were burning and how ashamed he was about the wreck, David felt lighter inside. Excited. He had a plan. Invite Brigitte here. He couldn't tell Christine, though, no matter what his grandmother said. If everything went well, no one would ever know.

"WHAT HAPPENED?" Christine asked her mother, watching Carl hook a winch to the back of a truck stuck against a mesquite. David had jumped in to ask Carl how he could help, which she was glad to see. At least he was showing an interest in something.

"I had a little accident," Aurora said, her cheeks bright red. Aurora was *embarrassed?* Unheard of. "I got the urge for a beer at Toad Tavern, so I jumped in the truck—"

"You *jumped* in the truck? First off, no driving for six weeks. I would have driven you to town, you know."

"Hold on." Aurora held up her hand. "So I had the car in Neutral, and it was rolling downhill, but it wouldn't start right off and—bam—I hit the tree." Her mother's eyes flitted back and forth. There was more to the story than that.

"Carl, watch the bumper now," Aurora said, moving closer. "David, get out of the man's way."

Christine had a terrible thought. "Did you black out?"

"Black out? Of course not. I was *going* for a beer. I hadn't had any yet."

"Not that kind of blackout. You might have had a stroke. Do you have any loss of feeling?" Her heart raced at the possibility. A stroke would be terrible. "Make a fist. Smile, too. I forget the tests to see if you've had one."

"Cut it out. Honest to God, if you stab me with a pin to see if it hurts, I'll knock you to the ground."

"She's fine, Mom," David said. "Don't worry." Was he limping?

"What's wrong with your leg?" she asked.

"I scraped it in the gravel. No big deal."

"You know kids, clumsy as hell," Aurora interjected. "And I did not have a stroke. I misjudged. A dumb mistake. Jesus."

"We should have your doctor check you out. Aren't you due for a checkup anyway?"

"Calm down," Aurora said, her expression softening. She looked Christine straight in the eye for once. "I'm fine. I really am. Please stop worrying about me." Her mother smiled.

What the hell? Her mother was being gentle and kind to her. This was new. Christine felt warm all over. "If you're sure…"

"Can I get your tools?" David yelled to Carl, who was pounding open the bent hood. "Or do you want water? I could get lemonade."

"I'm glad to see David being helpful," Christine said.

"He damn well ought to be," Aurora groused. "He doesn't always use his head, does he? Jumps in without thinking?"

"Sometimes, yes."

"That could really get on your nerves." Without looking at Christine, she added, "You weren't like that. You always had good sense."

"Why, thank you, Aurora," she said, amazed at the compliment and the sympathy over David.

"But if you don't let a kid make mistakes, he can't learn from them now, can he?"

With that her mother walked off. A compliment with one hand, a smack with the other. But what stayed with Christine was the tenderness in her mother's face, the kindness. For that moment, for that look alone, the trip to Harmony House seemed worth it. That wasn't why she'd come, of course, but it was something she longed for. Down deep inside, where the old hurts were buried.

CHAPTER EIGHT

"I'M GOING INTO TOWN with Todd and Robert to hang out," David said to his mother, his heart beating wildly in his chest. Brigitte was coming tonight and he could hardly stand it.

"That's so nice to hear," she replied, all happy. "I'm glad that worked out with them after all." She'd actually believed him when he'd told her the twins had quit smoking pot. He felt bad about lying to her, but he had no choice. She would not get it into her head that pot was no big deal.

David had bumped into the twins in town a couple days after the porn-and-pot shout-fest, and they'd practically kissed him on the mouth for saving their asses. Since then, he'd hung out with them a little. It killed the boredom somewhat.

The only annoying thing was how much they hounded him for some of Bogie's bud. First off, that would be stealing, and, second, these two were too obsessed with getting high. Which was insane with their parents, Mr. and Mrs. Social Nazi, who didn't know David was back in the sacred circle of their holy boys. They needed to chill out.

He liked Todd and Robert. They weren't bad for doofus jocks. Besides, since David had found out Brigitte was coming, the whole world seemed kinder and everyone in it more interesting.

After all the planning and dreaming, the big day had arrived. Friends of Brigitte's who were going camping were dropping her off at the New Mirage highway exit tonight and the Barlows were driving him there to meet her.

"I've seen you playing your guitar with Marcus a lot, too," Christine said, looking way too happy about that.

"Yeah." He rubbed his fingers together, feeling the calluses that had begun to form. With so little to do, he'd gotten more into his music. Whenever he played he felt like a hot wire burned from his brain to his fingertips to the strings.

That kind of embarrassed him and he'd almost asked Marcus if that made him lame or weak, but he wasn't sure the guy would understand what he meant.

Marcus didn't say a lot. Every question David asked him, he turned around so David ended up answering it himself. The dude was tricky that way. But he never jumped on David. He listened and asked questions that made sense without digging at him the way his mother's always did. Also, Marcus had said he wouldn't tell Christine what they talked about.

He didn't think Marcus liked his mom much.

Since the Barlow dinner they'd both acted strange, looking the other way or avoiding each other. That was fine with David. He liked Marcus being his friend alone.

"I can't believe you cleaned your room and changed your sheets. And were those flowers I saw on your desk?"

"Yeah. Bogie told me which ones I could cut." He'd set up an ice chest with sandwiches and juice, and the best commune food—fresh strawberries, tomatoes, snap peas and Bogie's cinnamon rolls. He'd bought two candles scented with sandalwood— Brigitte's favorite. He'd backed off on weed, too, to have some for when she came.

Close as the time was, it seemed forever away— like Christmas as a kid, where every minute of waiting was an hour, every hour a day, every day a year.

"I'm proud of you, David. You're trying. You finished your schoolwork without me getting after you."

"Not that big a deal." He'd wanted to be free of duties this weekend, so he'd done his last assignment the day before.

"Yes, it is. I mean it." God, there were tears in her eyes. She was building this up too much, making him feel guilty over his true reasons for everything he'd done.

"I know it's been hard for you being away from

Brigitte, but I appreciate how mature you're acting about it now."

Ouch. "It's not that big a deal, like I said."

"Not too late tonight, okay? Midnight?"

"I'll come say good-night when I get back." That way there would be no reason for her to knock at his door and interrupt his time with Brigitte.

"Wow. Great. I would like that." She looked so startled and so thrilled. The puniest things made her ridiculously happy. He got a stab of regret about lying. Like Marcus had predicted, once he started doing what she wanted, she'd gotten nicer to him.

She loved him. He knew that. He sure wasn't scared of her the way Todd and Robert were of their show-off parents, who pushed them to be captains of every stupid-ass team and were way more paranoid about pot than Christine.

He was half-planning to go back to Phoenix with Brigitte. If he did that, his mom would be sad, for sure. *It would kill your mother if you left.* That's what his grandmother had said.

The idea made his stomach sink. But, really, it was just like when kids left for college, the parents ended up relieved not to have to worry about them anymore. She'd be sad at first, then she'd see how right it was.

AFTER SUPPER, CHRISTINE NOTICED Marcus heading off to his room, Lady at his side. She wanted to thank him for helping David turn the corner so she half ran to catch up to him. "Marcus?"

He turned. "Christine." She did like the light that came into his eyes when he saw her. He smiled more, too, she thought, than when she'd first arrived.

They hadn't been alone together since that night on the hammock and standing this close to him made her nerve endings tingle and her muscles tighten.

Lady brushed her leg in greeting.

"I don't want to keep you from your book, but I wanted to thank you for what you've done for David." Every time she saw them with their heads together, talking or playing music, her heart surged with gratitude and relief.

"I enjoy David. He's smart and he has a good heart."

"You've really helped him, I'm not kidding. He's turned the corner. He finished his schoolwork, his attitude's better... It's a miracle." That alone had reassured her that not getting involved with Marcus had been the right decision. What mattered was Marcus helping David. Anything between her and Marcus might interfere with that.

"I'm glad to hear that," he said. "But don't be surprised if he relapses some. Progress is usually two steps forward, one step back."

She groaned in mock dismay. "I thought we were beyond the folk sayings. All I know is David's got a new light in his eyes. He cleaned his room and put flowers in it, for heaven's sake. He's fine with the curfew I gave him tonight. He even offered to come tell me good-night when he gets back from New Mirage."

"Like I said…"

"Two steps forward, one back. Yeah, got it, Doctor Downer. I don't care what you say. It's like I have the old David back."

"I'm glad, Christine." He smiled.

"So…good then… That's all I had to say." It felt lovely to stand with him, though. "You probably need to get to work. You pushed through your writer's block?"

"I did, yes. Largely thanks to you."

"To me?"

"After the Barlow dinner, on the porch that night, uh, I got kicked out of my stall. I went back to my room and wrote."

"You mean because we made out? Really?" She laughed.

He gave her a sheepish look. So cute.

"Wow. Because I got you…stirred up?"

"The dynamic concerns enzymes that control energy, focus and the sense of well-being."

"God, way to ruin it with science." She slapped playfully at him. "I was all excited about being your muse."

"You were," he said. "And, seriously, I also think it helped when you reminded me of all the blows I absorbed last year. Talking it out, I could see why

I might have been, well, less productive, and that helped break the block, too."

"I'm so glad, Marcus." Tenderness and pride filled her, but she couldn't get all emotional about it. "So you'll mention me in the acknowledgements? For *stimulating* your…thoughts? *Arousing* your interest?"

He laughed, low and deep and rich.

"Your eyes twinkle when you laugh, did you know that?"

"I didn't. No."

"You should do it more. Laugh, I mean."

"Then I guess I'll have to spend more time with you, Christine, since you make me laugh more than I have in a long while." He searched her face. "I've missed you."

"I've missed you, too." There was a moment of silence while the ribbon of connection tugged them together again. It was sexual attraction, sure, but it was more than that. She felt good with Marcus. Talking and joking with him cheered her up. She liked the way he listened so closely and accepted her without judgment. She liked the way his mind worked, so different from her own thinking. Hell, she was as hot for his personality as she was for his body.

Lady ran a few yards toward the cottonwood grove, then turned to bark at them, as if to urge them to come along.

"Looks like Lady has a plan," Christine said. "Could you spare time for a walk to the river?"

"Sure," he said.

They set off slowly, talking comfortably, bumping arms as they walked. Marcus was so handsome against the dusk sky, sturdy and strong and all man. Lady loped ahead, then circled back, seeming delighted they'd come along with her.

As they entered the cottonwoods, the evening breeze picked up, lifting her hair from her shoulders. The toads and crickets were tuning up for their nightly performance.

At the edge of the river, they sat on broad, smooth rocks. Lady ran off to explore. "When I was a kid, this was my secret place," she said. "And, believe me, with all the madness at Harmony House, I needed it. Not to mention all the arguments with Aurora."

"You both have strong opinions."

"But only one of us was right." She laughed. "How does she seem to you these days? Healthwise?"

"Stronger and her color's better. How about to you?"

"Better than when we got here three weeks ago, that's for sure. The truck crash worries me. What if she had a stroke?"

"Have you seen any behavioral or physical changes?"

"Not really. For a second there, she seemed loving

and kind, but that passed." She smiled. "I guess she's okay."

"How are you feeling about being here now?"

"Not bad. I like what we're doing at the clay works. It's satisfying. And I'm getting a kick out of making ceramics. I made this great set of goblets the other day. Aurora helped me glaze them and didn't bitch at me at all about my technique."

"Maybe she did have a stroke."

"You're funny, too."

"Only around you." He smiled, looking at her with affection.

Embarrassed, she gazed out across the water, which slid silkily downstream. "It's nice to use my hands, I guess. I've enjoyed being in the greenhouse with Bogie, too, planting things. Something about the air in there feels good to me."

"Sounds to me like you're enjoying yourself."

She turned to him. "I guess I am. I've been so fixated on the problems with David and the work at hand, arguing with Aurora and all, that I haven't really noticed." She thought about that for a second. "I dreaded coming back here so much, I just hoped I could gut it out without going to war with Aurora."

"And now…?"

She threw a stone at the river. "Now I don't mind being here so much."

"Not exactly high praise."

"Okay, I like it here. There, I said it." And she realized it was true.

"Enough to stay?"

"What?" She jolted at the question. "No. Of course not. Why would you say that?"

He shrugged. "Just wondering."

"Aurora keeps making comments like that. It's so weird. Not like her at all. I figure she's anxious about her health."

"A brush with mortality sometimes makes people want to redress past failures. She may be trying to resolve your conflicted relationship."

"So why doesn't she say that and get it over with?"

"She seems to be indirect about her needs and feelings."

"You got that, did you?" She smiled. "My theory is that once she's stronger, she'll shove me out the door."

"And you're eager to leave?"

"Once Aurora's back on her feet, yes." She shrugged. "Besides, if I were to stay, there'd have to be major changes around here."

"Like better water pressure?"

"Oh, absolutely. DSL Internet, too."

"That goes without saying."

"We'd have to paint the place, get some landscaping done. Do something about the smell."

"Sell the goats?"

"No can do. The cheese is *heaven*." She laughed

again, then looked at him. "What about you, Marcus? How much longer will you be here?"

"Long enough to finish the book. A couple months at least. For now, I'm about to send off a proposal to some agents."

She was pleased he'd be here as long as she would. "And after that? Back in L.A.?"

"I'm not sure. I'm looking into some public health funding for Carlos's clinic."

"Really?"

"Yes. My ex-wife has some leads for me on rural health grants."

"You're on good terms with her?"

"We've always been civil."

"That's very mature of you."

"Or it means I didn't allow a deep connection between us."

"It takes two to tango, Marcus."

He laughed. "A folk saying? I believe you could have a future in the mental health field, Ms. Waters."

"Thank you, Dr. B., but, really, no relationship is one-sided. Both people contribute to the problems. Even I, complete relationship screwup that I am, know that much."

"That may be true. But, as I was saying about my plans, I'm looking into funds for Carlos and working on my book. And, frankly, I'm glad to feel awake and alive again."

"And all thanks to me getting you turned on."

"Whatever works." His smile was swift.

"You know, afterward, I almost ran after you."

"Really?" He lifted his eyebrows. "To what end?"

"To what end? Jesus. To jump your bones, what else?"

"I see. Interesting."

"Interesting? That's all you can say?" She shifted closer and he leaned in, too. She took in his features, his mouth so close, a hunger in his eyes she recognized because she felt it, too.

"What made you stop?"

"Bogie, actually. On my way to you, I noticed him in the greenhouse and remembered that I hadn't spent time with him the way I'd meant to, that I didn't know how he was doing."

"So, you felt guilty?"

"At first. Then I remembered David was next door to you and what if he saw me at your door? Plus, I figured you'd be asleep and think I was an idiot."

"Oh, I doubt that."

"What would you have done?" she whispered, her mouth very near to his. This close, she noticed swirls of darker color in the crystalline green of his eyes.

"If I were smart I'd have declined." He cupped her face with his strong palms.

"But...?"

"But I would have welcomed you with open

arms," he said in a rush. He leaned in to kiss her softly.

"Marcus," she said, kissing him back, putting her arms around him and holding on. Waves of desire crashed against the breakwater of her good sense. Marcus was struggling, too—his fight for restraint obvious in the tension in his body.

They both began to shake.

Marcus broke off the kiss, cradling her face in his warm hands. "I can't stop wanting you. No matter what I do."

His words sent a white-hot ribbon of hunger twisting through her body. She needed this. She needed him.

"Let's go to my room," she said. "We can slip in without anyone seeing."

"What about David?"

"He's in town until midnight. It's perfect."

He watched her, clearly dying for a way to justify succumbing to the heat and need racing through them both.

"We're adults. We can keep it simple, can't we?"

"We can try," he said, crushing her against him, burying his mouth in her neck. "We can sure as hell try."

MARCUS COULD NOT believe he was sneaking into Christine's room like a teenager with parents down the hall. But he realized at the moment that he would do anything to get Christine naked and in his arms.

He held all judgments in abeyance, put all analysis on hold. He would be fully in the moment. With Christine that somehow seemed possible, even right. His desire for her was a drumbeat in his head, a haze of need, an ache in every part of his body.

When she let him into her pink room, he threw her on to the bed, then landed over her body, making the ancient springs squeal. She had to interrupt him to get condoms from the cupboard over the sink in her room. Elizabeth had been on the pill so he'd had no need for protection. Talk about not thinking ahead. He was clearly lost here.

When she returned, he went for her lush mouth, catching sight of her gray eyes, her pupils wide and gleaming with arousal. He plunged deep with his tongue, his senses slammed with awareness of her scent, her sounds and panted breaths, the brush of her hair, her breasts against his chest, the way she squirmed and bucked beneath him.

The drive to tear away her clothes and get between her thighs almost overpowered him, but he forced himself to slow down, take his time, absorb all of her.

"For God's sake, Marcus, do not slow down," she gasped.

"I want to enjoy you," he teased, kissing her throat.

"Oh, *no!*" she said, shoving him to the side so

she could whip off her top and bra. "Here. Enjoy." She flopped onto the mattress, arms over her head, offering her breasts to him.

"Mmm," he said, cupping the soft flesh, then tasting one.

She arched into his mouth. "Finally."

"That's right. Patience is not one of your virtues, is it?" He suckled her, making her buck and moan and rub herself against him so that he had to fight for control.

"We have to get *naked* now," she said, breathless and desperate, going after his belt.

He got her out of her jeans too roughly, but she didn't seem to mind, and she shoved his pants out of the way. Then they were nude, bodies pressed together. He held his weight off of her with his elbows and paused, letting them adjust to this new intimacy, the heat, the need, the anticipation of the act to come.

"You're doing it again," she moaned. "Making… me…*wait*." She ripped open a condom packet with her teeth. He took the condom and slid it on. Christine opened her thighs, and dug her fingers into his buttocks, urging him to enter her *now*.

So much for being tender. With a quick stroke, he buried himself deep.

"*Ohhh*, so…*gooood*," she said, clutching his back.

He groaned at her slick heat, the slide of her

muscles, her curves and swells and swollen velvet flesh.

It was as if they'd waited for this from the moment their eyes met in the Harmony House garden, as if *I want you* had been a pulse between them all these days and weeks. Maybe it had.

CHRISTINE LIFTED HER HIPS to meet Marcus's thrusts, deep and slow and *soooo* right. She could not believe how good this felt, how much she needed this. She'd been starving for this. *Starving.*

In sex, she was usually careful with timing, speeding up or slowing down to match her partner, but with Marcus she just let go. Wherever and however Marcus chose to take her, she knew she'd enjoy the ride. She trusted him, she knew him and he knew her. She let herself slip into pure sensation, reveling in the roller-coaster hitch upward toward the joyous drop to come.

This, this is what sex was supposed to be. This precious physical connection with another person, this intimate joining of need and yearning and lust and love—or at least affection.

Even as she bucked and tightened and rocked toward release, she wanted to hold on, make it last forever, take all the time Marcus could manage. Emotions clotted her throat—gratitude, amazement and joy. Tons of joy.

Then Marcus tensed, nearing orgasm, she thought. She sped her movements, catching up and holding on until she was flying with him through space and time, shivering, feeling spasm after spasm, Marcus's along with her own.

This was good…. *Sooo* good.

When they both stilled, Marcus rolled onto his back and Christine rested her cheek on his chest, feeling his heart beating fast and hard beneath her own, which was also racing.

She became aware of the moment-to-moment miracle of being alive—brain waves, energy transfer, circulation, breathing, her trustworthy heart pounding away, 24/7.

The moon gleamed through the window, giving them both an otherworldly glow. She snuggled into the cocoon they'd created, their limbs tangled, their skins sweaty and slippery, so close they seemed to be one body, not two. She felt so relaxed, so relieved, so good. This had to be right.

Marcus rested his hand on the side of her face. "You okay?"

"I'm amazing."

"You certainly are." He chuckled, running his fingers through her hair, soothing her. He hugged her closer. She loved that. She'd loved how they'd been together, how she'd felt. Fully *there*. Not worried or scared or swamped with memories or regrets. Just enjoying it all.

She was settling in, relaxing, when Marcus patted her arm. "I'd better go," he said, sliding away and sitting up.

"Not yet," she moaned.

"Didn't you say David would be saying good-night?"

"Oh. Yes! That's right." She'd forgotten. She checked the clock. It was barely ten. Whew. David's curfew was midnight. That had been careless of her. She'd gotten too lost.

She watched Marcus pull on his jeans, slip on his shirt, button each button with those strong fingers she wanted to feel on her body again.

"With that look on your face, you're not making it easy to leave." He leaned down to kiss her, cupping her cheek. He gave her a look so tender it took her breath away.

She wasn't done with him. Not at all. In the bed still warm from their lovemaking, she wanted more. "Can we do this again?" Next time they could slow down, discover the touches that pleased each other the most.

"Is that what you want?" he asked.

"I haven't felt this good in such a long time. I really needed that. If we're discreet around David…?"

He smiled at her, then opened his mouth to speak.

"Do *not* give me a folk saying, Marcus."

"Like *all good things must come to an end?*"

"Exactly like that."

"It sounds good to me," he said on a sigh. "But let's think about it before we decide."

"You are terminally sensible, aren't you?"

"Most of the time, yes. Not around you, it seems."

She smiled, loving that she'd made him lose his self-control.

He went to the door, opened it a crack to peek out. "I can't believe I'm sneaking out like a teenager."

"It's worth it, Marcus. Remember that."

"I will. You can count on that." He gave her a last smile, then slipped out the door.

Restless, Christine dressed and went for a glass of rose-hip tea, deciding to wait out front for David. She felt so good, her body relaxed, her joints loose and graceful. She didn't remember the last time sex had felt this good.

Maybe it was being in this offbeat place, away from the daily pressures and rush. Or maybe it was Marcus and her together. Some people set each other on fire, didn't they?

She took her glass to the porch and lay back in the hammock. She *loooved* the hammock. She *looooved* the cool breeze, the summer sounds, the smell of the river in the air. Tonight, she *looooved* everything she could see, smell, taste, hear or touch. Her mind was clear and her worries gone. David was better, after all, and she'd had great sex for a decent reason. Tonight, all was right in her world.

Headlights woke her as a car pulled up to the house. She blinked, then realized she'd fallen asleep in the hammock. Evidently the twins had brought David home early.

Maybe she and David would have a chat like in the old days. No pressure, not too many questions, so she wouldn't exasperate him. No point pushing her luck.

David stumbled out of the backseat, slammed the door and staggered toward the stairs to his room. Was he drunk? Christine's heart sank to the dirt.

CHAPTER NINE

"DAVID?" CHRISTINE CALLED. He didn't acknowledge her, just kept weaving toward the stairs.

She trotted to catch up with him. "David! What's wrong?"

"Leave me alone," he said, waving her away.

She stayed with him. "What happened to you?"

"I'm drunk, so *beee* 'appy. Alcoholz bedder, right? 'S legal." He lifted his face to hers. She saw that blood had clotted on a raised bruise on his forehead.

"You're hurt." She tried to look closer.

"Quiddit." When he lifted his hand to block her she saw his knuckles were scraped and swollen. He ran then, but lost momentum at the stairs and collapsed on the bottom step.

She sat beside him. "Were you in a fight?"

"I lost Brigitte," he groaned. "She was 'sposed to come."

"Brigitte was coming…*here?*"

"Grandma told me to invite her."

"She what?" God, Aurora. How was that backing Christine's authority? She'd okayed a secret visit from Brigitte?

"You got what you wanted," David said. "I can' gedder back." He lay against the steps, which had to be digging into his spine.

"I'm sorry, honey."

"No, you're not. Don't lie. You're glad."

"I didn't want you to get hurt." She'd hoped he'd lose interest in Brigitte, not get dumped. She'd give anything to take away his pain. "I know it doesn't seem that way now, but there will be other girls. You're so young and Brigitte is—"

He jerked upright. "Don't you dare trash Brigitte." His eyes blazed at her, his face pale in the moonlight. He had so much heart and he was so vulnerable. "Brigitte sees whoIam, not like you. You wan' me perfec'. You don't see me at all." Then, abruptly, his body tensed, and he threw up into the dirt beside the stairs.

She tried to hold his forehead as she'd done when he was little, but he pushed her away and retched again. When he finished he lay back on the stairs, gulping air. "Brigitte's my life," he said. "I…miss… her…so much."

"How did you hurt yourself?" she asked gently.

"I punched a wall…rammed my head. So what? Forgeddit." He pushed himself to his feet and tramped up the stairs, his hair flopping against his back, his boots thudding unevenly.

She followed him upstairs, even though she knew he'd shut her out. Sure enough, he slammed and locked the door. "Go away!"

She stood outside, helpless as ever. David wasn't better. He'd cheerfully cleaned his room and set out flowers because Brigitte was coming for a secret visit. Invited by Aurora.

Marcus had warned her. *Two steps forward, one back.* Except David was not only not better, he seemed worse. He'd gotten drunk—possibly gotten the twins drunk, too—slammed his head and hands into a wall and was even angrier at Christine. If anything, he'd taken three steps back and no steps forward at all.

DAVID SWAYED ON HIS feet, surrounded by the evidence of his broken heart—the flowers he'd cut, the candles on the window ledge he'd used to prop up the curtain so Brigitte could see into the courtyard, the ice chest of food he'd hoarded.

When she hadn't shown on time, David figured they must have left late, so he had called her—the cell signal from the highway was decent—to find out when they'd arrive.

But it turned out they'd never left Phoenix. Brigitte was at a party. A *party,* with laughter, music and yelling in the background the whole time they talked.

Her friends had had last-minute car trouble. She hadn't been able to call him because she didn't know the Harmony House number. *I figured you'd call,* she'd said, like it was no big deal. *Another time... Later... Whatever...* She'd just shrugged it off, happy to skip seeing him and party with her friends instead.

She was pulling away from him. He knew it then for sure. The twins had been nice about it, given him the vodka they'd swiped from their dad for themselves. They hadn't made him feel stupid for crying, either.

He'd hoped the liquor would numb him out. Instead, he felt raw, like someone had ripped off his skin and left him a blob of jelly on jiggling legs.

He heard a howl right outside his door. Lady. It was as if she sensed his sorrow and echoed it with her own. He opened the door and she trotted inside. She'd never been in his room before. He crouched down and she walked right up to him and licked his wet cheek, then sat on her haunches, watching him. That was nice. *She* cared, at least.

David rolled a joint with some of the bud he'd saved for Brigitte, hoping it would settle his stomach and make him sleepy. Then he lit the candles for the flicker and glow and the good Brigitte smell. His brain was thick, his body heavy, his limbs like blocks of wood. He wanted to drift off and never wake up again.

But the pot didn't zone him out. It got him thinking, wondering, scheming. Maybe he should call her again. If he could get to the highway where there was a signal…

He had to fix this, get her back. But how? His thoughts twined and twisted like the pot smoke hovering in the air before him. Maybe the problem was he wasn't aggressive enough with her. Maybe he had to grow a pair, be a man. She'd prefer a guy who took action, didn't pout or whine, just went after what he wanted. Sure. He'd been too passive. He knew what he had to do now. It was all so clear. What had taken him so long?

MARCUS AWAKENED TO THE sound of loud, rapid barking. Lady, of course, but he'd never heard her so frantic. He stumbled out of bed, then smelled smoke. Smoke? He yanked on his jeans and ran outside. On the terrace, Lady was scratching at David's door, barking and whining. She glanced over at Marcus, then back to the door, her bark changing to a high, urgent yip.

He realized the smoke was coming from David's room. "David!" he shouted, banging on the door with one fist, while trying the knob with the other. Locked. No answer.

Was David inside, overcome by smoke? Smoke killed in minutes, he knew. Marcus's body went electric. Not again. He would not lose someone else he cared for.

That meant breaking down the door. He slammed his shoulder against the wood, but it was too solid. "David!…Fire!" he shouted. Every second he wasted, the flames consumed more of the oxygen David would need to survive.

He needed a prying tool. Shouting "Fire" and

banging doors as he ran, he raced down the stairs, across the terrace to the utility shed, where he grabbed a crowbar and headed back.

Bogie met him at the bottom of the stairs. "What is it?"

"A fire in David's room. Call 9-1-1. Wake everybody. Get Carl up here to help me with the door."

Upstairs, Lady was still barking and scratching, but she backed away when he jammed the crowbar between the door and the jamb at the level of the knob. He threw his weight against the far end of the bar. Once, twice, but no good. He brushed sweat from his eyes, threw all he had against the metal rod, his skin tearing from the force of the blow. The door popped open, wood splintering, and smoke and heat exploded out.

Coughing, his eyes running, Marcus covered his mouth with his shirt, held his breath and pushed into the room. His skin tightened in the heat, but he moved forward, praying he wouldn't find David's body sprawled lifeless on the floor or in his bed.

The fire crackled at the back wall, yellow-white through the smoke. He felt as though his eyeballs were boiling in his skull.

He banged into a chair, shifted to the left, feeling his way toward the bed. When his shin hit the frame, he patted the mattress, praying the bed was empty.

It was. Thank God. David wasn't in the room. He rushed out to haul blessed air into his lungs.

Tears streamed down his cheeks and he was coughing hard, but he had to make sure everyone was outside and safe. Carl met him on the terrace carrying a fire extinguisher. "Mitch and Louis are bringing the water sprayer. A hundred gallons."

"It's a start. Do what you can with that." He nodded at the extinguisher. "We'll start a bucket brigade."

The fire crew would be volunteers and would likely take some time to get here.

Downstairs, he called to the milling residents, "Help me grab buckets," then led the way to the greenhouse. At the entrance, he found Christine. "What happened?" she asked. It was surreal to think that only a couple of hours ago, they'd been in bed together. Since then all hell had broken loose.

He took her by the shoulder. "David's not hurt, okay? There was a fire in his room, but he wasn't in it."

"He what? There's a fire? How did—" Her eyes were wide. "Where is he then?"

"I don't know. Right now we've got to put out the fire. Come and help."

She nodded, instantly focused on what had to be done, and hurried after him into the greenhouse.

HALF AN HOUR LATER, Christine handed Marcus another water-filled plastic bucket. Her back and arms throbbed from the strain. "Have you seen

David?" She'd kept an eye out but hadn't seen her son.

Marcus shook his head, handing the bucket forward, breathing hard, his face and bare chest streaked with sweat and ash.

"He was so upset. Where would he go? Do you think he would run away? Try to go to Phoenix for Brigitte?"

"How would he manage that?"

"I don't know. Maybe the twins came back for him." She felt sick thinking about it.

The whine of a siren made everyone pause to listen, then cheer with relief.

"We've contained the fire at least," Marcus said, looking over the billowing smoke. "Hopefully, the damage isn't too extensive."

"What caused it? Surely not David, do you think?" The idea horrified her. "He's not destructive." She gulped, remembering the bump on his head and his beat-up fists. Surely he hadn't done something as awful as start a fire.

"Marcus, I've got to find him," she said, handing him the next bucket. "I'm sorry." Without waiting for his response, she ran back to the house for her car keys.

When she returned to the yard, two fire trucks were pulling up, followed by a pickup bearing a *New Mirage Fire Department* insignia. The truck parked and David got out of the passenger side. Thank God he was safe. Relief flooded her.

"David!" She ran over. She wanted to hug him, but first she needed some answers. "Where were you?"

"Trying to get himself killed." The driver of the truck, a woman in fire gear, glared at David. "You his mother? Because this young man needs a serious talking to. He was backing onto the road from the shoulder with no lights. I nearly T-boned him into next week. Real, real stupid." She shook her head, then loped off to join the fire crew.

"You were *driving?*" Christine demanded. "How could you drive?"

"Mitch showed me. I swerved to miss a deer and slid down the shoulder," he said, pale and shaken, no longer sounding drunk. "I couldn't get back on the road. I kept trying."

"With no lights on? You could have been killed. What were you thinking? Where the hell were you going?" She tried to keep hysteria out of her voice.

"I had to get home," he mumbled.

"To Phoenix? You took a truck in the middle of the night. What is wrong with you?"

He hung his head.

"The fire started in your room, you know."

"My room?" He looked in that direction. Two fire hoses played over the far end of the second floor.

"Do you know how that could have happened?" she asked, praying he hadn't done the unthinkable, holding the memory of the sweet helpful boy he used to be in her heart while she waited for his answer.

"No. I mean I didn't start it. I just…left…." His eyes went even wider. "Oh. It might be—" He grimaced. "I might have left candles burning in the window."

"Near the curtain?"

"Sort of. I…forgot…. I was…freaked out." He looked angry now. "It was an accident. People light candles. So what?"

She grabbed him by his shoulders and shook him. "Listen to me. You could have killed people. Marcus. Carl. Mitch and Louis. The whole house could have gone up in flames due to your carelessness."

"I'm sorry, okay?" He looked suddenly bereft, bony shoulders slumped, hair hanging down. "I didn't know. I didn't mean…what happened." His voice wobbled and he started to cry.

"I know you didn't," she said, feeling his pain, her anger fading. He hadn't set the fire. He'd only caused it. As if that weren't horrible enough.

"Let's go see how they're making out," she said. Together the headed to the residents watching the fire crew work. As they approached, Lady noticed and ran to David, jumping up to put her paws on David's chest. David dropped to his knees to hug the dog.

"Everything okay?" Marcus asked. "David?"

He glanced up at Marcus, then back at the dog.

"David was driving to Phoenix when he swerved

off the road and got stuck. One of the firefighters almost hit him in the dark. He left candles burning in his room. That's what caused the fire."

"I see." Marcus looked down at David.

"I don't know for sure," David mumbled, keeping his gaze on Lady.

"Marcus risked his life breaking into your room to save you. He thought you were inside. He could have *died,* David."

"You did?" David looked up, horrified.

"Lady noticed the smoke and woke me up with her barking. She was scratching and whining at your door."

"She was? Oh." He blinked, and pressed his face into the dog's side. "Thank you, girl," he said.

"And what about thanking Marcus?" Christine demanded, her voice shrill. "And apologizing for what you did? His room is burned, too. What about that?"

"Thank you." David stood, unable to meet Marcus's eyes. "I'm sorry…I didn't mean…what happened." He spun away and ran toward the cottonwoods.

"David!" she yelled, tears in her voice.

"Let him go." Marcus took her arm.

"He has to face what he did," she said.

"Take a moment to breathe, Christine," he said in a low voice that caught her attention, settled her panic a little.

"You could have been killed," she said. "We all

could have." She could barely speak around the lump in her throat.

"But I wasn't. No one got hurt and only a few rooms were damaged. Don't make this worse than it is."

"What about your book, all your research?" As if risking his life weren't enough, he might have lost all he'd worked for.

He patted his jeans pocket. "I've got a backup thumb drive on my keychain, which, luckily was still in my jeans. As for the research, we'll have to see. No one was hurt. That's what matters."

"How can you be so calm?" Then she had a horrible thought. "You had to break down the door… like with Nathan— David might have been— Oh, I'm so sorry, Marcus. So sorry and so grateful." She felt tears on her cheeks. She wiped them away.

"I'm glad I was there," he said, but she saw the flash of pain in his face. He'd paid a price for his heroism. "Come here." He pulled her into his arms, his bare chest smelling of smoke and clean sweat and she accepted a brief moment of comfort before pulling away. She had to stand on her own feet, no matter how weak and shaky she felt.

"I have to handle David right," she said, but her brain seemed to freeze. She didn't have one clear thought, only a rush of bad feelings—regret, fear, failure. "I don't know what to say to him. Do I lecture him? Try to make him feel worse? Punish him? How?"

"You'll know what to do and what to say. You love David. You know him very well. Trust your instincts."

"My instincts? You mean the ones that told me David had improved, when he was really plotting a tryst with the girl who messed him up in the first place?"

"You might have been excessively optimistic for a moment, but your gut feelings are solid. David's struggling with intense emotions right now. Give him a chance to sort them out. Give yourself a chance, too. You'll know what to say and do."

"I'm not so sure."

"I have faith in you both." Marcus stood so broad and strong, silhouetted against the darker sky, she almost believed him. Standing with him, she felt protected, taken care of, safe.

That was different for her. Christine took care of herself, her son and her world and always had. This felt good, but also risky.

After the fire crew hacked into the walls of the three rooms damaged by the fire to be sure they'd missed no embers, they permitted everyone to return to the unharmed portions of Harmony House.

Christine gathered bedding for Marcus and David, the only residents who'd lost rooms. David helped her shift furniture out of the way in the spare room next to hers, where he would stay. Marcus took an empty room on the far end of the second floor.

Once the bed was made, David sat on it, his head

in his hands. He looked so bereft, surrounded by stacks of chairs, boxes, old lamps and battered tables.

"You got what you need?" Aurora's gruff voice came from the doorway. "Don't be lighting any matches in here, David," she said, nodding at the tower of cardboard boxes beside him, clearly trying to make a joke. It fell flat.

"I'm so sorry, Grandma," he said, gulping air.

"What did I tell you about calling me that?"

"Whatever. I'm just…sorry."

"Accidents happen," she said. "Get some sleep and we'll sort it all out tomorrow."

He nodded miserably.

Christine followed Aurora out into the family kitchen. "I don't suppose Harmony House has fire insurance?"

Her mother laughed. "What do you think?"

"Worth asking, I guess. I'll pay to rebuild the damaged rooms. We'll get a couple of estimates."

"No need."

"Of course there's need. We're taking full responsibility." It would take a serious bite out of her savings, but it had to be done. "I am very sorry David did this. I know this is the last thing you need right now."

"The place is old. Fires start. Forget the estimates and keep your cash. We'll fix it, or we won't. And forget the blame. Blame means guilt and guilt is pointless."

"But we are to blame. David was so drunk he left candles burning near a curtain. If it hadn't been for Lady and Marcus, Harmony House might have burned to the ground. And I'm to blame for allowing him too much freedom—that room off by himself for one thing—and, for…I don't know, thinking he was doing better. We're taking responsibility and we're paying for the repairs. Period."

"Things happen for a reason, Christine."

"What? David was *supposed* to nearly kill us all?"

"No one died. Don't blow this out of proportion."

"Excuse me? David ran off the road and was nearly hit by a fire truck. He was on his way to Phoenix, barely able to drive, no permit and drunk."

"I told him not to do that."

"Excuse me? You told him not to do what?"

"I…oh, hell. I caught him trying to practice driving. And I told him not to drive because you didn't want him to. He was the one who hit the tree."

"David crashed the truck? Why didn't you tell me?"

"I didn't see the point. And he learned his lesson."

Christine remembered something else. "David said you told him to sneak Brigitte here. Is that true?"

"I told him to talk to you about a visit."

"Why didn't you say something to me?"

"He didn't want me to."

"So what? You're the adult. After all the trouble he's been in, you didn't think I should know this?"

"It was up to him," Aurora said stubbornly.

"So, if he'd taken off for Phoenix tonight, that would be okay with you?"

"It's his life, Christine," she said, jutting out her jaw, defensive now.

"That is so typical of you. *If you love something let it go,* right? That's just an excuse to not do the hard parts of parenting. I will not abandon my son to the fates or the universe or whoever you think runs the show." Christine was furious.

"That's what you think I did? Abandon you?"

"That's sure as hell how it felt." The words were out before she could stop herself. She was so tired and scared and worried. "I waited for an hour at the bus station, thinking you'd come get me, but you didn't. You let me go. I will never do that to David. I will always reach out to him."

"If you want to blame me for every zit and hitch in your life, Christina Marie, you go right ahead, but whatever I did or didn't do, you turned out pretty damn good if you ask me." Her mother's eyes flashed at her. *Christina Marie.* Her mother hadn't called her that since she'd changed her name to Crystal.

Christine's anger dissolved. What was she doing? Instead of apologizing to her mother about the fire, she'd picked a pointless fight. "I'm sorry I said that. I'm upset."

"Well, don't be. The fire doesn't change life around here and it's not the end of the world. And as for David, the kid's not perfect, but then neither are you. Nothing is. You keep forgetting that." With that Aurora turned and headed down the hall.

Christine leaned against the sink to catch her breath—something she should have done before losing it with Aurora. Christine closed her eyes. She was exhausted and shaky scared. Maybe Marcus had faith in her, but she didn't deserve it.

Heading to her room to try for sleep, she looked in on David. He lay on his back, one arm slung over his eyes, the way he had as a little boy. For a moment, she saw him as he'd been—sensitive and eager, helpful and loving. How had the boy who was now so big his feet nearly hung off the bed ever been tiny enough to fit inside her body?

What if he'd been in that room with the fire? What if he'd wrecked on the road? Icy terror washed through her. Looking at him, she swore it again: *I will not lose you.*

As if he'd heard her thought, he sighed and dropped his arm. He was awake. What should she say to him? *Trust your instincts,* Marcus had said. For now that would have to do.

She went to sit on the side of the bed. "You okay?" She brushed the hair out of his eyes, startled anew by the ugly bump on his forehead.

"Don't." He turned away and pressed his face into the pillow, as if to hide from her. She noticed his knuckles again.

"Can I get ice for your hand?"

"No." He looked up at her, his eyes desolate. "I know you hate me. I'm a shitty son."

"No, you're not. I love you, David."

"I should leave you alone, quit messing up your life…."

"My life is fine. It's yours that needs some work."

"I belong with my dad. I miss him so much."

"You hardly knew him, David." She fought the panic that always arose when he brought up Skip. David wanted to run from what he'd done, so he'd jumped to his imaginary perfect father as his escape hatch.

"We used to have fun." He hesitated. "Was he mad at me? Because of that fire in his apartment I started? And now I did it again. Started another fire. I'm such a loser." His face crumpled and he began to cry.

"It was an accident, David. And the fire at Skip's was not your fault." She'd thought David had forgotten that. He'd been barely five. Her heart lurched. "Skip should never have left you alone. I should never have left you with him."

She'd known better than to trust Skip for an entire weekend, but she'd had a last-minute commercial shoot in LA, and no place else for David to stay.

"You were trying to make oatmeal." But he'd put a metal bowl in the microwave, which sparked and set off a fire. Luckily, neighbors heard the smoke alarm and called 9-1-1.

"We were lucky you weren't hurt." She'd never forget the terror she'd felt pulling up to the apartment to find fire trucks and police parked there, then the sight of David sitting on the bumper of an ambulance, wrapped in a blanket, his eyes blank with shock.

"I remember the alarm screeching and screeching and how bad the smoke smelled, then a fireman pulling me out from under the bed."

They'd told her it was common for children to hide from a fire they'd lit.

"Is that why he never invited me over again?" David demanded now, his eyes wild. "He didn't forgive me for that?"

"You did nothing wrong. He was playing poker instead of keeping you safe. He knew it was his fault. After that we moved to Phoenix, remember?" David had had nightmares for weeks and clung to her at night. Christine had left Skip and his bad habits in Albuquerque. Skip had neither objected nor asked for visitation rights. He knew he didn't deserve them.

"This time it's all on me," David said, desperation in his eyes. "I was so stupid. I hate myself."

"It was an accident, David. No one was hurt. We'll get through this. We'll fix it. We'll rebuild the damaged rooms. You'll help. You can hammer nails or paint. Whatever is needed." It would be cheaper if the commune residents did the construction themselves for sure. She might have to fight Aurora to even do that. "And you'll try harder around here—be better, do better, right?"

He nodded, still miserable. Maybe David's horror over what he'd done would jolt him into changing, or was that also excessive optimism on her part? She thought of something else. "You and Marcus have been talking, right? What about if you get his ideas on how to do better? Talk with him?"

"You mean be his patient?"

"Not in a formal way, no." Marcus wouldn't want that. But their talks could be more directed, more purposeful, with David fully involved in the process. "You would discuss your problems and he'd suggest ways to do better. Would you do that? Talk to him? Get serious about it?"

"Marcus is okay, so I guess."

"I'll ask him then. We'll figure it all out tomorrow. Get some sleep now, all right?" This time when she touched his hair, he didn't turn his head away. She smoothed the locks away from the bump. "The swelling's going down. You won't have a scar."

At least not on the outside. She hoped Marcus would agree to more talks. David needed all the help he could get.

Marcus… His name made her go hot and cold all

over. He'd been her rock tonight, comforting her, reassuring her.

And before that? They'd been in bed. She couldn't believe that mere hours before David got drunk, started a fire and tried to run away, she'd been blissfully making love, acting as if she hadn't a care or concern in the world.

There was a lesson there. Clearly, they had to stop. The sex had been lovely…heavenly…achingly good, but it was over, especially now that she would ask Marcus to spend even more time with David. Believing David was better, she'd allowed herself to be selfish and shortsighted. Marcus had figured it out, she realized, suggesting they think about it. He wanted to let her down gently. Sex was not worth the risk, not even sex so good the thought of never having it again made her almost cry.

CHAPTER TEN

PART WAY THROUGH THE DAY after the fire, Lady's woof made Marcus look up from dragging his charred desk onto the terrace. The dog was galloping toward Christine and David, who were heading his way.

Seeing David jolted Marcus back to the night's crisis, to prying at David's door, the scream of adrenaline in his head, the burn in his gut, his terror that the boy had died while Marcus slept heedlessly next door.

As he'd worked, he'd felt the painful déjà vu of breaking into Nathan's bathroom, finding him slumped against the tub, his skin gray, the needle still in his hand, the belt around his upper arm. While Nathan had been giving himself a lethal injection of drugs, Marcus had been oblivious, working at his computer. He would never forgive himself. Never.

Marcus shook himself clear of dark regrets. Now, in the sunlight of the present, David was unharmed. And there was work to be done. That was where he should focus.

"Oh, dear. It's bad, huh?" Christine asked, surveying all that Marcus had brought onto the terrace to dry—furniture, books, papers, clothes, his computer, the mattress on its side, too wet to salvage.

"It could be worse," he said, rubbing his eyes, which felt as though they'd been scraped by sandpaper from smoke and lack of sleep. "It's mostly water damage. The walls got ripped up pretty good. The smoke smell should fade. I haven't tried the computer, but it's pretty wet. The books will dry. I can get copies of most of the research." The pages and files had been soaked, trampled and torn. "My net book survived so I can keep working."

"What about your guitar?" David asked, looking at the case braced against the wall.

"Safe and dry. How about yours?"

"I had it in the truck, so it's okay." He hung his head, evidently feeling guilty about his attempt to run away.

"Can we help you?" Christine asked.

"Want me to carry out more stuff?" David asked.

"I've got it, David. Go ahead and start on your room."

David nodded glumly, then turned for next door.

Christine followed Marcus into his room. "We'll pay for everything you lost. I feel so bad we did this to you."

He shook his head. "The computer's outdated.

Nothing else is worth replacing. I brought very little here."

"I have to do something, Marcus."

"It's all right. I have what I need and a place to stay. No real harm done." He wanted to take her into his arms to reassure her, except David was nearby.

"Mitch and Louis have worked construction, so they're going to give me an estimate on supplies. If we do all the labor, with their help, it shouldn't be too expensive." She bit her lip.

He wished he could slow the churn of her worries. Hell, he wanted to hold her again. So much for taking time to think about it. Just seeing her made him want to make love with her. "How are you feeling? Did you sleep?"

"Not much. You?" Their voices held the tenderness that came from physical intimacy and closeness.

"Not bad. How did your talk with David go?"

"Surprisingly well," she said, brightening a little. "He's agreed to work on the repairs and to try harder. Perhaps I'm being excessively optimistic again, but he seems motivated this time."

"That would be a reasonable reaction."

"Actually, Marcus, I have another favor to ask you. I know that sounds outrageous after what we did to you—but…well, it's important." She searched his face, her eyes hopeful and anxious.

"Yes?"

"I asked David if he would talk with you about his problems. Not like a session or anything. I know you don't want that. But more direct and specific than before. And he'll take your advice, he says. Is that okay with you?"

She wanted him to go deeper with David, uncomfortably close to therapy. Feeling as he did about the boy, Marcus no longer had a shred of professional neutrality. "You might be happier with a formal therapeutic relationship. Now that David's willing to work on his issues, the therapist could create a full treatment plan and truly—"

"But he trusts you, Marcus. And we'll be leaving soon. Starting new with a therapist doesn't seem smart."

Would he truly be able to help David or would his feelings blind him to the boy's needs? He was now far too enmeshed in both their lives. If he wanted to back away, this was the time.

"Mom! Help!"

David's shout brought them both running next door, where a set of bookshelves had toppled onto his back and shoulders. He was struggling to hold them up. Marcus and Christine lifted the shelves away.

David stood, looking shaken and pale.

"Are you hurt?" Christine asked, a black streak on her cheek from grappling with the charred shelves.

"No," he said, rubbing the back of his head. In

his other hand he held a photo in a blackened frame, the glass cracked. David and a girl. Brigitte, no doubt.

"Let me see," Christine said, checking his skull through his hair.

David pulled away. "It's okay. I'm fine. Just quit."

Watching the two of them, Marcus's heart went tight. They looked like war refugees, lost and shaken and scared. He would do whatever he could to help them, no questions asked. "Your mother tells me you'd like to talk with me," he said.

David's gaze shot to his. "Yeah, I guess. If you want."

"This has to be something *you* want. For yourself. Not to appease your mother or out of guilt."

David considered that for a moment. "I want to be…a better person. So, yeah, I want that."

Christine heaved a relieved breath.

"Then we'll start tomorrow," he said, hoping to hell he was doing the right thing. He'd sworn to do no harm. Could he do some good? He wanted to very much. More than he'd wanted anything in a long time.

AFTER CHRISTINE HELPED David salvage what he could from his room, she got the repair estimate and headed over to talk to Bogie about it. He might have tips for how best to approach Aurora.

Her vision was blurry from exhaustion and she

had that hungover feeling of not having slept. Everything threatened and loomed and ordinary tasks felt monumental, but stepping into the moist, loamy air of the greenhouse, and seeing all that life, she felt much better.

Bogie stopped his soft whistling and smiled. "Hey, girl. You doing okay after last night?"

"I'm fine. It's the house I'm worried about. We made quite a mess of it."

"It's nothing we can't handle. No worries about that."

She smiled. Bogie did make her feel better, even if he was completely wrong. "I want to get it fixed up. And I talked to the guys who know construction—Mitch and Louis?—and they said it won't be too difficult." About three grand in lumber, wiring, insulation, wallboard, plaster and paint. "I'd like to get started right away while they're still here. I figure we can let some chores slide a bit, borrow people for the labor. If we have to, we can hire extra help, too."

"What does Aurora say about that?" he asked, rearranging some seedlings in small clay pots on the slats of wood.

"That's where I hope you can help. We kind of argued about it already."

"Aurora can get scratchy about changes. Why don't you take a look at those anemones you planted." He pointed down the row. She walked over and saw slivers of green poking up in every square. "They're coming up!" She felt ridiculously proud, though she knew it was just nature doing its thing. Trees sprouted from sidewalks, for God's sake. She'd merely picked the place and offered soil and water. Still, it seemed so brave of the seed to send up a shoot, come what may. "That is so cool."

"Make sure the soil's damp, not soggy now." These minor miracles were everyday events for Bogie in his greenhouse.

She checked. "It feels right."

"When the leaves touch, we'll thin them out. These lilies are ready to go into bigger containers. How about we repot them? Grab me three of the mediums." He gestured to the stacks of graduated containers.

She brought them over. "So what about Aurora? How do I approach her? Or should we buy the supplies and go for it?"

Bogie didn't answer, just gently shook the lily out of its clay pot. "See how the roots are twisted and crammed together? It's maxed itself out."

"Yeah, I see that." She forced herself to calm down and focus on what he was showing her.

"Always use the very next size up. Not too big or the plant exhausts itself absorbing food and water." Bogie braced the plant in one of the pots she'd brought, then nodded for her to pour in his special formulation of loam, peat and sharp sand.

They repotted the rest together, working in

peaceful silence. "Did I do this one okay?" she asked him.

Bogie nodded. "You did it just right."

"You always were a good teacher." She remembered he'd been so patient with her and the other kids, tolerant of silliness and mischief. He'd taught her to pick strawberries without bruising them and to set the irrigation tubes in the big fields.

"I just show what I know." He shrugged, finishing the last lily. "Aurora won't let you spend your savings on this, you know that. She's got plenty of cash."

"But it's our responsibility, Bogie. We—" She stopped. "What do you mean, plenty of cash? We're bringing in more from the clay works, but I don't see that as *plenty*."

"From her parents. When her mother passed, an attorney tracked Aurora down with quite a pile of dough. She didn't want to take it, but I said we might need it for emergencies. I was right, what with her heart surgery and all. But there's thousands left."

"*Thousands?* Why hasn't she spent any of it on the commune? I mean, at least paint the house. Fix the plumbing, the wiring, put in some landscaping. Harmony House could be so much more appealing. You said you wanted more residents, right?"

Bogie stopped working and looked at her closely. "Is that what you want, Crystal? To fix up the place?"

"Me? I don't know. I'd love to improve things.

Who wouldn't?" She remembered joking with Marcus about what fixes she'd need to stay here. Then she realized what Bogie might be asking. "Wait. It's not my soul's work or anything, if that's what you mean, but it would be fun for sure."

She'd love to give Harmony House a fresh face. Abruptly, she remembered Winston talking about "experience" vacations. Harmony House would be perfect for that—*experience life in the oldest continuously inhabited commune in the west.* Travelers would eat that up. Especially a new and improved commune. One with clean towels and hot showers.

Her advertiser's brain was spinning with plans. They would place ads in travel venues, pitch themselves to travel agencies and travel writers…. This could be great.

Then reality set in. "Aurora would never go for it," Christine said. "She had a conniption over buying a computer, which, by the way, she never leaves alone now."

"Your mother listens when you say something she believes in her heart, but won't let into her head." He deftly pushed some seeds into a flat of potting soil. "How do you think I talked her into keeping the money in the first place?"

Hmm. So Bogie knew how to work around Aurora after all.

"Of course, doing all that construction and painting and landscaping will take more time," he said, shooting her a wily look. "That might appeal to your mother."

Uh-oh. More time would not work. David had school and she had her job.... But if they started immediately, it should be easy to make her mid-August departure time.

"If this is right, you'll find a way." He looked her straight in the eye, no humble ducking or shuffling at all. Bogie had surprised her. Maybe her mother would, too.

THAT EVENING AFTER SUPPER, Marcus handed Christine another stack of plates to rinse, but she didn't seem to notice. She'd been talking to him nonstop about her plans to fix up Harmony House and how she would convince Aurora to go along with them.

Only a day after the fire, she'd charged past her despair straight into ways to make things not only right, but better. She amazed him with her energy and optimism. She wore him out, too.

And turned him on. Right now, watching her lips and flashing eyes, the sway of her hips, the swell of her breasts, he wanted to take her into his arms and kiss her to silence. He couldn't wait to take her to bed again.

"What?" she demanded. "You think I'm crazy to ask Aurora?" She'd misread him entirely.

"Not even close." He leaned in. "I'm thinking about getting you naked."

"Oh…Marcus…" She closed her eyes, clearly feeling the same bone-melting lust he did. But when she opened them again, she wore an entirely different expression. Sorrowful, but resigned. "I think it's better if we stop," she said.

"You do?" He was startled. She'd seemed pretty eager to keep going at the time. His heart sank.

"Not that I don't want more. I do. *Lots* more. But since you'll be spending more time with David, I'm afraid to risk it. I lost my focus, I think. Plus, there's so much to do now because of the fire."

"I can understand that," he said, swallowing hard.

"It was lovely, escaping for a while. I'll never forget it, but I think we should leave well enough alone. I mean, why risk complicating things or possibly hurting each other or—"

"You don't need to convince me, Christine."

"I guess I'm convincing myself." She put a hand on his arm and looked up at him. "I want you almost more than I can stand."

Heat shot through him, nearly buckling him with desire, but he held himself in check. "That seems the wisest approach," he said, managing to look sober and serious. "Better for everyone."

"I'm glad you agree." Did she look a little hurt? That made no sense.

They were both right. It was sensible, sound and smart to quit. But Marcus felt hollowed out, let down, *hurt*.

What the hell was wrong with him? Sex was great, but hardly life-altering. He and Christine had had one frantic encounter that was more of a collision than an act of love. How could ending it cause him so much pain? Perhaps waking from his numb fog wasn't all it was cracked up to be.

WATCHING MARCUS CROSS the courtyard away from her, Christine wanted to chase after him and take it all back. Which was ridiculous, since Marcus had been so quick to quit on them. *The wisest approach... Better for everyone.*

If she did chase him, he'd raise an eyebrow. *Get hold of yourself, Christine. This reckless behavior does not become you.*

It kind of hurt her feelings, really, that he could brush her off like so much lint off a jacket.

She kept thinking about it, reliving it. Marcus's mouth on hers, his knowing hands, the way he'd whispered her name, how safe she'd felt in his arms. Every time she looked at him, her knees turned to water.

Never mind. She had vital work to do at the moment: convince Aurora to spend her inheritance fixing up the commune. She braced her back against the kitchen wall and took several deep breaths, readying herself to enter the dragon's lair...well, go out onto the porch and face her mother.

Aurora was in her usual spot—the rocking chair

near the hammock. "Nice night," Christine said, sitting in the hammock.

"I can still smell smoke from the fire," she said, crinkling her nose, then glancing at Christine.

"Not for long, I hope." She took a deep breath. *Here we go.* "Especially if we get started on the repairs right away, while Mitch and Louis are here to save us labor costs."

"There's no rush, Crystal."

"But I think that if we get on this, we could make some improvements to the place. Simple things— paint, landscaping, electrical, plumbing, like that. While I'm here to supervise."

"Harmony House is *fine.* Are you never happy with anything?"

The words felt like a slap, but Christine made herself smile. "Maybe not. And, actually, Bogie has been asking me about what will make me happy here. He wants me to figure out my 'soul's work.'"

She was surprised when her mother's face softened. "That man has always been a pest about that. When he let me move into the place he was renting—it was after the miscarriage—anyway, there were a bunch of people living there, mattresses all over the place, and he was always after us: *Are you happy? What do you need to be happy? What speaks to your soul?* Lord God above."

Her mother usually only talked about her past to illustrate some point in one of her lectures, so

Christine didn't know many details beyond the fact that after her parents refused to let their pregnant daughter back home, Aurora had stayed with friends, slept in cars, sometimes worse. Three months in, she'd lost the baby. Not long after that, Bogie had invited her to become one of his shifting set of housemates.

"So *were* you? Happy, I mean?" Christine asked.

"I was sixteen. All I knew was I was free. Happy takes time. I had to learn that."

"What about now? Are you happy now?" That was a nosy question for her very private mother, but she wanted to know.

"I'm still learning." She turned to look straight at Christine, both feet planted on the porch boards. "I promise you that slapping a coat of paint on Harmony House and planting some hedges will *not* make you happy, Crystal."

"What if it's my soul's work?" she said, half-joking. "Isn't that worth a try?"

Her mother began rocking again, silent for a while. "You don't have the kind of money to pay for all that."

Christine decided to say it straight out. "Maybe not. But you do. Bogie told me about the inheritance."

"He what? That was not his right!" she snapped. "Dammit!"

"He wanted to help me. He likes my idea." She

realized her heart was racing. More and more she wanted to do this. It felt like fixing her past, smoothing out the rough spots, making Harmony House neater, cleaner, organized and steady—a place Christine might not have minded living in as a child.

"You can approve every nail, paint color, tree or bush if you want. And I will see it through to the end, until you're satisfied, no matter how long it takes." That was a gamble, of course, and she crossed her fingers that she wouldn't be pushed beyond her planned departure date.

There was a long silence while Aurora thought this over. Christine focused on the crickets and toads singing happily, and on the soft air on her skin, the sway and creak of the hammock.

Finally, Aurora spoke, her voice soft. "My parents were spiteful people. Cold and hard and mean. They didn't love me or understand me or even try. I never forgave them. Not that they asked me to. They didn't care enough." She gave a half smile.

"I didn't want one dime of their money. Not one dime. Bogie hammered me about it and I finally gave in. The medical bills ate up some, but there's a lot more hanging over my head."

Her eyes took on a faraway look, almost sad, then she came back to Christine. "Hell, what you're planning is as good as throwing that cash down a hole anyway, which suits me just fine."

"So you're saying yes?" Christine's heart lifted.

"But you run it all past me and you'll stay until I'm ready to boot you out. I'm holding you to that." She glared at Christine, as if reading her own doubts.

"Absolutely," she said, hoping for the best. She couldn't wait to tell David they were getting DSL.

CHAPTER ELEVEN

IT HAD BEEN A HOT AND sunny day, but David felt ice cold under gray clouds. Brigitte had broken up with him. Four days after she'd blown off her visit and he'd nearly burned down Harmony House because of her, she'd cut him free like an annoying string dangling from her sweater.

It was after supper and David was due for his first talk with Marcus. He carried his guitar, which Marcus had suggested, but he felt too low to play a note.

These talks sounded stupid to him, but he figured it was better than going to some stranger in Preston, with his mother grilling him the whole way there and back each time.

Lady was with him, sitting at his side like his bud. Lady helped. Lady was a friend. He ran his hand down her back, taking comfort in her soft fur, the appreciative thump of her tail.

The sound of feet on the stairs made him look up to see Marcus with his Martin and a wad of guitar strings. He sat and started changing out his strings. Whew. They would just sit quietly for a bit. He did get a feeling of peace and calm whenever he was around the guy.

After a minute or so, David got bored and found himself playing some chords for something to do. He felt so restless now. He couldn't focus or think. He ran hot and then cold. He wanted to crawl out of his skin, explode into a million dots of nothingness in the air.

When he'd finished with the strings, Marcus strummed through a series of chords to test the tuning. "So what's up with you right now?" he said suddenly, his gaze sharp on David.

He was so startled, he blurted it out. "Brigitte broke up with me. Over the phone."

Marcus watched him. "You sound angry about it."

"Yeah, I'm angry." He thought he was mostly sad, but red flared in his head now. "She threw me away like we had nothing."

"I notice your hand is scraped." Marcus nodded at the oozing scabs across his knuckles.

"I punched a wall." He studied his hand, which still hurt.

"That happen often? Hitting things when you're angry?"

"Sometimes." His mind went red and he just swung. That bothered him some, he had to admit.

"Rage always seeks an outlet. Hitting something is a natural way to handle it, though it's usually better to choose something that won't hurt you back."

"I guess." He shrugged.

"Unless that was what you wanted? To hurt yourself?"

His eyes darted to Marcus's. "No. I mean, I don't know. I wanted to stop feeling like shit. I wanted to *do* something."

"And physical pain is better than emotional pain?"

"Sometimes. Yeah."

"Would you like some ideas for how to handle your anger in ways that won't, say, put you in a cast?" Marcus smiled.

"I guess."

"Next time, we can go over that. For now, what else is going on with you besides anger?"

"Nothing. I feel empty. And stupid. I mean, we were in this together. This being apart and how much it hurt, like we were climbing a mountain together and Brigitte got tired and let go of the rope, letting me crash to the ground."

"People handle separations in different ways. Some hold on tighter. Others withdraw."

"She's not even going to Europe. She's going to ASU and living at home. It's because of Rocky, this guy we know I think she likes." David felt choked up inside, helpless and ruined.

Marcus didn't speak, so David's thoughts rolled on, deeper into scary areas. "When I go home I'll look like a fool who got dumped. She'll mock me behind my back. That's what she does to people she feels superior to." His voice cracked. "It hurts *so much*. Like it was all fake from her."

Marcus still didn't speak, just let David settle down. When he felt calmer, he said, "Should I call her? Try to work it out?"

"Is that possible?"

"No. She'd say I'm being immature." He shook his head, miserable. "It's over. I know that."

"What are you telling yourself about the kind of person you are because of this?"

"I don't know...." He paused, thinking. "That I'm a loser. That I'm boring. Too boring to stick in Brigitte's head."

"Were you boring when you were with her?"

"No. I was smart and funny and interesting."

"Have you changed?"

"No. *She* changed. She stopped caring about me."

"It's good that you realize that. It's common for people in a breakup to judge themselves harshly based on the other person's behavior."

"I still feel like shit."

"Are you eating normally? Sleeping?"

He shook his head. "Not really."

"Eating regularly will help stabilize you. Get plenty of protein, fruits and vegetables and avoid sugar, which puts your insulin into overdrive and can cause mood swings."

"Food makes me feel like puking."

"Try small amounts throughout the day. Also, stay with your usual bedtimes. Don't nap to catch up. You'll get back on track eventually. Exercise raises your endorphin levels, which creates positive feelings, so doing chores should help."

"Great. Can't wait." He didn't really care about all that "eat, sleep, exercise" crap. "I feel so hopeless."

"The hurt is new, David. That will pass over time. For now, you'll have to ride it out as best you can. It helps to stay busy."

"With what? Chores?" He smirked.

"Play music maybe? Hang out with friends. Learn to make pottery. Read. Go for hikes. Swim in the river."

"I don't feel like any of that."

"As the days pass, the waves of sadness won't hit so hard. You'll gradually feel better and more like yourself."

"Are you sure?"

"That's the pattern with most people. If a month passes and you feel no better, you might want to see a therapist about medicine to boost you to solid emotional ground for a while."

"Okay, I guess." Marcus made it sound so easy.

"How are things with your mother?"

David shrugged. "Not great. She's holding the fire over my head, to prove I'm a loser and a screwup."

"Has she said something to that effect?"

"No. But that's what she thinks."

"What do *you* think?"

David stared at Marcus for a long moment, then he admitted the truth. "That I am a screwup and a loser." He dropped his head, feeling the wash of horror from that night—his crazy drive to Brigitte, stoned and drunk, losing control of the car, almost getting hit by that truck, then learning he'd nearly killed people.

"How about we reframe that? You got upset and took some unwise actions. How about we say that you did some screwed-up things, but those actions don't define you."

"Means the same thing to me."

"It's a subtle difference, but it's important."

"Whatever."

"So you feel that you made some serious mistakes. What are you doing to make up for them?"

"I'm helping with the repairs is all."

"And you apologized, correct? To me, to your mother?"

"And my grandmother, yeah."

"And you're talking to me, right? What else?"

"I'm going to try to not do stupid shit again."

"It sounds like you've had some insights, David, and that you have a plan to do better in the future."

"Yeah? I guess so."

"That sounds responsible to me."

"It does?" He felt a little lighter and blew out a breath.

"Anything else on your mind at the moment?"

He remembered that Marcus had busted down his door to rescue him, risked getting burned up to save him. That made his nose sting with emotion. He wanted to say something, to thank him, but that felt babyish. "Not really, no."

"Then how about we play some guitar?"

"Okay." Relieved, David hit a chord. That hadn't been so bad, after all. Maybe he'd feel like writing a song later. Maybe it would be about Brigitte, maybe not. Music could be an escape like Marcus said.

A WEEK AFTER THE FIRE, Marcus sighed and pushed away from the desk. While he waited for copies of the ruined research printouts to arrive, he'd been reading over the three hundred pages he'd completed, making notes as he went. He was not happy. The book was too bogged down in research, too repetitive. He'd gotten too caught up defending his ideas. Making it shorter would help, but that wasn't quite the whole problem. Something about the book felt dead to him.

He rubbed his tired eyes and looked out the open window. The moon was bright and a light breeze blew in, carrying the scent of the water. He liked the view of the cottonwoods from the room he'd moved to after the fire.

His talks with David seemed to be going well,

so that was good. Christine, however, was making him crazy.

He couldn't get her out of his mind. He kept remembering holding her, touching her, how right it had felt to be with her. He'd taken his own advice and kept himself busy, but in quiet moments, Christine filled his head.

In fact...was that her in the yard? He rubbed his eyes. Yes, it was—in a pale sundress, Lady at her side, walking toward the cottonwoods. She looked like a ghost from some Gothic mystery.

As if she sensed his gaze, she turned and looked up at him, wiggling her fingers in a hesitant wave. Heat poured through him. He wanted her so badly. This was pure torture.

Lady let out a howl, as if channeling his frustration.

MARCUS HAD CAUGHT HER staring at his window.

She did this every night on her walk with Lady, testing herself. Would she run to him or could she stay strong?

She could feel the scratchy edge of the condom packet she'd tucked into her sundress. She carried it with her each night in case she lost her fight against temptation.

She waved at him. He waved back. Electricity seemed to jump between them, eating up the distance until she could almost see the green of his eyes in the moonlight.

Lady let out a terrible howl, as if giving voice to her own longing. Christine's heart hammered her ribs like hail on a window.

He'd seen her, she might as well go talk to him. About David. About his book. About anything. Where was the harm in that?

She just wanted to see him, feel his eyes on her, his mouth against hers—no, that was wrong.

Of course, David was in town with the twins, so there was no danger of him seeing her slip into Marcus's room....

Lady jolted forward, toward the house, and Christine followed, as if pulled by a leash she did not hold.

The door was open when she got there. Marcus took her hand and pulled her inside. He paused, waiting for Lady to enter, but the dog dropped to her haunches, as if on duty, so he shut the door and took Christine into his arms. *Thank God.*

They stood there, holding each other, for long minutes, as they had that night in Dylan's old room, the night of the mosquito salve and Marcus's tragic story. She felt as she had then, as if she'd taken warm shelter from some terrible storm.

"I missed this," she said against his neck, smelling the woods-and-fresh-laundry smell of him. He was breathing hard and holding her as if he would never let her go.

"Me, too." He leaned back to look at her. "Is it safe for you to be here? What about David?"

"He's in town."

"That's good then."

"I know we had good reasons to stop," she said. "For David and so I could stay focused."

"Very good reasons."

She swallowed hard. "But this seems important, too. I just…can't stop thinking about you. It's making me crazy. It's making it so I *can't* focus."

"I understand completely." His eyes swirled with held-back emotion, shining in the golden lamplight of his new room.

"Is it selfish? Shortsighted?"

"Perhaps." He gave a quick smile, but held her gaze.

"Then I should go." But her body seemed to have a mind of its own and her arms tightened on his broad, strong back.

"You probably should," Marcus said. Christine's heart sank. Why did he have to be stronger than her? "But I don't want you to." His voice was rough with need. "I want you to stay."

Then he lowered his mouth to hers and kissed her, long and slow, letting the desire build and swell into a wave they could surf all night long.

Hurray. At last. She could give in, stop fighting this. And Marcus was right there with her, giving in, too.

He cupped her breasts through the soft jersey fabric, then frowned. "What's this?" He patted her breast, then reached under the top and pulled out the strip of two condoms. He raised an eyebrow.

"I always carry them. In case of emergency."

"Good girl," he said, his eyes merry with humor. But beneath the laughter, heat simmered steadily.

"We really didn't get a chance to see how we could be together, you know?" she said. "The fire happened and I panicked. Do you think we can keep it simple?"

"I have no idea. This is new to me. I never behave this way or feel this way or get so…overwrought."

"*Overwrought?* Good God, Marcus, that's not very sexy. How about *insanely turned on? Passionately aroused? Utterly obsessed?*"

"All I know is that whenever I see you I want to throw you against the nearest wall and take you standing up."

"That works," she said, his urgency making her even hotter. To drive a man as restrained as Marcus to such passion was a thrill. "Being together seems inevitable."

"Nothing's inevitable, Christine. We have choices here."

"So I can't use the we-got-swept-away excuse?" She couldn't believe she was joking when she was electric with desire for this man, desperate to have him inside her.

"Not with a wad of condoms in your fist, no."

"I guess not."

He lifted her off her feet and walked her backward to his bed, lowering her to the mattress.

"We're good for each other, don't you think?" she said, trying for one more good reason. She tugged his shirt from his pants and over his head.

He pushed the strapless sundress to her waist, his eyes flaring at the sight of her breasts.

"I mean I wake you up and you calm me down, right? That's good, isn't it?" He'd been so wounded—by Nathan's death, his professional crisis, the media mess, his divorce. Maybe she was helping him heal. He was helping her with David, giving her comfort and safety and friendship, erasing the loneliness she hadn't realized she felt.

"What's good is you're here," he said, tugging her clothes down her body and away, "and you're naked."

She could only gasp, having lost all her reasons along with her panties.

MARCUS WAS BEHAVING LIKE a lust-driven Neanderthal, but he didn't care. Something about Christine stripped away his civility, left him bared to the bone, to basic drives. He wanted this woman and she wanted him. That was all that mattered.

He wanted to make her gasp with pleasure and buck wildly in release. He wanted to feel her convulse while he did the same. He didn't care about any of her excuses. He knew one thing: This felt right. She belonged in his arms and in his bed.

He hardly recognized himself. He was flying without a net here. Whether he needed one or not remained to be seen.

He rid himself of his clothes and had Christine's soft flesh in his hands, her gasps and cries in his ears. She yanked him into position and locked her heels into his backside, telling him in no uncertain terms where she wanted him and how hard and fast.

This time he didn't resist. He filled her in one stroke, making her cry out in sharp pleasure. He pulled back and thrust again. Her eyes went wide and she lifted her hips, matching each push with a welcoming one of her own. He watched her face, so alive with heat and happiness and hope.

He wanted to make this last, to never stop, to look into her eyes forever. He was experiencing a biochemical short circuit, of course, as every pleasure enzyme in his brain fired at once, but he would enjoy it all the same.

They rocked together, slow at first, then faster, moving together, two halves of a whole until they broke open together in climax, gasping for air.

Afterward, he pulled her onto his chest, his heart thundering beneath his ribs. He didn't speak and neither did she. Once their breathing had normalized, he turned her on her side and spooned himself behind her, one hand on her breast, soaking up the quiet peace, resisting all doubts or analysis.

This was supposed to be simple. But he knew already it would be complicated as hell.

Two weeks later, Marcus stepped back from hammering Sheetrock in David's old room to take a swig of water from the jug David handed him.

"Can I take a break?" David asked. "Just fifteen?"

"Go ahead," Marcus said, wiping sweat from his forehead. David had turned out to be decent with a hammer and he worked hard, clearly determined to make up for what he'd done.

Though David had continued to be hostile with Christine, Marcus had seen improvement. He was a good kid who felt emotions intensely, very much like Christine herself.

He decided to take a break, too, and make Christine take one, as well. She worked nonstop if no one intervened. Hell, he just wanted to be near her.

He filled his water jug from the container on the terrace, grabbed two peaches from a basket and headed downstairs.

Christine had turned Harmony House into a swarm of activity. Residents wielded rollers of bright yellow paint or brushes of white for the trim and terraces. The Barlow twins and some friends were painting the room doors in colors and designs sketched by art students from the high school and approved by Christine and Aurora.

Trenches had been dug for a Xeriscape sprinkling

system in the front yard, which meant minimal water use. Desert trees and cacti rested in truck beds waiting to be planted.

Heading for the clay barn, due to be painted red, Marcus noticed David talking to one of the art students, Delia Dominguez, the daughter of Carlos's nurse. Marcus smiled. David seemed to be moving past his grief over Brigitte just fine.

Inside the earthy-smelling barn, light filtered gently through the high windows, making dust motes swirl and dance around Christine, who was unloading clay items from the kiln.

She noticed him and smiled.

"Need a break?" He held out his water jug.

She drank thirstily, heedless of the rivulets escaping her mouth to spill down her pretty throat. He wanted to kiss her there, taste the water on her sweet skin.

She handed him the jug, and he held out one of the peaches. "Too busy. A bunch of orders came in yesterday."

"Take a break with me," he said. "Come see what you've set in motion." He gestured outdoors.

She smiled her thousand-watt smile. "All right, I guess." Clay dust covered her hair and he reached to brush it away.

"Careful," she murmured, stepping back, darting glances in all directions to be certain no one had noticed his move. They'd kept their affair secret from everyone so far.

"There's dust in your hair."

She shook her head, then roughed her curls with both hands, sending her scent his way.

"I want to touch you so bad right now." He could not get enough of her. When she wasn't in his arms, she was in his head.

She shut her eyes, trembling a little at his words. "I know," she whispered. "Tonight after supper."

"Dammit, this computer's busted!" Aurora yelled from the office area, which they'd protected from dust with heavy plastic sheets since the computer had arrived.

"It's not broken," Christine called to her. "Read the instructions I wrote down about the database program."

Aurora grumbled, then said, "There. I fixed it."

Christine rolled her eyes. "She acts like the Web site and the computer are a pain, but she spends hours glued to the screen. Yesterday, she told me all about Google searches."

He smiled at the tenderness in her voice. "You're not as irritated as you're trying to sound."

"That's only because she's occupied back there, not railing about how landscaping violates the spirit of Harmony House. I promised she could approve every hedge and paint chip, but I didn't think she'd take me up on it."

"Better than being an armchair quarterback after the fact."

"Oh, she'll do that, too, just you wait."

"But you're smiling, Christine. Not gritting your teeth."

"I am?" She paused. "Maybe I'm getting used to her." She took a bite of the peach Marcus held out to her. Juice dribbled down her chin. She wiped it with the heel of her hand.

"You missed a little," he said, running his thumb across her lower lip.

"Oh, don't," she breathed, stepping away. "You'll make me faint dead away."

He led her out to the yard and they sat on the top rail of the fence. Around them they could hear the chuff of shovels and friendly chatter, punctuated by bursts of laughter.

"This is going great, huh?" She looked out at all the work being done. "We're going to paint the kitchen and dining room and furnish more sleeping rooms. I've got ads in some travel magazines and bookings are up already."

"Sounds very promising."

"It is, I think."

"And you sound happy."

"I'm enjoying this a lot. It's like giving the place a fresh start...with the Internet." She grinned.

"You're making the changes you joked about needing if you were going to stay here. Are you thinking about that?"

"Thinking about it? Not really. I mean...I'll miss it, I know...." She seemed to suddenly realize something and looked directly at him. "It will be hard to leave." She meant hard to leave him.

"It will be," he said, letting that fact sink in.

"But there's no point planning the end when we're in the middle, right?" She seemed to force herself to brighten.

"No," he said, wishing he were better at dealing with loss.

"Looks like David's talking to Delia again," Christine said, nodding in that direction. "I'm going to hire her to take bookings and market us with travel agencies." She paused. "You think that's okay? She's a year older than him."

"He's making friends. That's a good thing."

"I just hate to see him laying his heart on the chopping block for another girl's ax. I want to grab her by the shoulders and say, *please don't hurt him.*"

"You're assuming the worst."

"The worst happens. Better to be prepared." She sighed. "He's braver than I am, I guess. More hopeful."

"Hey, now, where's your excessive optimism?"

"When it comes to love, I'm a hard-bitten realist, baby."

Don't give up hope, he wanted to say. Talk about excessive optimism.

CHAPTER TWELVE

THAT EVENING, CHRISTINE was finishing the whipped cream while Aurora took out plates for the strawberry shortcake dessert they would be serving the residents and high school workers who'd been invited to supper.

After the long day of scraping, painting and planting, the dinner had been a delight, full of talk and laughter and great food, with Aurora so cheerful she'd entertained everyone with commune stories from the old days.

"Assembly line or plate-by-plate?" Aurora asked her now.

"You're asking me?" Aurora never asked her opinion. "Uh, assembly line, I think, would be easiest."

"That could work, I guess." Aurora clearly preferred plate-by-plate, but she was being kind for some reason. "I'll do the cake, you do the strawberries, then we can start at both ends slapping on the whipped cream. How's that?"

"Sounds great." She was touched by her mother's gesture.

Aurora began laying the plates in rows on the counter.

"Supper was nice, huh?" Christine said.

"Except for the eggplant. It wasn't seasoned right."

She smiled. Marcus had added garlic to Aurora's recipe and it had tasted wonderful, but Aurora would always be Aurora, even when she was making an effort to be kind.

"I meant the way everyone was enjoying each other after working together so hard. It reminds me of the good times here."

"I didn't know you had any." Christine heard the sadness beneath her mother's stab.

"I was a kid. Kids complain. The point is I see why you and Bogie stuck it out all these years. There are good things here."

"So why are you painting and planting over it all?" she said, but she was smiling, and her eyes were lit with pleasure.

Feeling a surge of affection, Christine almost hugged her, except Aurora would go stiff and the moment would get awkward. Then a better thought hit her. "What about a party?"

"A party?" Her mother's forehead creased. "Celebrating what?"

"You and Bogie getting better, finishing the face-lift we're giving Harmony House. We'll do it on the Fourth of July. How's that? We could make it an open house. Invite people from town."

"That's a hell of a lot of trouble to go to," she said, but she was clearly pleased.

Together they carried the cream-topped strawberries to the dining room to cheers and applause. Christine told everyone about the party, her heart so full she couldn't stop grinning. After supper, David joined Christine to do the dishes.

Delia helped David clear, then left the kitchen. "She seems nice," Christine said.

David only shrugged.

"She designed some of the doors, didn't she?"

"Mom." He stopped washing and turned to her.

"Okay, none of my business. Sorry." They worked in silence until she asked, "How are things going for you lately?" David rarely talked to her and continued to be sullen and moody.

"Fine."

"Is that all you can say?" She sighed. He seemed so far away. Like he was on a raft and when she reached for him, the motion sent him sliding farther out to sea.

"I'm not playing Name Three Things, so don't even try." The rule used to be when she asked him about school he had to name three things that had happened or that he'd learned.

"You still talk with Marcus, right?" At least that.

"Mostly we play guitar."

"And you sound good," she said. "You've been practicing."

Another shrug.

She had a sudden idea. "Maybe you and Marcus should play at the open house."

"Yeah?" He stopped washing and looked at her. She'd actually surprised him. "You mean like a gig? For pay?"

"Sure. For pay." Why not?

"Okay. Yeah. That would be cool."

"We'll be having a lot more guests in the future. Maybe we could have a happy-hour thing on the weekends where you and Marcus could perform. Or you could solo."

"And you'd pay me?"

"You'll probably get tips, too."

"Yeah. I'll do it. I'll tell Marcus. Thanks." He nodded his head in that ostrich-bob way he had.

"I'm glad, then." *I love you.* She was about to say it when David frowned at her.

"Don't get all weird. Here." He thrust the colander he'd been washing at her. "Rinse."

AFTER TAKING AURORA to Preston for her checkup, Christine left her mother in the clay barn and went to talk to Bogie. She found him in the garden supervising two couples and their kids as they harvested cabbage. "Is this the right way, Mr. Bogie?" asked a little girl.

Bogie squatted and watched as she snapped off the leafy ball. "It's perfect. You have a knack for this," he said.

The girl beamed, spun and hurried to her mother three rows over, holding out her prize. "I have a knack, Mommy," she called. "Mr. Bogie says I have a knack."

"Put it in the basket," the mother said. An older son, probably thirteen, pulled plants a few rows over. He was working on a report about intentional living and his parents spoke fondly of their year at a commune in Michigan.

Catching sight of Christine, Bogie approached the fence. "What did the doctor say?" he asked.

"According to Aurora, clean bill of health. Though she wouldn't let me go with her to the exam room. She insisted on driving home, too."

"Now that's good news, isn't it?" Bogie said, beaming with relief. "You're looking pretty healthy, too, these days."

"Thank you."

"I remember those tired eyes of yours when you came. Now they're just shining bright."

She smiled at him, warmed by his affection.

"So that settles it. We'll be having those fireworks for the party. I don't care what Aurora says. In honor of you both."

"That's sweet of you, Bogie."

"It's not sweet. It's right." He paused. "What do you say we enlarge the greenhouse this fall, make the aisles wider?"

"If that's what you'd like to do…" Her stomach tightened. Already, Aurora was talking about things they would do "this fall" or "next winter," and now Bogie was at it, too.

"Mr. Bogie? Check me, please?" the little girl called.

"I'll let you get back to it," Christine said, easing away. She didn't want to disappoint Bogie, but she had to return to Phoenix. Things were getting… *complicated.*

She headed for the house. A *baa* made her pat Ruby, her favorite goat. In the courtyard, she gently suggested two little boys ought not to chase the chickens or they wouldn't have nice eggs in their omelets.

After supper that night, once she was sure that David was in town with friends, Christine headed to Marcus's room, dying to be in his arms. It was ridiculous how she longed for these private hours with him. They were careful about the timing so they never risked David finding out. Marcus's room's location helped. It was near the far stairs, easy to slip up and down without being seen, and far from the owners' quarters, where David stayed.

More than once she'd thought about tapering off, so that it would be easier when they parted ways in six weeks, but she couldn't seem to even bring up the idea.

She knocked at his door, her heart in her throat, and Marcus welcomed her into his arms, his hair damp from the shower, smelling clean and sweet, and she was so glad to be with him again. She noticed soft music playing and saw a boom box on the bookshelf.

When Marcus released her, she noticed he'd cleared the papers from his desk. One of the commune's beeswax candles glowed beside a jar of bright flowers and a bowl of fresh blackberries. Next to that was a bottle of red wine and two ceramic goblets.

"These are the ones I made," she said, picking one up, admiring the even shape and graceful stem.

"Why do you think I chose them?"

"This is so lovely, Marcus." She indicated the table, the music, the goblet in her hand.

"I'm glad you like it. I wish we could risk going out to Sammy's or Toad Tavern, but here we're close to a bed, and that's crucial." He held her gaze, hunger in his eyes. "Take off your clothes. I'm thinking dessert, then blackberries."

Christine went weak in the knees. How she wanted this man.

Afterward, Christine rolled onto her side to look down at Marcus. "That was so great. I feel like we invented it."

"Sex, you mean?" Marcus gave a low chuckle, and ran his finger along her cheek. "We are pretty good together."

"Good? Are you kidding. We're *amazing*." They were, too. She'd never felt this physically delighted and satisfied and comfortable. Of course, that made her wonder about Marcus, so she had to ask.

"How were you with Elizabeth? Physically, I mean?"

"I'm not sure how useful that would be to discuss."

"Screw useful. Just tell me. Or, okay, I'll go first. Skip was good. He had the moves and all, though it kind of felt like a performance a lot. But it was never like it is with you, the way you hold me with your eyes the entire time, completely with me, together, you know? Totally in *tune*."

"How could I not be?" he breathed, kissing her forehead. "I can't take my eyes off you."

She sighed. "That's what I mean. You look at me that way and you say shit like that. I just…I don't know…I feel so lucky." Tears sprang to her eyes. "I mean, you're perfect."

"Perfect?" He frowned. "I'm hardly perfect. We both know that. We're in a unique situation here, with a limit on our time together, so that intensifies our reactions."

"Maybe." She knew emotions ran high when sex was new. This felt different, but she'd tricked herself in the past, seeing more than was there. She'd certainly done that with Skip.

"You'd get bored soon enough, Christine. Trust me. I get distant and preoccupied. I disengage. Just ask Elizabeth."

"You think it was all your fault, right? That you let her down emotionally. Did you ever think that maybe she let you down?"

"Christine, I don't think that's—"

"I'm no marriage expert, of course. I mean with Skip, I think I fell in love with the idea of him. But you haven't been distant at all with me or with David. You've been completely here, absolutely present."

"I want to be. I want to be exactly what you need. But wanting is not being, so let's not get carried away."

He was probably right. Maybe she'd get bored with him and all his quiet restraint. Certainly, she would be too much for him. Too much emotion, too much intensity. Simply too much. Still, she couldn't help wanting them both to be wrong.

CHRISTINE SMILED AT THE crowd that filled the Harmony House parlor listening to David and Marcus perform. A surprising number of New Mirage residents were here, including the mayor and Susan, and lots of media—travel writers from national and regional magazines and *USA Today,* style reporters from Phoenix and Tucson, even some Arizona TV crews.

Up by the fireplace, David and Marcus sat on tall stools, lit by clusters of candles on stands. Christine had insisted they wear the Harmony House tie-dyed T-shirts she'd had printed up to be sold at the front desk.

David was nervous, she could tell, and her heart went out to him. She'd taken Marcus's advice and given him space, stopped pushing him to talk to her, though it was against her instincts. Maybe Marcus knew best.

Marcus noticed her watching them and winked, which sent a sexual charge through her. She couldn't wait for after the party when they would rehash what happened and make love.

She leaned on him more and more, sinking into his steadiness, the ready comfort of his arms. This was risky, she knew. She had to stay strong and independent, take care of herself and her son, not get lazy. Because things went wrong, people failed you. That's just how it went. And afterward it took a while to pull up your big-girl panties and move on.

But here she was, hooked on Marcus. When she left and he went back to L.A., she'd end up with a huge hole in her heart for sure. So much for keeping it simple.

They began with Dylan's "Blowin' in the Wind," Marcus's rich baritone beneath David's tentative tenor, supporting, not overshadowing. David looked so handsome and grown up her heart ached with tenderness and pride.

When the song was over, everyone clapped and the Barlow twins whistled their approval. She'd hired them and some of their friends to pass appetizers and clean up.

When they stopped for a short break, Christine went up to David. "I'm so proud of you," she whispered. She was dying to hug him, but she knew that would embarrass him. Already, he was glancing side to side to make sure no one saw him with her. "I'll disappear, no worries," she said, stepping back.

"Thanks for the gig," he blurted, giving her a shot of his old sunny smile.

"You're very welcome," she said, her heart full. She'd been right to bring David here, she thought, hoping she wasn't being excessively optimistic again.

On her way to the kitchen to check on the appetizers she ran into Aurora. "I swear to God if I hear 'Michael, Row the Boat Ashore' one more time I'll explode," she said.

Christine laughed. "Come on. You can't even pretend not to love the way they sound."

"David's not bad," Aurora admitted. "He seems pretty settled in around here. Not so moody and lazy."

She noticed Marcus smiling at her from across the room, so she nodded in his direction.

"You and Doctor B. seem settled, too."

Christine jolted, turning to stare at Aurora. "What?"

"Come on, the man turns three shades of pink when you walk into a room. And look at how jumpy you are this minute."

"That's not—I mean I—" She went hot all over. How embarrassing that Aurora had noticed.

"Relax, I won't tell anyone."

"We're spending time together, but that's all."

"You're settled in…like I said. Both of you." Her mother looked straight at her, digging in with her brown eyes, more direct than she ever looked, except when she was furious.

Now Aurora wanted *Marcus* to stay, too? This was bizarre. For all the ease with which Aurora had let her run away, she sure as hell was holding on tight now.

And there was no need anymore. Her mother was back to her usual feisty self, with a clean bill of health. The clay works was doing fine at its higher productivity. Harmony House looked great and any glitches due to the higher occupancy rate would be settled long before it was time for Christine and David to leave. And they had to leave. David had school and she had a job.

"Everything's shaping up," she said, avoiding the issue. "I need to check on the food." She hurried away.

As she walked, her eye was caught by the gleam of the freshly polished wooden floors. The parlor walls were now burgundy with goldenrod trim, dramatic and warm at once. The common areas all looked historic and cared for instead of ancient and neglected.

The kitchen was full of people, which pleased her, and kids were carrying out full trays of snacks showcasing the commune's food—goat cheese puffs, hummus, honey-crusted tofu.

She'd had the tattered 60s posters patched and framed, along with the commune rules, and she'd made the task chart into a white board with erasable markers.

Everyone sharing and caring. A noble goal. Now that Harmony House had fresh paint, some order, water pressure, and serious Internet access, it seemed more possible than ever.

MARCUS WATCHED CHRISTINE glide through the party, lively and laughing, somehow arriving just in time to answer a reporter's question, clear a server snag or gather a group for the next tour of the grounds led by Aurora or Bogie.

She'd changed Harmony House in a big way. And him. She'd stripped off his protective insulation, leaving him feeling a little raw, exposed, almost too alive.

Sometimes he was glad. Other times, he felt like a rabbit in a dog's mouth—shaken, hurting and exhausted.

He hoped he'd been useful to her, too. She seemed more relaxed, less anxious, more centered and confident, and less overbearing with David since he'd entered her life.

They'd be together just six more weeks. Christine would go and he'd leave Harmony House soon after. He hated to think about saying goodbye to her, but at least he had plenty to occupy himself after she was gone. That afternoon, he'd met with Carlos to go over the grant applications Marcus was submitting, thanks to some advice from Elizabeth.

He'd managed a meeting with Winston Barlow and a rural health grant from the state of Arizona was in the works. He'd also talked with a few colleagues in L.A. His fund-raising mission helped break the ice. He could see that returning to L.A. would not be difficult.

Elizabeth had recommended some face-to-face meetings with key people. She'd sounded calm, self-possessed, back in charge of her life. They did not speak one word about their divorce or Nathan or even Lady. Probably for the best. It struck him in the end how little lasting impact they'd had on each other.

Marcus caught up with Christine as the fireworks were about to start. People were seated in lawn chairs in the front yard, eating the Harmony watermelons and goat-milk ice cream.

"Great party, Christine," he said, standing close, but not close enough to raise eyebrows.

"I know." She smiled at him, her eyes shining with pride. "You and David sounded great. Thank you so much."

"It was my pleasure." They were still staring at each other when the first Roman candle streaked the sky, bursting into a blossom of gold and green light.

The crowd exclaimed its awe, faces faintly lit by the glow. He couldn't take his eyes off Christine as she reacted to each burst of fire. She meant so much to him. Simply seeing her made him smile. He felt good around her, better than he'd felt in longer than he could remember.

Looking into the color-brightened sky, he had to admit the truth to himself: He'd fallen in love with her.

When she turned to him, lips parted, face expectant, he almost said so. But what good would that do? Ultimately what could he offer her? Not enough. Not even close.

"What is it?" she asked him.

"I'm just enjoying the fireworks," he said.

The flash and crack of a rocket made Christine look up. A ball of blue stars burst into the sky. Watching its reflection in her eyes, Marcus realized it was true what Christine had said about him. He was in. All in.

WHEN THE PARTY WAS finally cleaned up, it was so late and Christine was exhausted, but she ran to Marcus's room all the same, eager to see him, to make love, to rest in his arms.

When he let her into his room he hugged her so tightly she could hardly breathe, as if he'd rescued her from death.

She pushed out of his arms. "Are you okay?" He'd looked at her strangely during the fireworks, too.

"I'm happy to hold you," he said, kissing her with the heat she expected. Desire wound around and through them, a hot ribbon binding them tight. Their hands moved on each other's bodies in the now-familiar dance, touching skin, pressing muscle and bone, sparking a need that built and built and built.

Once in bed, Marcus entered her like a deep sweet breath. Oh, how she loved this. Marcus was fire and calm. Exactly what she'd always needed, but never found—or even known to look for. They moved together, climbing toward release. Marcus looked at her with such tenderness she wanted to cry.

He made her feel so cared for, important, almost vital to him. He listened to her, calmed and stead-ied her, helped her see her own strengths more clearly.

This thing between them was supposed to be sim-ple—meet each other's physical needs and enjoy a friendly intimacy—but it had become far more than that. Too much more. And in six weeks, it would all be over.

Marcus stopped moving. "What is it?" He'd no-ticed her distraction. The man never missed a twitch or a sigh.

Don't ruin this, she warned herself. "Nothing. Just don't stop, okay?" She locked her heels onto his backside to show him she meant business.

A few minutes later, after their personal fireworks had burst open, hot and bright, inside her body, as wonderful as ever, Christine knew she had to tell Marcus the truth. She braced herself on an elbow, lying on her side facing him, as he mirrored her position.

"Here's what it is, Marcus," she said. "I'm in love with you." She felt like crying. "I'm sorry. I didn't mean to be. It just happened. It got complicated."

Marcus laughed. "That's a hell of a thing—to be *sorry* to be in love." He leaned close and kissed her, keeping his lips close when he spoke. "I'm in love with you, too."

"So, you're saying it's a good thing?"

"I wish to hell I knew." His eyes brimmed with the same mixed feelings she was having.

"I want it to be." Maybe she knew what she was doing this time. She was so tired of being scared and lonely, of guarding her heart from another stupid mistake. Maybe Marcus was sturdy enough to put up with her. "I don't know how we'd be together. I could be too much for you."

"Oh, you already are." He smiled.

"I'm serious." She searched his face.

"So am I." He linked fingers with her and kissed the back of her hand. "I want this, Christine. I want to be with you."

"So maybe we'll be all right," she said. He loved

her and she loved him back. Why couldn't this work? She felt strangely light and hopeful and excited.

And something else, something new. It came to her in a burst, like fireworks in the sky: She felt *happy*.

CHAPTER THIRTEEN

FOR THE FIRST TIME since he'd come to Harmony House, David felt good. Or at least not totally bummed. Last night had been great, with everyone clapping and whistling for him when he performed with Marcus. Best of all, Delia had said he was good.

In fact, back in his room, he'd been so fired up he'd started writing a song. When he finished it and knew her better, he'd play it for Delia.

She made him smile. He'd been so lonely here without having one person who understood him. Delia gave him hope. He needed hope because he dreaded seeing Brigitte again in Phoenix. Delia was like cool medicine on that burning sadness.

A bunch of kids, including Delia, were going to Preston tomorrow for a music festival. The twins had an extra ticket for him they wanted to trade for some of Bogie's bud. No way, he'd told them. He'd pay with the money from his gig.

They thought he was joking when he told them they were too obsessed with weed. The truth was that he hardly smoked at all anymore. He no longer wanted to throw away the hours. Besides, weed sent him into sad and paranoid thoughts about Brigitte, which did not help one bit. Marcus was right about keeping busy.

At the moment he was sweating like a fiend, since he'd had to run out to the far garden to ask his mom for his pay.

He had a ride to town with Mitch if he hurried. He had to buy some blank CDs to make a copy of an album Delia said she liked and he wanted to give it to her on the way to Preston.

His mother was annoyed about the rush, but she told him to go ahead and take the emergency fifty she kept in her address book. Sometimes she did get him. And she *had* thought up the gig idea, which he was pretty happy about.

There was a door between his room and hers, so he used it to get into her room. It was the saddest, silliest-looking room in Harmony House. It made him feel kind of sorry for her as a kid stuck in this weird, fake-princess space.

She'd been going to fix it up but Aurora said to leave their living quarters alone for the time being. Instead of being mad, his mother had actually laughed. Bizarre. She'd been acting bizarre in general, all happy and cheerful for no real reason. But, whatever, she wasn't hassling him that much and that was fine with him.

He found her address book on the bureau. He flipped it open. She said *in the flap,* but which one?

The front flap had receipts, so he flipped to the back of the book. No cash. Just a pink message slip that said *Skip* in black Sharpie.

Skip? His father? Adrenaline slammed through David like an electrocution. He saw there were two phone numbers and an address in San Diego.

His father had called? The message was dated in April—a month before they'd left Phoenix. That made no sense. Christine had told him she didn't know where his father was.

David's blood roared in his ears. He had his father's number in his hand. He could call him. Right now.

First, the money. He found a clear plastic pocket and saw the folded-up fifty inside. He took it, then headed for the kitchen, the message slip trembling in his fingers, his stomach a hot ball of nerves.

He dialed the area code, his heart in his throat, glad no one was around to overhear. What would he say? *Hey, Dad. Long time no see. What's up?* What if his father didn't want to talk to him?

But he'd called, hadn't he? And left a message. It had to be David he wanted to reach, not Christine, who hated him. He dialed again. One…six…one… nine…

He slammed the receiver. He needed to plan his words first. This was too important to blurt whatever was in his head. Plus, he had to catch a ride with Mitch.

Okay, he figured it out. He'd take his cell phone

with him and get the twins to drive him to the highway so he could call his dad on his cell phone in
privacy.

He folded the message slip into a small square
and tucked it into his pocket. What had happened
was *huge*. His father had called to talk to him, but
Christine had refused to let him. How could she?
When she knew how much this meant to David?

Outrage boiled in him, higher and hotter every
second. How dare she do this to him? Deny him his
own dad? He was so mad he wanted to hit something. Maybe even her.

Marcus's tips for anger popped into his head. *Walk
away from the situation. Take five slow breaths, in
and out. Match the speed of your thoughts to your
breaths, slow, slow, slow. If you need a physical
release strike an object that won't break or hurt
you.*

Okay, David told himself, *do this right.* He took
the breaths, slowed his thoughts. Gradually, his fury
eased. The main thing was he would get to talk to
his dad soon. He would get to know him, plan a
visit. He had the key to the biggest mystery of his
life in his right pocket. He patted the spot. It was
all good.

An hour later, David left the twins in the car listening to tunes at a rest stop while he sat at a picnic
bench where he had a solid signal. He clicked in
the digits, his breathing jerky in his ears. *Please
be there. Please.*

"Yeah?" An impatient male voice answered on the first ring.

"*He-e-ello?* Hi, um, is this Skip Scanlon?"

"Who is calling?"

He closed his eyes and blurted, "David. Your son, David."

"David?" There was a long pause. "David. God. How are you?"

"I'm fine. Fine. I'm good." Relief rushed through him like wind. His father sounded shocked but glad. "How are you?"

"I'm good." There was a pause. "It's great you called."

"I just found your number. I didn't know how to reach you."

"I left the deets with Chris. Actually, I was in Phoenix the first of May and wanted to maybe hook up with you, but Chris never called back. I figured you weren't interested."

"*Sure* I'm interested." He wanted to scream in frustration and disappointment. "I would have wanted to see you. Definitely."

"That's good to hear, David. Very good. So how are you? You sound so grown up. You're…what? Fourteen now?"

"Fifteen and a half. I'll be a junior."

"That's great. Wow. You know, the last time I saw you, you were, what, five? You probably don't remember me much."

"Yes, I do. I remember everything. We played

hide-and-seek and shot Nerf arrows and ate cookies for breakfast."

"We did? I guess so." He laughed. "I bet you're tall now."

"Kind of. Five foot seven, I think."

"I need a photo of you." He probably carried a sad, cracked preschool shot in his wallet. Christine was so mean she probably hadn't sent him any school pictures ever. The thought made David's throat hurt so much he was afraid he couldn't speak.

"I bet the girls are all over you," his dad said.

"Not really. No. I mean, I had a girlfriend. And we broke up. But there's this other girl I like." He felt his scalp heat. "I wish I could have seen you when you came to Phoenix."

"We can get together, no problem. My schedule's hectic, but we can work it out. We'll do that one of these days."

"That'd be great," he said, feeling hot all over, happy and lonely and sad at once. He was afraid he'd start bawling like a baby.

The line went dead for an instant. "Can you hold on? I'm expecting an important call."

"Sure." David was actually relieved for the break. It was almost too much to have his actual father on the line, happy to hear from him, wanting to see him.

There was so much he wanted to tell him—about his music, about who he was, what he wanted in life, about Brigitte. It was all bottled up inside, dying to burst out in a flood of words.

"You still there?" his father asked a few seconds later.

"Sure." Did he think he'd hang up?

"That was the guy and I gotta jet. Give me your number and I'll call you back tonight maybe."

"I'll have to call you. We're at Harmony House for the summer, out in the boondocks with no cell reception."

"Oh, okay. *You* call *me* then when you can. We'll catch up."

"Yeah." There was so much to catch up on. Years and years.

"'Bye, son. It feels good to say that…*son*."

"Yeah, it does. It feels—" But the phone went dead before David could say it felt good to say *Dad,* too.

It didn't matter. It was all good. He was so proud he'd made the call. He felt stronger, bigger, whole, like he fully existed in the world for the first time in his life.

Back in the car, he told the twins what his dad had said and by the time they got back to town, David was mad again at his mother. He'd spent years afraid his father didn't even *want* him, especially after all the crap Christine had told him.

Instead, the guy had called and called and Christine had said no-no-no, while David begged her to look for his dad. Christine knew where he was all along. *All along.*

By the time the twins dropped him off, he was full-on, red-brained furious. He wanted to scream at Christine, shake her, hit her even. That scared him a little.

He tried the anger process a couple times, but this was too much, too awful. He needed help. He needed Marcus. Marcus would walk him through the bad stuff. He would be on David's side against Christine, too. Maybe he'd even tell her off.

He'd told David that his father should be in his life. Well, not exactly. More like that it was confusing to not have contact with a parent. Then some B.S. about the risk of investing too much energy on imagined perfection or whatever.

Marcus could be full of it at times. And he never said what he thought, always turned it around to David.

He scanned the yard, the garden, the animal barn, looking for the guy. Then he spotted his tall form at the far pump under the mesquite trees. He was filling up a bucket.

Christine was there, too, dammit.

David started walking that way, then noticed the way they were laughing. Too friendly, almost like they were—*no,* not that. To his shock, Christine leaned in and kissed Marcus on the mouth. Worse, Marcus pulled her into his arms and kissed her back.

David felt glued to the spot, electrified into stone. His mother and Marcus were…together. That meant sex, too. They'd hidden this from him. Scammed him. Marcus probably told his mother everything David said and the two of them laughed at David behind his back.

He felt like he had to puke. He'd been betrayed, lied to. First about his dad. Then about Marcus. Marcus had lied, too. That hurt worse. Marcus had been his friend. *His*. Not Christine's. Nothing was his. Nothing and no one.

Even worse, Lady was lying in the shade beside the two of them. Even the dog had abandoned him. Before they could see him, David spun away and headed for his room, sick with hurt.

Except, as he ran, a golden idea came into his mind. He had his dad. His father would understand this betrayal more than anyone, since Christine had betrayed him, too.

His dad *wanted* to see him. Anytime, he'd said. Anytime. So how about now? After the lies Christine had told him, it would serve her right if David went to live in San Diego, which was a great place. He'd learn to surf and fish, water-ski, maybe sail. David had a ride into Preston tomorrow with the twins. Did he have enough cash for the bus fare from there?

It was a possibility, at least. Just thinking about it eased his agony a bit, enough to keep him from smashing his hand into a wall, his head through a window. For now anyway.

CHRISTINE HEADED FOR THE house to take a shower. She'd taken a chance, kissing Marcus right out in the open. David was in New Mirage, but still, they'd sworn to be discreet. Were they losing control? It seemed that way at times. They loved each other and they wanted more time together. But they'd avoided discussing how that might work out, just floated on this cloud, which was not smart at all, not like either of them. She had this scary feeling in the pit of her stomach that they were making a big mistake, that there would be a huge crash at the end, but then she'd kissed him like it was the right thing to do. Worse, he'd kissed her back the same way.

Her biggest worry was David's reaction.

Marcus wanted to tell him, but Christine thought it was too soon. David had bonded with Marcus. Learning that Christine and Marcus were a couple might damage his progress, cause him to backslide. Christine couldn't bear that.

In the back of her head, she was thinking, *What if the affair didn't last?* What if their love burned itself out in the weeks before they both headed home, or even after that, while they tried to hold on to it from separate cities? If it ended, they would have upset David for nothing.

She didn't say that to Marcus. He would think she wasn't "all in" the way he was. And maybe she wasn't. The thought made her heart sink and her stomach burn. She didn't know what she felt. This was so new for her. She didn't trust it at all.

Being with Marcus in any permanent way felt so impossible. How would they manage it? Would he move to Phoenix? Would she drag David to L.A.? That seemed as insane to her as Aurora and Bogie expecting her to stay at Harmony House.

It made her head hurt, so she tried not to think about it, focused on enjoying the moment, though more and more gray worry clouded her sunny days. She was holding her breath to see what happened, praying no one would end up heartbroken.

When she got to her room, she heard David's music very loud, then saw the pass-through door was open. He must have left it like that when he got the money.

When she went to close the door, she noticed David was lying on his bed. Not in New Mirage. Huh? Immediately, she picked up spicy smoke, like a basket burning, and knew what it was. Sure enough, David brought a skinny cigarette to his lips and took a drag. He was smoking marijuana.

Electricity shot through her and she marched into his room "David!" she said, scared and worried and mad.

He sat up, startled at first, then he settled into angry defiance. "Don't you knock?"

"The door was open, but so what? You're doing drugs!"

"I'm not *doing* drugs. I'm sucking in a bit of herb," he said in a fake cool voice. "After what you did to me I deserve a big fat blunt and then some." His eyes were red and puffy. In fact, he looked like he'd been crying, too.

"Where did you get the dope? Did you buy it from the twins? Is that what you wanted the money for? To buy drugs?"

"I didn't buy it. I got it from Bogie. Free."

"Bogie gave you marijuana?"

"No. And don't go yell at him. I took a few buds from his grow room without telling him. No big deal. He wouldn't mind."

"You *stole* from Bogie? That's his medicine." She was horrified, shaking with outrage. David was completely unapologetic. He'd never been this defiant.

"He's got plenty. He doesn't care. And pot's no big deal." He took a deliberate, slow puff, daring her to object.

"It's a big deal to me. A very big deal. You promised me you quit. You promised Aurora no drugs. You *lied!*"

His eyes flashed sudden fury. "No, *you* lied. You lie to me every day of my life." He lunged at her, looking like he wanted to strike her.

"What are you talking about?"

He was breathing hard, staring at her, making his hands into fists. "You and Marcus," he finally spat out. "I wanted to talk to Marcus about something important and I saw you out at the pump with him." His face twisted with disgust.

"Oh." Embarrassment swamped her. He'd seen the kiss. "I'm sorry, David. We shouldn't have done that. We thought it was best not to say anything to you at first."

"So, did he tell you everything I said to him? Am I a big joke to you?"

"Of course not. Your talks with Marcus are private."

"Yeah, right. Like I can believe a word you ever tell me." His voice cracked. His face flared with fury, his eyes burning at her. "You take away everyone I have ever cared about. You took away my father, you dragged me from Brigitte and now you stole Marcus. You're sick, you know that? Twisted! What do you want? To lock me up in a box? Control me and everyone around me?"

"Of course not. I only want—"

"I don't care what you say. It's too late. I'll live where I want and love who I want and you can't stop me! It's *my* life! *Mine!*" He was shrieking now, his face red, a vein bulging from his forehead, spit flying.

"What are you talking about?" This was too extreme a reaction. There had to be more. "I can see why you'd be upset about me with Marcus, but where is all this hate coming from?"

"Like you don't know," he said with a bitter smile.

"This doesn't sound like you at all. Is it the marijuana? Is it because you're high?"

He snorted. "I don't sound like me because you don't even *know* me. You made up some kid I'll never be. No matter what I do. It's too late." Now his voice shook with tears. "Just leave me alone," he sobbed. "Leave!"

She started to refuse to go, but she remembered what Marcus had said about how to handle David's anger. She took a slow breath, fighting her alarm, her urge to talk this through, to force a fix, resolve it.

"I can hear how furious you are right now. I'll leave, but not for long. We need to talk about this. For now, you need to know that what happened between Marcus and me doesn't change how I feel about you. And Marcus is still your friend. We both care for you and we both want the best for you—"

"Yeah, right," he said, his sarcasm sharp as a blade. "I bet you do. You want the best for me because you're the perfect mother. Thanks so much. I'm *sooo* glad."

She retreated from his room and shut the door, sick inside and so scared. She'd let her own selfish needs take precedence over David's problems and look what happened. She'd been right to expect a crash. It was even worse than she expected.

David was smoking pot again. Not even hiding it. Because of her being with Marcus. She'd never seen him so angry. What had she done?

THE FIGHT WITH HIS MOTHER had made David feel even more certain of his plan, full of fire and confidence. He wouldn't wait for the ride to Preston in the morning. He would leave now. He'd practiced driving with the twins, so he'd take his mom's car to Preston and catch a bus to San Diego from there.

One last thing. He needed more cash since he'd spent too much on that stupid festival ticket. He knew who to ask.

He found his grandmother in the clay barn working at one of the wheels. He dropped onto a stool beside her, forcing himself to sound calm and easy.

"What's got your boxers in a twist?" she said to him. How did she know he was upset? She hadn't even looked at him.

"Christine. We had a fight."

"What'd she do now?"

"Everything. She lied to me about my whole life. About my dad. Just…everything." He couldn't talk about this or he might cry like a baby. "She wants me to be someone I can't be and I'm sick of it. I'm sick of her."

Aurora nailed him with a look. "You two are so alike."

The idea horrified him. "No way. I'm not one bit like her."

"You have strong ideas about how things ought to be and when they're not, you get mad as hell."

"I'm not like her at all," he repeated. "She's hopeless."

"Christine never cut me any slack, either." She sighed.

"This is different. Way different."

"Wait until you're on your own, David. You'll understand things a lot better about your mother and about yourself."

"When I'm on my own, sure," he said softly. Had she guessed he was leaving? His grandmother could be spooky psychic.

She ran a wet piece of sponge over the rim of the bowl she was working on, widening it evenly, making it look so easy.

"Grab some clay. We'll work on your technique," she said. "Cool your jets some."

"Not today." He'd ended up with a messy blob of sloppy clay the last time she tried to show him. "But can I borrow some money? I'll pay you back." When, though, he had no idea.

She didn't look up. "How much you need?"

"Just a hundred." That should cover the bus ticket and maybe some for a cab to his dad's place if his dad wasn't able to get to the bus station right off. He had some of his gig pay for food.

"Grab it out of the cash register. Key's under the pad," she said.

He felt a flood of love for her. She'd said yes without demanding to know what it was for. She was a great person, no matter what Christine said.

She was as wrong about his grandmother as she was about his dad.

He got the money, then came back to say goodbye. He watched her run her fingers lovingly over the wet gray curve of the bowl. He thought of all the love she rubbed into the dishes and mugs and cups and bowls they all used and didn't appreciate, carelessly tossing them around, banging them in the sink, not even caring if they cracked or broke.

But Aurora kept on, no matter whether or not anyone appreciated what she'd created. A strong tangle of feelings twisted through him—love and pity and guilt and sadness. He wanted to hug her, but Aurora wasn't like that, he knew. "Thanks," was all he could choke out. He turned and ran.

He would miss her a lot. Now that he knew Marcus was a traitor, she was the only one who understood him. Bogie was cool, but he shrank back so much, like he wasn't good enough to talk to you or something.

David fought past the choked feeling in his throat. He should be dead-on thrilled. Soon he'd be with the person who would understand him best of all. His dad, who would love David for who he was, not some made-up perfect kid like with his mom.

All he had to do was throw crap in his backpack, grab his guitar, the keys and the Volvo, and he'd be out of there. Off to his real life at last.

CHAPTER FOURTEEN

SUPPER WAS READY AND David was not at the table.
"I'm going after him," Christine said to Marcus,
shooting him a glare. He'd refused to talk to David
right after the fight, even though she'd told him
she'd never seen David this hateful.

He needs time to regroup and process this,
Marcus had said. So maddening. Sometimes time
was the last thing people needed. Marcus hadn't
even been that flipped out about the marijuana. He
seemed concerned, not alarmed.

On top of that he'd done everything short of say
I told you so about keeping their relationship secret
from David for so long. In short, Christine was as
frustrated with Marcus as she was scared and worried about David.

"Would you like me to talk to him?" Marcus
asked quietly.

"Not if you think he needs more *time,*" she said.
She noticed the residents had reacted to her sharp
tone. "If you wouldn't mind, that would be great,"
she said more politely.

But before he left the dining room, Aurora stuck

her head in from the kitchen. "The Barlow kids are out here. Something about David? They want to talk to you."

Christine headed into the kitchen, Marcus behind her.

Todd and Robert stood inside the door, looking nervous. "This is weird," Todd said, "but David wanted us to come over and tell you some stuff." He dipped his head.

"Like what?" she demanded, taking a step closer.

"He, um, left. To go to his dad's. He said your car will be at the bus station in Preston with the key in the magnetic box under the wheel well."

"What? He's going to— He knows where his father is?" She sucked in air, feeling dizzy. "That's not possible."

"He found the number you had and called it."

But where— Then she remembered the message slip with Skip's contact information. She'd left it in her address book where she'd sent David for the money he'd hounded her for.

"Oh, God."

"He said not to call or e-mail 'cause he won't answer."

"When did he leave?" she asked, fear pouring through her.

"He's on the bus by now. Almost there. He said we had to wait until suppertime to tell you so you can't stop him. Sorry." Todd shrugged.

"He was just really pissed," Robert added, "so he'll probably call and say he's sorry and all."

"If he calls you, will you let me know?" Christine asked, her throat so tight she could hardly get out words.

The boys nodded solemnly. "He sort of flipped out, so maybe he'll change his mind when he calms down," Robert said.

The boys turned and left.

"I guess that's what the money was for," Aurora mused.

Christine jerked to look at her. "You gave him money?"

"A hundred bucks. He came into the clay barn."

"Did you ask him what it was *for?*" she demanded.

Aurora shrugged. "He said he was mad at you, that you lied to him about everything, that he couldn't please you."

"And that didn't give you a *clue?*" she said. "He's mad at me, he asks for that much money and you don't inquire as to his plans?" She tried not to sound as outraged as she felt.

"If he wanted to tell me, he would have told me. And if he wanted to leave, I couldn't have stopped him."

Which was exactly as careless as she'd been with Christine all those years ago. Now Aurora had let her grandson run away.

"I can't believe this." Christine made her hands

into fists and squeezed to keep from yelling or crying.

"He'll figure it out, don't worry," Aurora said.

"Figure it out? And what might happen to him in the meantime? He's fifteen years old, Aurora."

"I'll call the bus station and sheriff's office and see what we can find out," Marcus said, going for the phone.

"I can't even call Skip. David has the message slip."

Her helpless feeling got even worse when she learned the bus company would not confirm if or when he'd taken a bus to San Diego and the police wouldn't look for him unless he was in imminent danger.

David's cell phone went straight to voice mail, so Christine left as calm a message as she could manage, then sagged into the desk chair in her alcove office. "I've lost him," she said to Marcus, who sat across the desk. "He's gone."

"He will call or his father will," Marcus said. "You just have to wait a little while."

"This was my last chance and I blew it. What if he won't come back?"

"I'm sure he will. And in the meantime, the visit might be valuable for him."

"*Valuable?* Are you nuts? With Skip? He's a terrible person and an awful influence. He'll break David's heart."

"The absence of a parent can distort a child's view of himself and his place in the world."

"What? You're giving me a psychology lecture now? My young son, who can barely drive, took my car and may or may not have made it to Preston, found the bus station, got on the right bus to San Diego where his flaky father may or may not meet him—or even know he's on his way."

Just saying that out loud scared her even more.

"Of course you're worried, but it does no good to create worst-case scenarios, Christine. For now we're waiting." In the face of her distress, Marcus seemed to have turned into some distant, neutral stranger.

"Even if he makes it there safely, Skip is a disaster."

"David has created a fantasy father in his mind. Meeting the man will be a reality check for him."

"A reality check? You're saying he *should* visit?"

"The research indicates more positive outcomes when a child experiences a disappointing father than when he has no contact with him."

"You're quoting research now? And, what, saying this is my fault? That I should have let him be with Skip? I'm a bad mother, is that it?"

"That's not what I'm saying," he said calmly, looking at her as though she was being silly. "You seem to have had an extreme reaction to the idea of David spending time with his father. Are you afraid

David would choose Skip over you, because that's highly unlikely given your—"

"Just stop! You're not helping me," she snapped.

"My point is that David will discover his father's flaws and stop mythologizing him in his absence. That's a good thing."

"So you think it's *good* he ran away?" she said, laying on the sarcasm.

"It's not ideal, no, but trust your son, Christine. You've raised him with love and taught him your values. He'll sort this out and make good decisions."

"It's easy for you to be so wait-and-see about it. He's not your son. You don't know him like I do. Your heart's not breaking in two with worry."

"I do care about David. I've had extensive conversations with him and I believe he's mature enough and sensible enough to handle this situation."

"Do you realize how smug you sound? How all-knowing and God-like? Marcus knows best and I'm just the silly mother."

"That was not my intent at all, Christine."

"Well, that's how it feels. You didn't talk to him, Marcus. You didn't see his face, the hatred there. He was so angry. Last time he got this upset he drove drunk and almost got in a wreck."

"He's come a long way since then."

"Oh, yeah? Is that why he's still smoking pot? I should have been in his face about drugs, searching his room, making him take drug tests. Don't all those drug prevention people say you have to be assertive?"

"I believe the thrust of the argument is to be watchful, to have open communication, to discuss drugs regularly and frankly. All of which you've done."

"I should have put him into rehab. I should have made him go to a therapist in Preston."

"That's extreme, Christine."

"Extreme? That's *extreme?* Then how about if you'd talked to him when I asked you to? Instead of copping out with 'give him time, be patient.' You could have talked him out of leaving. He trusted you."

"Yes, he did. And I betrayed that trust by sleeping with his mother in secret. At least that's how he would see it." He looked at her steadily, coolly. "Under those circumstances, I doubt he would take my advice about anything."

He sounded so clinical, so wooden, but what he said made her realize a terrible truth. "David said when he saw us kissing that he was looking for you to talk about something important. It had to be about finding Skip's number. He went to you for help, to sort it all out, but I kissed you and ruined it."

"It was unfortunate timing."

"I knew better. I knew better all along. I should never have been with you. I put my own desires above David's well-being and this is the price I'm paying."

"You're being overly dramatic. You get to have a life, if for no other reason than to give David space for his own. This was a case of bad timing, not the proof you've failed as a mother, Christine. There's no point assuming the worst."

She just looked at him. He'd dismissed her feelings and concerns as so much hysteria. "Well, maybe that's how I deal with a crisis. Maybe it helps me to assume the worst."

"I don't understand that."

"Of course you don't. You're quiet and logical and reasonable and I'm loud and emotional and irrational. We're different, Marcus. Too different."

"What are you saying, Christine?"

"I'm saying we made a mistake." She swallowed hard. "We can't make this work. And not only because of David. In bed we're fine together, wonderful even, amazing. But in life? Dealing with the day-to-day issues, the problems? We'd never stop fighting."

Marcus seemed stunned. He opened his mouth to speak, then closed it again. "I don't know that that's logical."

"It's my fault. I asked too much from you. The minute we arrived I started leaning on you, asking you to fix David, to fix me. You did your best, but it wasn't your job. It was mine. I've made up a little fairy tale, after all. Aurora was right. I'm living in my princess room waiting to be rescued by my prince. That's not fair to you."

"I don't agree, but I can see I've disappointed you. I never intended that."

"We got carried away is all, making more of this than could ever be." She felt sick inside at this new loss, inevitable as it was. "At least we know now, before we turned our lives upside down for each other."

"I'm sorry, Christine," he said, pale as death. She thought she caught a flash of wild pain in his eyes, but it was gone so quickly she might have imagined it.

"However I can help, I'd like to," he said. "If I can drive you to Preston for your car or assist with David in any way, please let me know."

And with that, he was gone.

Christine stayed in her office until after midnight waiting for a call from David or Skip that never came.

When she finally went to bed, her head was tight as a drum, her eyes wide open, and she couldn't seem to take a full breath. She didn't even know if David had reached San Diego or found his father when he got there. If he had made it safely, she wouldn't be surprised if Skip had deliberately left her hanging as payback once David laid out her crimes against him.

She longed to run to the comfort of Marcus's arms, but she was strong enough to resist. Deep inside, she'd known better. She took care of herself, her son and her life and always had.

She'd gotten so caught up with Marcus, she'd let her son slip away. She would never forgive herself. Never.

ALL MARCUS WANTED WAS to be numb again, as he'd been before Christine landed in his life. Now all his synapses were firing, every sense was wide awake, and he felt an agony he wasn't sure he would survive.

He'd known better than to get so involved. He wasn't what Christine needed and could never be. Hadn't his marriage to Elizabeth taught him anything?

And as to David, he regretted hurting him. He should have insisted they talk to him, but he'd sensed that Christine believed, deep down, that their relationship wouldn't last long enough for it to matter.

He should have found David a therapist in Preston when Christine asked—not jumped in to be the big hero—then left Christine the hell alone. Instead, as he'd done with Nathan and Elizabeth, he'd let his feelings override his judgment and screwed up royally.

If he had any doubts, all he had to do was remember how he'd acted after they learned David had run off. Christine had needed him to take her in his arms and comfort her, but what had he done? Offered smug advice and a ride to Preston for her *car*.

He son was missing and he offered her a *ride?*

He was a psychiatrist, for God's sake. How could he have bungled human emotions so badly? Because this wasn't therapy, this was life, where his success rate was dismal. Where he was completely at sea.

And Christine was correct. The silver lining to this black cloud was that they knew now, before they'd turned their lives upside down to be together.

But, oh, how he ached to hold her again.

Sleep was hopeless so he went to his computer, searching for the distraction that would keep him from dwelling on his misery.

His book had been untouched for weeks. He skimmed the first few pages of each chapter to remind himself what he'd intended. There was the research overkill he'd already noted, the dry listing of data and rationale. Who would read such a book? Other psychiatrists and mental health professionals perhaps. And what was the point of that exactly? Preaching to the choir or falling on deaf ears.

Abruptly, he saw what else was wrong. The book had no heart. No emotion. No stories. No people. It was an intellectual exercise. Human beings appeared as data points, not flesh-and-blood patients and their families and therapists struggling against a system that cared less for them than actuarial tables.

His book should to tell those stories. Of course.

That would bring these issues to life. So how would that work?

He could interview his own former patients, his colleagues and their patients and write a book with heart, with life, with people and feelings. He would write a book that people would want to read, one that ultimately might lead to action.

Hesitantly at first, then more quickly, Marcus began to outline a new book. He owed this epiphany to Christine. Without her, without the feelings she'd awakened in him, he might never have figured this out. One day, he would tell her so.

THE NEXT DAY, WHEN Marcus met Carlos for lunch, he found his friend looking worse than Marcus felt after the sleepless, heartsick night he'd had. "You look like hell, Carlos."

"Feel like it, too. I just treated a rancher who needs dialysis he'll never get because we don't have the equipment. After lunch, a little girl's coming in with a misshapen arm because the fracture went too long without a cast."

"When the grants come through, that will change."

"Not soon enough for the people I see now."

"I'm going to L.A. next week and I plan to have some personal meetings with leads Elizabeth gave me. Maybe that can speed up the process."

"You're going next week?"

"For a couple of weeks, yeah. I need some interviews for my book."

"I thought you were about done with that."

"I'm starting over. I decided last night."

"Your muse let you down?" Carlos winked.

The smile he gave Carlos hurt his face. "Not at all. She helped me figure this out. However, we're not seeing each other anymore." He tried to sound matter-of-fact, but he knew Carlos would not let that slide.

"You what? You broke up? What did you do, *jefe?* Apologize, for God's sake. You know she's right."

"She is, and that's the problem." He told Carlos the basics of what had gone wrong.

"So, just like that? She flips out over her son, you go all cerebral, she gets pissed—as well she should—and breaks up with you? And you let her? Jesus."

"We were dreaming and we woke up. We'd end up hurting each other, so this is for the best."

"Right. Because you're a soulless automaton and she's a drama queen and neither of you deserve each other or love?"

"Mock all you want, but you're close to the bone here."

"Rethink this, *jefe.* You're wallowing in ancient history. She's not Elizabeth. I know you loved the woman, but she was pretty much an ice queen. You seem so much happier with this one. Give yourself a chance, *hombre.*"

He shook his head. Carlos was as excessively optimistic about love as Christine was about everything else.

"If I were a true friend, I'd go all intervention on your ass. But for now, how about we drown you sorrows in tequila after I close the clinic at five?"

"Sounds good," Marcus said immediately. It was an escape and that sounded good to him. As good as his new book, which saved him from complete despair. He owed Christine his thanks. She'd awakened him to the world again, opened him up to things he could do, like help Carlos with his clinic. Christine had reminded him to use his heart, as well as his head and hands. He would be grateful to her for the rest of his life.

AFTER A TERRIBLE NIGHT, Christine dragged herself out of bed to help cook breakfast. "Why don't you take it easy today?" Aurora said, her concern touching Christine.

"I need to stay busy," she said, grateful when Marcus didn't appear at the breakfast table. She wasn't sure she could stand the pain of seeing him again so soon.

She was elbow-deep in dishwater when the phone rang, so Aurora answered it. "Harmony House… Oh! Yes! She's right here, Skip. Hang on."

Thank God. Relief washed over Christine as she wiped her wet hands on her jeans, took the phone and rushed into the alcove. "Is David all right?" she asked, holding her breath.

"He's fine, Chris." Then he lowered his voice, as if not wanting to be overheard. "Jesus, you made me out to be some kind of psychopath."

"That's not true." But it was close, she knew, and she felt guilty about it. "I'm sure he's exaggerated because he's so angry at me."

"He's got good reason to be pissed at you."

"Will you send him back, Skip? Please."

"He seems to think he belongs here, since you say we're so alike, what with our terrible tempers and all."

She cringed. Skip was furious with her. What should she say? Marcus's advice about acknowledging strong emotion with David popped into her head. "I can hear that you're angry that I kept David from you," she said slowly.

"You're damn straight I am. You pretended you didn't know where I was to him. I called you when I moved most of the time. You know that. Maybe once or twice I couldn't make a visit, but that's no excuse to lie about me."

Once or twice? Try five or six or seven. "I'm sorry, Skip. That was wrong of me." She gritted her teeth.

"People change, Chris. And no one's as perfect as you want them to be."

"I'm sure that's true. So will you send him back?"

"David needs to get to know me, not the monster you told him about. He's fine right where he is."

Click.

"Wait!" But it was too late. He'd hung up without giving her a phone number, leaving her still stuck with no way to reach David. Worse, *David wanted to live with Skip*.

She felt as though she'd been slammed into a wall. That was what had scared her most. Marcus had her dead to rights on that one. She'd been protecting David from his terrible father, but she'd also been protecting herself. She was afraid David would love Skip more than he loved her. How pathetic was that?

Whatever failings Marcus might have in a relationship, he had read Christine like a book. She owed him an apology. When she could be near him without bursting into tears, she would give it to him.

CHAPTER FIFTEEN

FIVE DAYS LATER, Christine sat at a potter's wheel shaping the lip of a vase she'd been fussing over far too long, but now had just…about…perfect.

Working with her hands, in clay or potting soil, was about all that pleased her lately. The ooze of the clay through her fingers, the creak and spin of the wheel, the moist, earthy smells in the greenhouse, watching life emerge, eager and green from Bogie's special soil, all soothed her, eased her sadness and worry and regret.

The days and nights blurred. She slept fitfully, moments with David and Marcus playing over and over in her head, conversations she wished she'd had ringing in her ears. She missed them both like parts of her body had been carved away.

She restricted herself to one e-mail or phone message to David each day, forcing herself to sound easy and warm. Inside, she was dying of sadness. She rarely saw Marcus, which was a relief, and his car was often gone.

Through it all, she kept working and somehow, day by day, time managed to pass.

"Anything from David?" Aurora asked, taking a seat on the adjacent stool. Aurora had treated her with surprising gentleness, for which Christine was grateful.

"Nothing," she said, then saw that her momentary distraction had caused her to collapse the vase. "Dammit!" she said, her voice cracking. "I worked and worked this. I had it perfect. Now look what I did!" Her hands were shaking and her eyes burned. She wanted to *cry*, for heaven's sake. She was ridiculously emotional. "I'm hopeless."

"You'll throw another one, bunny. Not a biggie."

Startled and touched, Christine stared at her mother. "You haven't called me 'bunny' since I was in kindergarten."

"Your problem is you let it get too wet," her mother said, ignoring her words. She cut the mangled clay from the wheel with a wire scraper, then dropped a mound of newly prepared clay onto the wheel. "How about a fresh start?"

"I miss him so much," she said, her voice breaking, her emotions too high to ignore. She'd almost added *Mom*, she'd forgotten herself so much.

"Of course you do," Aurora said. Her gaze slipped away from Christine's, but she seemed to fight to pull it back, to keep eye contact. Her mother was truly trying to help her—and in a way Christine recognized.

"I chased him right to Skip. I should have let him

see his father, even if he got disappointed. I was afraid to lose him. I was selfish and stupid."

"Stop that right now," her mother said in her usual blunt tone. "You did what you thought best." Her mother's face softened and to her surprise, she reached out and gave Christine's thigh a tentative pat, then quickly pulled her hand away and cleared her throat. "Now get going on that."

Christine sponged some water on the clay and began to spin the wheel slowly.

"It hurt like hell to let you go, you know," Aurora said.

"Yeah?" Christine knew better than to look up or her mother would never finish the story.

"My parents wanted to lock me in my bedroom and throw away the key. I swore I'd be better than them, so I had to let you go if you wanted to leave. That was the promise I'd made to myself."

Christine was startled. So it hadn't been a case of out of sight, out of mind for her mother when Christine ran away. Aurora had struggled and been sad.

"You always have doubts as a mother," she said. Christine had sworn to be a better mother than Aurora, too. She hadn't done as well as she'd intended. Perhaps Aurora hadn't done as poorly as Christine had always thought.

"I swear if we'd stayed in that apartment, you'd have suffocated," Aurora said. It took Christine a second to follow her mother's train of thought. Then she realized Aurora was still talking about the choices mothers faced.

"I loved our apartment. It was cozy and tidy and perfect."

"No place is perfect, Christine. That's why Harmony House was good for you. You needed to break out of that cookie-cutter crap. Being different made you independent."

"It didn't feel that way at the time."

"And I'll tell you something else. If I'd been as strong as you, I wouldn't have been so scared when my folks locked me out. I panicked. I didn't take care of myself like I should have. I didn't eat or see a doctor. If I'd been stronger, you would have a big brother or sister this very day." Her mother swallowed hard and shook her head, clearly fighting emotion.

"You didn't cause your miscarriage," Christine said, startled to realize that was what her mother believed. "One out of four pregnancies fails. A miscarriage means something was wrong with the fetus. That's all."

"I don't think so." But hope flared in Aurora's eyes before she firmly put it out.

"Losing that baby was not your fault. And as to being scared on your own, well, you did your best," she said, repeating her mother's consoling words to her.

Aurora seemed to think that through, then dismiss it. "You're getting me off track. My point is that you would have taken charge. You wouldn't have been wimpy and weak like I was. And why was that? Because I brought you here."

"Okay…" she said, though her mother's reasoning was seriously flawed. She was flattered that her mother thought she was strong and brave.

"I knew you needed to escape the nuns and the rules and those bossy girls you liked so much. You were getting boxed in, your whole soul stifled. I wanted better for you, Christina Marie."

Emotion made Christine's nose sting. All these years, Christine had assumed she was an annoying burden to her mother, not her reason to come to Harmony House.

"From the moment I got pregnant with you I did everything right, too. I took every vitamin, got plenty of rest, saw the doctor once a month. At first I was living at Bogie's place, then in Colorado with friends, but I stuck to my promise."

Movement made them look up to see that Bogie had come into the barn carrying a jug of water and two Mason jars. "You should try for a nap, Aurora," he said, filling both glasses and handing them each one. "You know how you are after too much heat."

"I have a clean bill of health."

"And you practically fainted yesterday. Drink up," he said more firmly than Christine had ever heard him speak to her.

"You almost fainted?" Christine asked.

"I stood up too quick is all. You both worry too damn much." But her tone was friendly. Aurora looked at Christine, then back at Bogie, who was turning to leave.

"Stay a minute," Aurora said to him.

Bogie looked at her. "All right." He sounded wary, but he dragged a sawhorse over and sat. "I just want to say again how sorry I am about that marijuana," he said to Christine. He'd apologized three times already. "He never took much and I just didn't want to rock the boat."

"That's your whole problem, Clancy Hampton," Aurora said, suddenly blunt. Christine hadn't heard her mother use Bogie's real name since she'd introduced him to Christine before they came to Harmony House.

"Sometimes you have to rock the boat. Hell, sometimes you have to tip the damn thing over. It's time to tell her."

"Tell me what?" Christine said.

A look passed between the two of them, heavy and slow, before Aurora continued. "We've been talking about the old days, so now's as good a time as any. You promised."

Bogie hung his head.

"Bogie?" Christine stared at him, hardly able to breathe for the way her heart pounded in her chest. "What is it?"

"Oh, Crystal." His eyes filled with sadness and shame.

"Hell's bells, do I have to do everything for you? Bogie is your father, Christine. There. It's done."

"What?" Her mind stalled out. "But my dad's a policeman—"

"I made him up for you," Aurora said. "Bogie was out of the picture and you wanted a hero so damn bad."

"But I remember him. His coat. His aftershave." She remembered him throwing her into the air, the brush of his stubble, the scratch of his badge when he hugged her close.

"You've always had a good imagination."

"You and Bogie were together?" She couldn't imagine. Bogie seemed so much older than her mother.

"It's only ten years between us. And Clancy was a handsome man. Jesus. Anyway, when I got pregnant, Bogie couldn't handle it and took off."

Bogie hunched his shoulders, but didn't look up.

"He was afraid is all. It was a different time." Aurora cleared her throat. "I went to stay with friends in Colorado."

Christine kept looking from one to the other. She felt as though she was in a bad dream, foggily fighting to wake up.

"When Clancy found me at that rally, I didn't want him to tell you. You had your hero, first off, and I was still angry at him." She shot him a look. "Talk to your daughter now. Here's your chance to explain."

"I'm no kind of father," he said huskily. "I knew it then and I know it now." He stood stiffly and walked away.

Christine's mind reeled. The universe had suddenly tilted on its axis and she felt dizzy. Her heroic father was gone, replaced by a humble hippie who had left her pregnant mother all alone.

"Don't let him chicken out now," Aurora said. "He has a side in this story, you know. He'll be in the greenhouse."

Dazed, Christine went after him. Sure enough, he'd escaped to his sanctuary. He looked up, startled, watering plants that clearly didn't need it.

"You left Aurora pregnant?" That seemed so awful and not like Bogie, who'd always been steady and loyal.

"I freaked out. I left her all the money I had and the house had a year's lease. And I was only gone for a week. When I came back, she'd gone. I hitched out to Denver—I heard that was where she was—but never found her." He lifted his shoulders in a tiny shrug, that passive, noncommittal Bogie move.

"When I saw her again at that antinuclear protest, I knew it was my chance to make it right, to fix what I'd done."

He smiled. "I'll never forget when I first laid eyes on you. You had on a pink dress and black shiny shoes, and I knew I'd do whatever it took to spend time with you. I was so honored to meet you. Honored."

Christine's throat tightened. She felt so confused and shaken. The beloved father she remembered had been replaced by the humble ghost of Harmony House. "Why didn't you tell me back then?"

"You talked a lot about your dad. You were so proud of his being a cop and a hero. I couldn't ruin that." Bogie's face contorted and she saw he was crying. "I couldn't take it if you hated me, you see."

"How could I? You were always good to me, Bogie."

He shook his head. "Then you got here this time with David, so I figured I could be a father to you even if you didn't know who I really was."

She looked into his gray eyes, watery with tears. Now she knew why they'd always seemed so familiar to her. They were the color of her own. She had her father's eyes.

It was all suddenly too much. Her emotions were crashing like waves in a storm—confusion, anger, sadness. She needed to sort them out, adjust her thinking, recast her whole life. She had to get away before she burst into tears or started throwing things or yelling.

"It will take me a bit to get used to this," she said. "I'm glad to know the truth…and I'll…just… We'll talk later."

She left, her heart tight in her chest. Her brain, which already swirled with worries about David and sadness over Marcus, felt as if it might burst wide open.

She needed to talk about this, get the words out in the air. There was only one person who could help her. He'd said if she needed anything…

Without stopping for a moment of doubt, she ran up the stairs to Marcus's room and knocked on his door, hoping he was there.

He answered, looking rumpled and foggy, as if she'd woke him from a nap. "Did you hear from David?" he asked.

"Not yet. Nothing more from Skip, either."

"David will call. Try not to worry."

She smiled, wishing she were as confident as Marcus seemed to be. "Did I wake you?"

"I guess I dozed off," he said, rubbing his face. "I'm not sleeping much at night. What's up?" He widened his eyes, as if trying to be more alert.

"I just learned something I need to talk about, so I wondered if you—" She hesitated. "Maybe you should sleep."

"No, no. Please. If I can help, I want to. Let's talk." He smiled, clearly pleased to see her, despite everything that stood between them. He motioned her inside, but there were too many memories there.

"Can we walk to the river maybe?"

"Absolutely." He pulled his door shut and they set off. Usually, she had Lady with her on walks, but the dog seemed to be waiting for David, staying in his room or standing guard outside the door, making Christine even sadder.

Marcus stayed silent, waiting for her to speak. But Christine just wanted to walk with him beside her, strong and tall and reassuring. Being near him settled some of the chaos in her head. The sun was warm on her face and arms. Crickets buzzed and birds twittered genially.

Soon they reached the cottonwoods and then the river and found the rocks they'd sat on the first time they'd come here, before they made love.

"So," she said, glancing at him, then away, suddenly shy. "Here's the deal." She took a deep breath and blurted it out. "It turns out that Bogie is my father."

"He's…what? But your father was a policeman."

"I know. Aurora made that up to give me a hero. It was a lie. A lie that she and Bogie stuck with for thirty-five years. I feel so stupid. Like a fool. And hurt and disappointed."

"What I hear in your voice is anger," Marcus said.

"Exactly!" He'd said what she needed to hear. "I'm furious. At both of them. For lying all these years. For lying in the first place. For...all of it."

"That's understandable, Christine."

"But it's more," she said. "I'm disappointed, too. Bogie's a great guy and all, but he's my *father?* I mean, I felt so lost and lonely and unloved as a kid and he just left me like that."

"What should he have done in your opinion?"

"Been a lion for me. Defended me against Aurora, protected me at school. I could have talked to him about Dylan that awful night. He should have hugged me, told me he loved me. All those years... nothing but silence and a lie." Tears clogged her throat.

"So he didn't do any of that. What *did* he do for you?"

She looked at him. "I don't know. He was just Bogie." She thought back, then sighed. "He bought me that Barbie doll I told you about. He used to show me things in the greenhouse and the gardens." She smiled, remembering something else. "He would pay for the junk food and *Teen Vogues* I swiped from Parsons that Aurora would never buy for me."

She paused, thinking it through. "I guess I felt him on my side whenever Aurora would get on my case. He looked out for me in his quiet way."

"But that wasn't how you expected a father to behave?"

"Of course not. My father was a hero, remember?" She managed a smile. "And exactly how could Bogie ever live up to that fantasy? He said he didn't tell me because he didn't want to ruin that for me."

Marcus smiled, too.

Sharing her outrage had eased some of it. "I always felt safe with him. He was always there. And he stuck it out all these years with Aurora, no matter how bossy she got."

"So he's loyal."

"Or maybe scared to leave. No, that's not fair. Bogie's a strong person. Steady. And you know he cares. But he's not—"

"Father material?"

"Huh." She paused. "He's not the father I would have chosen, but he's the father I *have*. Is that what you're saying?"

Marcus simply looked at her.

"Once a shrink, always a shrink, Marcus." She threw a rock into the water. "Okay, so Bogie didn't teach me to ride a bike, or make sure I did my homework, or grill my dates at the door like I wanted. He did what he could."

A child is big. You want your child to be happy. He'd said that when she'd told him her hopes for David and he'd looked so sad. Meanwhile, she'd been *his* child and he'd been afraid to tell her so.

"So I've been living in my fantasy bedroom with the canopy bed all this time, completely oblivious to reality."

"You had no way to know about Bogie."

"True, but I missed things I should have seen. About Aurora, too. She told me she moved to Harmony House for me, to help me be more independent. She said it was hard to let me go when I ran off. I always thought she was glad I was out of her hair. I guess she loved me, but I never felt it."

"She wasn't the kind of mother you wanted."

"Not even close. And I kind of told her so, I think. A lot." She grimaced, feeling sheepish. "Maybe I wasn't such an easy daughter, either."

Her mother hadn't hugged her much, but with a childhood like Aurora's, no wonder. Instead of affection and encouragement, Aurora had offered lectures and commands. But she'd worried about Christine, loved her, held her in her heart, let her go even when it hurt.

"I think I'm starting to get a handle on this," she said.

With Aurora, you had to read between the lines. That was where the love was. "At least I'm not so angry now."

"It's a lot to take in," Marcus said, his eyes kind. How she'd missed his eyes on her. "It will take time to adjust as you reexamine and reinterpret your past through this new lens."

"That makes sense. Thanks so much, Marcus, for talking to me. You helped a lot."

"I only listened, Christine."

"Not everyone knows how to do that very well. I need to apologize for dumping on you when David ran away. I panicked and flipped out. You were only trying to help."

"You needed comfort and support and I gave you arrogant analysis. I let you down."

"No. You did your best. And you helped me all along. To be a better mother, for sure. I used your advice to talk to Skip, if you can believe that. And it worked."

"I never meant to hurt you," he said.

"The situation had hurt built right into it, Marcus. And I think we both knew it." She missed him so much, the way he looked at her—deeply and with so much love.

"Perhaps you're right." He sighed. "I'm glad I was still here when you came by. I head to L.A. tomorrow."

"For good? You're leaving?" The idea panicked her, which was ridiculous. They'd broken up, after all.

"For a couple of weeks for now. I'm meeting with people about funding Carlos's clinic. And I'll be doing some interviews for my book. I'm starting over again, believe it or not."

"But you were almost done."

"I'm taking a different approach, thanks to my muse." He smiled, then explained the book he would write with patient stories and far more heart.

"You sound excited really about it," she said.

"I am. And I owe you thanks for that. You helped me break through the fog from last year."

"I'm glad. So, see, we've been good for each other."

"I just wish…" He touched her hair, a world of wishful thinking in his eyes.

"At least we tried, Marcus, you know? I'm not sorry we tried."

"That's good then," he said, looking so sad she wanted to hold him, though she knew better. Her throat locked up and she feared she might cry.

"Something else." He reached into his pocket for his wallet and took out a business card he held out. "When you do talk to David, would you ask him to call me? I'd like to sort out what happened and apologize. Here are all my numbers."

"Kind of sad we're down to exchanging business cards, huh?"

"And there's one more thing. Lady."

"That poor dog. Now she's started howling for David. I'm forever tripping over her outside his door."

"She's very attached to David. That's why I'd like to give her to him, if that's all right with you."

"Oh, wow. David would love that, but it's no-pets at our apartment. I'm sorry. It's a wonderful offer…."

"If anything changes, the offer stands." Marcus gave her a quizzical look. "You know, I wonder if you might want to stay here."

"What?" she said. "Are you kidding?"

"You've built something here and you seem to enjoy more about Harmony House than you hate. You're closer to your mother. And now this news about Bogie. A smaller school might be good for David, a fresh start with new friends. And of course, now you've got DSL and water pressure." He smiled. "Just a thought."

"I don't see that happening. I've got my job and David has school. And our lives are there." Though lately Phoenix seemed very far away and long ago.

"Anyway, I can't think about that right now. Right now I'd better go talk to…my *father*. Thank you, Marcus." She kissed him softly on the mouth. She couldn't help it. "For everything."

Bogie was still in the greenhouse, which didn't surprise her. "Crystal," he said softly, stopping his work to look at her, his hands loose at his sides. They were leathery and callused, the creases stained by dirt, the nails chipped and cracked. Everything about Bogie's hands declared that he worked the earth. The earth had marked him as its own.

"I've been thinking this through," she said.

Bogie waited silently for her verdict, his gray eyes

anxious. He had always been a man of few words. He let his hands speak for him. In his greenhouse, in the commune he'd looked after all these years, and in the love he'd given to Christine and Aurora and, since he'd arrived, David, too.

The kindly hippie in the background of her life had, all along, been her father, her own flesh and blood. His genes twined at her core, his blood ran in her veins and she saw the world through the same gray eyes.

She stood still, remembering all he'd taught her in this greenhouse—the right time to remove dead blossoms, when to trim things, when to repot, that plants need enough room to stretch, but not too much, or all the energy goes to the roots and the plant suffers.

He'd said he'd been *honored* to meet her, his daughter. It all balled up in a tangle of emotion inside her and she said, "I'm *honored* you're my father," and threw her arms around him.

He was stiff at first, in her arms, but she held on until he looped his arms around her back and gave her three gentle pats. Afterward, he ducked his head. "Well, now, that's just all right, isn't it?"

"Yes, it is...*Dad.*"

Bogie grinned.

After that moment with Bogie in the greenhouse, Christine felt like a new person, one who truly knew her place in the world for the first time ever. Big pieces in her personal puzzle had snapped into

place. Mainly, she'd let go of her perfect image of
what a father and a mother should be, in favor of
who they really were. And when David returned,
she would see him as he was, not as she wished him
to be. Princess rooms were fun, but reality was...
well...*real*.

CHAPTER SIXTEEN

TWO WEEKS AFTER DAVID had run away, Christine was gathering plates to set the table when the phone rang and Aurora answered it. She listened, then grabbed Christine's arm, mouthing *David*, her eyes wide. Christine's heart leaped into her throat.

"Hey there, chief," Aurora said to him. "You've got us all bummed out over here. No one's singing folk songs night and day, that girl Delia keeps asking when you'll be back and Lady howls us awake every evening."

She listened to David, then said, "Your mother has some news you might want to hear." She meant about Bogie being his grandfather. "You want to talk to her?" She glanced at Christine, listened, then frowned. "You sure? I promise I'll stop her if she starts to give you hell." She sighed. "All right then. Yeah, put him on."

She held the phone to Christine. "Skip wants to talk to you. David's not ready."

Her heart sank, but at least he'd called. "Hello?" She heard Skip tell David to go watch TV. "Hi,

Chris," he said into the phone, sounding weary, not angry.

"Skip, before you say anything, can I have your phone number, so I can reach you in an emergency?"

"Yeah, no problem." He gave her all his contact information and she scribbled it down, relieved to have a link at last.

"And I also want to tell you that I was wrong to keep David from you. I'm glad you're getting to know each other." The difficult words came out in a rush. She held her breath for his response.

It took a while.

"Well, yeah," he said finally, surprise in his voice. "I'm not like I was, Chris. You never gave me much credit."

"I realize that. I wasn't fair."

"Good, then." He cleared his throat. He must have expected an argument. "I just called to find out when his school starts."

"The third week of August."

"So, three more weeks." He sounded disappointed, which seemed odd. "The thing is I've got deals brewing and he wants to shadow me all the time. I do half my business in bars, Chris."

"That's difficult," she said, her heart lifting. It sounded as though Skip was ready to send David home.

"He just dropped in on me, you know. No warning."

"Oh, I do. And he can be intense."

"And judgmental as hell. He got that from you."

She didn't react to the insult. "It sounds like you've had a long enough visit. Am I right?" She desperately hoped so.

"I can't make him leave. He'd never forgive me. But there's school, so that'll be a good end time."

"It's up to you. There's plenty for him to do here, though, and obviously a lot more space. An entire boarding house."

"The apartment is tight, all right. And now he wants to go deep-sea fishing." Skip sighed.

"Even if he's not showing it at the moment, seeing you means a lot to David," she said, surprised that she actually meant the words. Skip was not the father David wanted, but he was the father David had. And that was better than one he'd dressed up as a hero the same way Christine had done.

A WEEK LATER, CHRISTINE was in her office when the phone rang. "Harmony House, may I help you?" she said.

"Mom?" David's voice was small and shaky.

"David?" She caught her breath, determined not to overwhelm him, even as she wanted to shriek with joy and relief.

"I want to come back," he said abruptly. "Dad's an asshole. He's never home and when he is, he acts like I'm in the way."

"I'm sorry to hear that." And she was. She could hear the hurt in his voice and wanted to ease it if she could.

"He hangs in bars all the time, smokes weed and then lies about it. Half the time he goes to bed to avoid talking to me."

"Remember, you caught him off guard dropping in on him and it's hard to have a guest for long, especially in an apartment. You're on vacation, with complete free time, but he's working."

Another long silence. "You're defending him?"

"Just trying to help you understand him. I was wrong to keep you from your father. I know that now."

"Yeah?" She could hear him breathing. Her change of heart had no doubt confused him. "Anyway, he said he'd buy me a bus ticket whenever I want, so I want to—" He stopped abruptly, then said, "Hey!" to someone in the background.

"What did he tell you?" Skip demanded of her. He'd grabbed the phone from David. "That I neglected him? Because I spent all kinds of time with him. Movies, the beach, we played Xbox 'til I had blisters—"

"I don't doubt it, Skip. Relax. You don't have to explain a thing. He's my son, too, remember? I know how he can be."

"Good, then," he said, sounding relieved. Then he lowered his voice. "He acts like *he's* the dad, waiting up for me, sniffing my clothes for smoke and booze."

"That's no fun." Christine grinned to herself. David might have Skip's temper, but he had Christine's perfectionist streak. He preferred how things should be to how they really were.

"But he's my son," Skip said on a sigh, "and I should be glad to have him around."

"Next time, we'll plan it for when you can take a few days off, so you'll be more relaxed for the visit."

"Next time? You're cool with that?"

"Of course. He needs to spend time with his father."

"Maybe a long weekend first. Build up my resistance."

She laughed. "He won't be a teenager forever. And next time he'll have more realistic expectations. He thought you'd be the genie in the lamp all wrapped up with a trip to Disneyland."

"Good one," he said. "You're still pretty smart, Chris."

"Thank you. And you're still…you." Moody and flaky and selfish, but not the monster she'd held in her memory. And he loved David. She could hear it in his voice, right through the complaints.

"David has two of us rooting for him now," she said. "And that's important." She'd been a single parent too long. It was time to share the pains and the glory. It felt damn good.

THREE DAYS LATER, Christine climbed into her Volvo to get David from the Preston bus station. The interior smelled like polish and she smiled. Carl, who'd given the car a tune-up "just for fun," had detailed the interior, too. He was a sweet guy, prison tats notwithstanding. Maybe Aurora was right about the karma at Harmony House.

As she turned the key, she glanced out at the House, then went still. In a couple of weeks she and David would leave here for good. She hadn't let that sink in. She climbed out of the car to take a good long look at Harmony House in all its glory—bright paint, colorful doors, restful landscaping, the front porch bright with hanging baskets of Bogie's flowers and vines. It looked so welcoming now, so fresh and homey and peaceful.

Christine's view of the place had changed, too, even without the superficial fixes. The place she'd seen as neglected and sad turned out to be sturdy and stubborn and full of happy secrets.

Aurora's prayer came into her head: *May we all find here what we need.* Christine had needed a fresh start for David and to help Aurora and Bogie. She'd gotten that and more.

She'd gotten back her mother and found her father. She'd learned how to love her son better. There was the constant ache of losing Marcus, of course, a pain so deep she feared she'd never recover from it, but, as some consolation, she had Harmony House and the people and work she loved. It felt like home.

What if she stayed?

There was David and school to consider, but returning to Phoenix held risks, too. What if he wasn't strong enough to resist his old friends and habits, including Brigitte? David had made new friends here—the twins, a few of their friends and Delia, who asked about him constantly.

Christine had heard that the high school had a great fine arts program. Hey, if New Mirage High was good enough for Susan Parsons' perfect twins, then it was pretty damn good.

There would still be drugs, of course. As Marcus had pointed out, drugs were part of the culture. But she trusted David more. On the phone, he'd confided in her that seeing his dad come home high had made him swear off pot. *You have to be awake for your life,* he'd said, and she'd almost burst out laughing at the delicious irony of David's fantasy father being an object lesson in why not to do drugs.

Marcus would love that. She'd tell him when he got back from L.A. *Marcus.* Just the thought of him made her heart ache. It seemed to get worse and worse as time passed instead of better.

What if they stayed?

Living at a commune meant hassles and sacrifice, but it also said something about the human spirit, about the possibility of becoming better through deliberate sharing, deliberate dependence, deliberate love.

She looked up at the fresh yellow paint, out at the

lush gardens, thinking about the tentative promise, the wistful hope that was Harmony House. Why *not* stay?

It would not be a cakewalk. She might understand and appreciate Aurora more, but they would still fight. The commune was old. Things would break and fail. Hell, the electricity was still fragile and the DSL signal hinky.

What about her career? She'd planned to start her own advertising agency, but the idea seemed less urgent now.

David might throw a fit. But there were lessons for him in staying: Sometimes you belonged. Sometimes you made the best of things. Sometimes not getting what you wanted made you stronger.

She sounded like Aurora, who'd dragged Christine kicking and screaming out to the middle of nowhere because Harmony House would be good for her.

The ironies kept piling up. Harmony House hadn't been *good* for her exactly, but it had helped shape her into who she'd become, in all her flaws, strengths and hopes.

For her, staying might give her what she'd told Bogie she wanted: to feel settled in, safe, surrounded by people she loved who loved her back, doing work that mattered.

Maybe, just maybe, staying here *was* her soul's work.

Christine climbed into the car again and started

off for David, but she watched Harmony House in her rearview mirror until it was out of sight.

In Preston, at the bus station, Christine's excitement about seeing David turned into anxiety. Would this be weird? What would she say to him? Would he be sullen, hostile? How would she handle that?

Then, there he was, standing on the top step of the bus, blinking in the sudden sun. Her son. Her David.

Her doubts dissolved. She would know what to do and say.

He'd gotten so big! He'd only been gone a month, but he looked so much older. He was becoming a man. For a moment she couldn't catch a breath.

He saw her, ducked his head, descended the steps and came to her. Before she could decide whether or not to try to hug him, he threw his arms around her and hugged her hard. She'd been a fool to think David would stop loving her just because he spent time with his father.

"You're taller," she said when he let go, her voice wobbly.

He seemed pleased by that. "Dad kind of cried when I left."

"He loves you, David. We both do."

"Whatever. Can we just go?" But he had to hide his smile.

The drive went fast. They talked nonstop. First, David unloaded on her about all his dad's flaws, on and on, until she gently coaxed him into talking about the fun stuff, too. Then she told him that Bogie was his grandfather.

He sat for a long silent moment before he said, "Bogie's cool." Then he paused. "So he's in my family now. Think of all the free weed I can get."

She jerked to look at him.

"Just messin' with you." It was so nice to joke again, Team Waters against the world. For the moment, at least. *Two steps forward, one step back,* as Marcus had said.

"Some summer, huh?" Christine said softly. "We both found our fathers."

David pondered that for a moment. "Yeah," he said finally. "I guess we did."

Soon they were at the New Mirage exit, and when they passed through town, she watched David scan the streets for friends. She smiled. Maybe he wouldn't hate her forever when she told him they were staying.

Before long, they were pulling through the gates to Harmony House. She felt so different from when they'd arrived. She'd been uncertain about being here and worried about David. Today she was more sure of herself *and* her son.

She turned to him. "Before we go in, I want you to think about something. What if we stayed?"

"Here? You mean for good?" He stared, jaw hanging.

"We could give it a year to see how it goes. The

school's decent. The classes are small. They have a great music program."

"Supposedly the band director did studio work in L.A., but that could be B.S. They're all a bunch of hicks."

"Which means you'd be the cool urban dude."

"God. Don't say *dude*." He shook his head, telling her how lame she was, but he wasn't angry. "I thought you hated this place."

"Not anymore." She explained the changes in her thinking, and she told him she trusted him more, that he could make more decisions for himself here.

"So I get my permit?" he asked.

"Why not?" She wasn't above a bribe.

"No curfew?"

"I said I trusted you more, not completely."

He sighed. "Whatever."

"You'll think about it then?"

He only shrugged, but that was good enough for now.

Bogie and Aurora met them at the door. "How's my grandson?" Bogie said, walking right up to hug David hard. Aurora just beamed. Had she ever seen her mother beam before?

Bogie and Aurora had arranged a welcome-home supper for David with balloons and a sign and his favorite dessert—store-bought ice-cream cake.

After supper, Christine went out to the greenhouse to tell Bogie that she hoped to stay. Until she was certain of David, she would hold off on telling her mother.

He didn't seem a bit surprised. "You're happy then, Crystal?" he asked, his soft gray eyes as intense as she'd ever seen them. She remembered Aurora saying Bogie had always been a pest about happiness.

"Getting there," she said. "Definitely getting there." Despite the hole Marcus had left in her heart, despite her worries about David, she was on the path. "Thank you for helping me figure it out."

She looked at his calm face full of quiet love—a love waiting for her since she was a seven-year-old in lacy anklets and patent leather shoes—and felt a rush of regret over all the lost years. "I wish I'd known you were my father before. We wasted so much time."

"Not wasted. Waiting. We were waiting until it was right. And now it is. And you're happy. What more could a father want?"

TAKING THE WINDING ROAD to Harmony House, Marcus was ridiculously excited to see Christine again. And David. It was stupid, of course. Nothing had changed. And it would only renew the pain he'd managed to tuck away while he'd worked in L.A.

He was back now and with a plan. He'd decided to create a foundation to support rural health care in Arizona.

He would name it after Nathan.

Carlos was his field consultant and Marcus would rent a house in New Mirage for when he wasn't traveling. He anticipated many twelve-hour days, welcomed them, in fact, since it kept him from dwelling on how much he missed Christine.

She'd e-mailed him when David returned and told him David would talk to him once Marcus got back to Harmony House. She'd changed her mind about Lady, which surprised him. Maybe her landlord had agreed to an exception. She'd saved the news for Marcus to tell David.

He'd barely unzipped his suitcase when there was a knock at his door. David with Lady. "Come in," he said, waving him inside. "I just got here."

"I saw you pull up. I told my mom I'd come by. You wanted to say something…?" He sounded uneasy and resentful.

"I do." Marcus sat on a chair and patted the bed for David to sit. He did, but reluctantly. Lady lay down at his feet.

"I wanted you to know that I value your friendship. Separately from how I feel about your mother. I enjoyed the time we spent playing guitar and talking. I believe you're a remarkable young man and—"

"Stop. It's no big deal. I was pissed at the time, but it's your business. And my mom's…whatever." He stretched his neck, his face flaming red.

"You have every right to be angry. I kept an important secret from you after asking you to be honest with me. I apologize for that. You deserved better."

"It's cool. Just stop, okay?" He seemed to mean that, so Marcus let it go for the time being.

"I'm here when you want to talk more about it." He hoped he hadn't completely destroyed David's trust in him. "There's one more thing. Would you like to have Lady?"

"You're kidding! You're giving me your dog?"

"She was never really mine. I know Nathan would want you to have her." His throat tightened. "And she clearly loves you."

"You hear that, girl?" David dropped to the floor and buried his face in the dog's neck. "You're staying with me."

"I spoke with your mother and she approves. I assume she cleared it with your landlord."

He looked up at Marcus. "There's no landlord. We're staying at Harmony House."

"You what? You are?" Marcus was stunned. Christine was staying? Stupidly, his heart leaped in his chest.

"Mom's making us. It's lame, but my old school sucked. The kids know about how Brigitte scammed me, so it would be humiliating." David shrugged. "Anyway, I'm stuck here now."

"I'm sure you'll make the best of it."

"Whatever," he said, standing. "If that's it, I'll go."

"That's it from me."

"Yeah, so here's what I want to say. I know I messed you up with my mom and all. She's a good person, even if she freaks over every little thing. So give her another chance, so it's not, like, forever my fault."

Marcus was so moved he had to swallow to get his voice under control. "It wasn't your fault, David. We care for each other, but we ended things for our own reasons."

"Like what reasons?" David was as nosy as his mother.

"It's complex, but basically, we're not compatible."

"So fix it. You were always after me to be a better person. Why not you?"

Marcus smiled. "It's not that simple, David."

"That's just bullshit."

Marcus burst out laughing. The boy had the same stubborn set to his jaw as Christine and the same way of locking on with his gaze. Marcus realize he loved this boy. And his mother.

And he wanted another chance with them both.

"You make a good point. I'll talk to her when I can."

"Soon, okay? I need her in a good mood so she'll take me to get my driver's permit. She's too grumpy."

"I'll see what I can do. Tell you what. If it doesn't work out, I'll take you myself. How's that?" Lady barked, as if in full approval.

Marcus felt like his chest would burst open. Why couldn't he try to be better? Carlos had mentioned he seemed different with Christine. Maybe he could be.

What was he afraid of? Hurting her. Failing. Getting hurt himself. Maybe that was just bullshit, like David said.

FROM HER SPOT IN THE HAMMOCK, Christine saw Marcus and David coming down the stairs, Lady beside them. They looked so right together, the three of them, that her heart throbbed.

She found herself standing, then bounding down the porch stairs toward them. When Marcus saw her, his eyes lit up.

"You're back," she said, breathless.

"It's good to see you," he said, holding her with his gaze.

"You, too." She felt grounded, suddenly in the right place at the right time.

"David tells me you're staying." He smiled.

"It feels right. I've done a lot of thinking and sorting things out and…" How she loved this man.

"As it turns out, I'll be staying in New Mirage myself." He explained about a foundation for health care he was working on with his friend Carlos, some travel, how excited he was, but she wasn't really listening. She was simply taking him in.

"So, the point is, we'll both be around," he said, studying her with his intense gaze. When she'd first met him, his eyes had pulled her in and warned her away, too. Not now. Now they held on tight. "It's so good to see you."

"You already said that," David said. "This is so gross. Come on, Lady." The boy and his dog took off toward the cottonwoods, leaving Christine and Marcus grinning at each other like a pair of idiots.

"Your son gave me quite a talking-to just now," Marcus said.

"He did?"

"Oh, yes. He told me I should give you another chance, even though you freak out over every little thing."

"He said that, did he? And what did you tell him?"

"That we weren't compatible."

"That's true." She'd thought she'd be too much for him. He'd thought he wouldn't be enough for her. Was it possible they could both be wrong?

"David said we should fix it."

"But that's not as easy as it sounds."

"That's what I told him. But he said that was, well, *bullshit*."

"Such language. What kind of mother lets her son talk like that?"

"One who loves and accepts him, swear words and all. And he made another good point, that I expected him to be a better person, so why shouldn't I make the same effort?"

"Good one, David."

Marcus cupped her face. "I need you in my life, Christine. To keep me awake and alive."

"I'll make you crazy, you know," she said, her heart in her throat.

"No doubt. And I'll disappoint you."

"Possibly. But it won't be because you aren't trying. You never let me down. Not once. You've been there for me with David, Aurora, even Bogie. And the rest of it…that's my job. I can stand on my own two feet and lean on you, too."

"So we'll fix it then? Like David suggested?"

"Start where we are and build from there, yeah." She smiled. "I can't believe I just quoted my mother."

"And I'm taking relationship advice from a teenage boy."

"If it works, it works." She smiled at him. "I've figured out a few things lately—mainly, that holding too tight to what you think about people makes you miss them altogether. If you let them be, who they are will shine like the sun. Bogie always did. And so did David. And you, Marcus. Definitely you."

"No one shines like you, Christine. You're the sun and all the stars to me." He kissed her, long and slow, as if they had all the time in the world. And maybe they did.

She would enjoy every minute, see it all through fresh eyes. She had a mother she'd begun to understand and a father she'd loved without knowing who he was. Never again would she miss what was in front of her because it didn't fit her picture of perfection.

She would hold on to this, her new life, her man, her family, with both hands and all her heart. Christine Waters had come home at last.